WHAT THEY FEEL

FALLING SERIES

MADI DANIELLE

Copyright © 2023 by Madi Danielle

All rights reserved.

No part of this book may be reproduced in any form or by any electronic or mechanical means, including information storage and retrieval systems, without written permission from the author, except for the use of brief quotations in a book review.

This novel is entirely a work of fiction. The names, characters and incidents portrayed in it are the work of the author's imagination. Any resemblance to actual persons, living or dead, events or localities is entirely coincidental.

Designations used by companies to distinguish their products are often claimed as trademarks. All brand names and product names used in this book and on its cover are trade names, service marks, trademarks and registered trademarks of their respective owners. The publishers and the book are not associated with any product or vendor mentioned in this book. None of the companies referenced within the book have endorsed the book.

Cover Design: TRC Designs

Proofreading: KMorton Editing Services

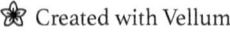 Created with Vellum

PLAYLIST

Villains Aren't born (They're Made) - PEGGY
You make a woman wanna... - Emlyn
Hate Me – Nico Collins
Super Villain - Stileto & Silent Child
Waiting – Breathe Carolina
Breakfast – Dove Cameron
How do you like it – Jynjo
Villains – TeZaTalks
Dark Side – Iris Grey
Die For a Man – Bebe Rexha
Dangerous To Know – Hilary Duff
HELP ME – Demi Lovato
Hurricane – Thirty Seconds to Mars & Kanye West
Last Call – Sadie
Dynasty – Miia
Music – Kelsea Ballerini
Silent – The Veronicas
I Don't Wanna Fall – Grey Zeigler
4 EVER 4 ME – Demi Lovato

"I like not fair terms and a villain's mind."
  -William Shakespeare

1

Trent

Present

I watch the gate slide open.

Finally.

Five years is a long ass time.

And I'm finally getting out.

I'm relieved, and I'm pissed.

The time locked up didn't lessen my anger, it just made me smarter. It made me consider a lot of things in my life, and I'm about to fix every single one of them as soon as this fucking gate lets me out.

I've kept contacts while I've been locked up, and I know the work I put in five years ago when my stepbrother, Zander, first got us to move to the shit show that is Portland, has been set back significantly since the feds got involved.

I had a good thing going in Phoenix, and I wanted to expand, but it bit me in the ass.

I won't trust anyone again. I will do what I need to do from here on out.

My dad taught me to take what I wanted. Do whatever I need to do to get shit done. He taught me to be successful no matter the cost, and definitely not worry about if it's legal.

That's what I was trying to do, then that fucker Zander got me locked up.

The gate is open enough for me to slip through, the brand new Ducati I had set up waiting for me outside. I hop on and speed away faster than I probably should considering I'm on parole for the next three years.

I have a check in with my PO in the morning, but I don't give a fuck. It's not going to stop me from doing what I want to do. The justice system is fucking stupid. They think just because you sit in a concrete box for a few years, get treated like shit by guards, fight, work out, get some tattoos, eat shitty food, and sleep on a fucking rock that you'll change.

Sometimes a person is just who they are going to be, and no amount of punishment will change that.

That's me. I don't give a fuck, I learn from my mistakes, but not what I *shouldn't* do. I learn how not to get caught.

I continue to speed down the empty streets because it's late as fuck, and I can't wait to get to my house and take a hot shower.

Zander and I lived in this house on the outskirts of Portland hidden away in the forest, and he left to get away from me in an attempt to protect him and his little girlfriend. I kept the house even while I was locked up. I managed to buy it before I was sentenced since money isn't a problem. Money still isn't a problem. I have plenty. Working my ass off over the years has earned me enough. *More than enough.*

Once I pull up to the house, I'm hit with the negative memories that took place here and with Zander in general. Everyone thinks he's so fucking perfect, and always has been, but only I know the truth. I wanted everyone else to see that too.

As much as I want to focus on my revenge, I have more pressing matters to deal with now that I'm back.

First, is that hot shower and sleeping on my memory foam mattress. Next, will be finding out what state my business is in, especially with the feds sniffing around.

Fucking feds.

I stomp up the steps to the front door. I had the place cleaned before I got here because I wanted fresh sheets on my bed and didn't want to choke on dust that's accumulated over the years.

Once I stepped inside, the simmering rage I was feeling while I was thinking about the past has lessened for the moment. I take in the fact that I'm finally fucking free, and don't have to sleep in a cell with two other guys tonight.

Without even a glance over at the hallway that led to Zander's room, I head to mine and directly into the bathroom. I strip down from the clothes I was arrested in five years ago that are now a bit too tight due to the muscle I gained from working out.

I glance in the mirror at myself once I'm naked, and take in how different I look. The mirrors in lock up are shit, so I haven't been able to really see myself. My arms are now covered in tattoos of various shit I liked. There were some guys who were actually decent at art, and those were the only ones I let tattoo me. The designs spread onto my chest.

My muscles are more defined than they were before. I've always been fit, but now the indents of my abs are deeper, and the grooves in my arms are more toned. I used to be leaner, but now I'm bulky, and I don't hate it. I would use Zander as the guy to fuck up people that needed to be fucked up. Now, I don't even need anyone for that, unless I don't feel like getting blood on me.

The hot water hits me, and I groan at the feeling. I missed hot showers more than I thought. I stand under the spray without washing any part of my body, just basking in the feel of the warmth enveloping me.

When the water starts to cool down, I quickly wash my buzzed hair, and body before stepping out with a towel wrapped around my waist. I open the closet to see fresh clothes already hung up and ready.

I can't remember who exactly I put in charge of handling all this shit for me, but I need to make sure I keep them around. I keep people around that are helpful and good at what they do. I only tolerate the best.

Pulling on a pair of brand-new boxers before I slide under the covers of my bed I think about the other thing I've missed since being locked up.

Sex.

I haven't fucked anyone in five years, and I used to fuck every night if I wasn't too busy with other shit. Lying in bed I think about the fact that I could have someone here in ten minutes or less if I wanted. And trust me, I want that, but do I want to deal with the potential of whoever she is overstaying her welcome? Not really.

Instead of calling anyone over I decide to enjoy the first full night of sleep I've been able to get in years.

Tomorrow the real fun begins.

2

Present

The buzzing smart watch on my wrist pulls me out of my deep sleep, but I can't be bothered to open my eyes yet. I smack my watch to make the buzzing stop. Once it does, I roll onto my stomach, grab one of my pillows, and put it over my head.

I don't even realize that I fall asleep again until I'm being poked by someone. I try to roll away from the source of the poking, keeping the pillow over my head. Suddenly, the blankets are ripped off my body followed by the pillow over my head.

I turn over to glare at the person bothering me. My sister, Mila.

"Don't you need to get up?" Mila signs to me.

"Why do you care?" I sign back with an eye roll.

"Fine, whatever." She turns her back to me before stomping out of my room.

We aren't really close with each other, and haven't been for a while. Not since our mom died. She truly was the glue that held our family together, and once she was gone, so was our close family. She died six years ago when I was fifteen, and Mila was seventeen.

Mila ran away shortly after she turned eighteen, then after a few months she returned, but she was a different person.

The good news was she was talking to me again.

The bad news was she's a shell of who she was.

She doesn't talk about where she went or what happened, but it was obviously something bad.

Our dad has barely spoken to both Mila and me since we lost our mom. He never signs to me anymore, so if I am in a room with him, he uses his voice, and I'm left out almost completely. I'm able to read lips, but that only works if he looks at me, which doesn't happen anymore.

I've basically been on my own since I was fifteen.

Now, at twenty-one I share an apartment with Mila because neither of us could afford to live alone and couldn't stand the thought of living with our dad. We tend to leave each other alone for the most part during our day-to-day lives. However, there are times, like today, we have to interact for one reason or another.

I'll be honest, I don't know why Mila had to bust in my room to wake me up today. I would rather not have to ask her about it either, but if it's something important then I'm sure she won't let me leave the apartment without telling me.

Or she just wanted to piss me off.

It could be either.

Or both.

I peek at my wrist to check what time it is and see it's only eight in the morning. Which is usually considered three in the morning to Mila since she works at bars or something. I don't even know. I usually wake up around this time since I am a rare college student that prefers morning classes so I can get them over with, and head to one of my various jobs in the afternoon and evening.

Since it's summer and I'm not taking any classes, I am able to have more jobs, the most time consuming being an ASL teacher at a transition home for juveniles who have recently gotten out of detention.

The program is designed for teenagers who need more time before going home. I learned about it through an internship search. I was an intern at first until they were able to offer me a part time position as an ASL teacher.

I'm not a certified teacher *yet*, so that's not my actual job title. The program has various extracurricular options for the teenagers to choose from that develop different skills. Second languages are really popular in the program, and my boss was excited to have someone able to teach ASL for the first time since the program opened.

I love it.

Plus, it solidified my desire to be an ASL teacher at a hearing school. School was shitty for me, and I want to do what I can to make it better for other kids, so they don't have to go through what I did.

Pulling myself out of bed I put in my hearing aids. They only help me with environmental noises, and most of the time I forgo putting them in anyway because sometimes I don't feel like dealing with them.

I get dressed in jeans and a light tank top because even though I live in Oregon, the heat is not my friend, and I don't like summer. I know other places get much hotter, but anything over eighty-five is unbearable to me.

Once I'm dressed, I throw up my blonde hair in a ponytail, so it doesn't stick to my neck once I inevitably start sweating.

With a deep breath I go out to face Mila and whatever she felt was so important she needed to wake me up.

Mila is standing in the kitchen with a mug cupped in her hands, it's probably filled with some herbal tea because she doesn't drink coffee. Mila is pretty, I've always thought so, though we don't look alike. We both have blonde hair and brown eyes, but that's where the similarities end. Mila is also shorter than my five-foot-six frame by about three inches.

I push past her without a word to grab my cold brew from

the fridge. I can live without certain amenities in life such as opting to live with my sister and sharing a bathroom. I draw the line at giving up my coffee.

Seriously, I've skipped meals to make sure I have it.

Mila waves her hand to get my attention before signing, "*Dad called.*"

I grimace. "*Why?*"

"*Wants us to come see him sometime,*" she signs with an eye roll.

"*Pretty sure you mean he wants to see you.*"

Mila tries to drag me along when our dad wants to see us, mostly because she doesn't want to be alone with him. He's never hurt us or anything, it's just awkward. Especially for me.

"*Why did you have to wake me up for that?*" I sign with a glare.

She shrugs. "*I didn't. You weren't up, and I figured you should be.*"

"*Wow, thanks for caring.*" I make sure to exaggerate my signs, and show I'm being sarcastic with my facial expressions.

"*It's what older sisters are for,*" she signs before prancing to her room, shutting the door.

I feel like I don't know anything about her life. That is the most words we've exchanged in months. We don't ask each other things about our lives, and just coexist in this apartment with the knowledge we share blood and that's about it.

But she's not wrong, I did need to get up. I don't have to be at the transition center for another hour since my first class isn't until ten.

I finish my coffee before reluctantly deciding to wash my hair after all since I have the time to kill, and nothing else to really do. Before jumping in the shower, I check my phone and see I have a text from my best friend Jenson from last night while I was already sleeping.

> Jenson: Please tell me you're up. I'm bored and need entertainment!

I chuckle to myself. He knew I would be asleep. He's the night owl, and I'm the morning person. We've been friends since freshman year of high school and he knows me better than my own sister.

He was the only person to stay by my side while everyone else thought it was funny to make fun of the one deaf kid in school after we moved.

It sucked.

But I quickly realized none of those people mattered to me anyway. They weren't worth my time or energy, so I got over it. I wouldn't even let Jenson stick up for me when he would try. I could fight my own battles, and I don't need anyone to do it for me.

I still don't need anyone else to fight my battles. People can adapt to be a part of my world if they want, but I don't have to change myself to fit into theirs. Which is why I choose not to speak with my voice most of the time, I prefer ASL. I will if I need to, I'm not against using my voice for any reason other than I just prefer to communicate in ASL.

I can read lips when necessary, and utilize that for both my own communication, and also just because I'm nosy at times. It can be fun to eavesdrop on conversations you have no business eavesdropping on. It adds an extra layer to people watching which is one of my favorite pastimes.

People always assumed Jenson and I were a couple, or that we like each other in that way, but it's just not true. We kissed once because, well, I wanted my first kiss to be with someone I trusted, and he agreed. It was weird, quick, and never happened again.

Plus, a couple years later Jenson told me he was never attracted to me because he prefers men.

I decide to text him back, since I know he's still sleeping anyway.

> Violet: I bet my next month's paycheck you're still asleep just like you knew I was last night.

I throw my phone down as I go into the shower; I know I won't hear back from him until at least noon.

3

Present

"No." I tell my parole officer sternly.

I knew I would have to do community service. It was a part of my parole to get released early. I figured I would get to pick, and honestly, find my way out of it somehow. Pay some guy to show up for me or something.

"Yes," my PO, Carrie, replies.

I was excited to learn I had a woman PO, until I saw her. That excitement faded quickly. She's at least sixty, and I'm not against fucking an older woman if I need to, but I draw the line at gangly teeth, and the smell of body odor so strong I can barely keep my eyes from watering.

Despite all of that I attempt to turn on the charm with a smile. "Look, Carrie, I thought I could pick my community service. Plus, honestly, I would rather pick up garbage on the side of the freeway than do what you're telling me."

She's unfazed, and my smile fades. "Mr. Moore, you will serve your community service at the Wright House for teens. It'll be good for you to see the kids headed down the same path as you and maybe make an actual difference for them. Show them change is possible."

I have to fight to hold back the scoff. *I haven't changed for shit.* And I really don't want to spend the next three years of my parole telling these punk ass kids not to do exactly what I'm still doing. I know what I was like as a teenager, and I don't want to deal with their fucking attitudes about it.

I'm not going to make a difference, so there's no point in sending me there to try.

"I will do anything else." I try to bargain.

"You'll do anything, and you're going to do this. You start today at eleven and remember, not showing up to your community service is a parole violation, which will land you back in jail to finish the remainder of your sentence."

I plaster on a fake smile again so I can just leave this place before I end up killing my fucking PO. That's another thing that will land me back in the concrete box for sure.

"Goodbye," I tell her before turning on my heel.

As soon as my back is to her my smile drops and I walk out the door. I didn't need more things to be pissed about, but apparently another thing was just added.

I PULL up to the Wright House exactly at eleven. I strongly consider not getting off my Ducati, and just see how far away I can drive before I get caught. I'd really rather not go back to lock up. That's the only thought that carries me off the motorcycle and up to the front door.

This place looks like a big, old house. There's a gate around the front, but it isn't locked, and doesn't look like any detention center I've ever been to. I know Carrie said it's a "transition home", but I don't even know what that means. Lucky for me, I never got caught doing shit when I was a kid, so I never had to deal with a place like this.

The front door isn't locked so I'm able to walk in. I wonder what the point of this place is if people can just come in and out.

Inside, the house opens to a long hallway with doors on either side, and I can see at the end of the hallway it looks like there's a common area. I'm supposed to find the manager's office, which is probably in one of these doors.

Walking through the long hallway I peek into every room, there's one that looks like an art room, one with padding on the floor like it could be used for exercise, then I get to a room that looks like it's a small classroom. When I peek inside, I see a woman standing at a desk at the front of the room. Her back is turned to me, but I take a moment to take in her amazing body.

Her blonde hair pulled up in a ponytail, which I'm a fan of. I can't stop the image of wrapping the long hair around my fist. She's in jeans that show the perfect curve of her ass right below her hips. She's in a tank top showing the skin of her arms which I can tell would be soft under my touch.

I haven't even seen her face yet, but I've convinced myself she's going to have the perfect pouty lips, large doe eyes and straight nose. I can't help but stick around to see the front of her.

Leaning against the door frame, I fold my arms across my chest as I wait for her to turn around. She's shuffling around papers, and I can't help but make my presence known.

"I think I'm lost and need someone to help show me around." I say jokingly, anticipating her to jump at the sound of my voice.

She doesn't move.

She doesn't even turn around to see who's talking to her.

I furrow my brow at her blatantly ignoring me. I continue to lean against the door frame watching her put things into her bag.

"Seriously, I think I'll get lost if I don't have you hold my hand to help me." I try again, and she still doesn't acknowledge me.

I continue to watch her as she finishes putting away her things before finally turning around. The look on her face when she sees me is shock for a moment then quickly turns to confusion.

I take the moment to finally see her for the first time. I was right that she's pretty. She's drop dead gorgeous. Her lips aren't as pouty as I pictured but look soft and would look good taking my cock between them. She's younger than me, probably in her early twenties, and that's just fine with me.

Her nose is small and straight, with deep brown eyes that look like they are examining me, but more under scrutiny rather than attraction. I give her a wide smile, which only makes her narrow her eyes at me even more.

"You want to make me work for your attention? I can do that...all night long." I wink.

Instead of smiling or giggling like I expect, she rolls her eyes, and starts moving her hands around quickly. She still hasn't said anything, and my smile slowly falls.

For one of the first times in my life, I don't know what to say. She is still moving her hands around while glaring at me and hasn't spoken a word. I decide to try one more time because I want to know something about this woman.

"Can I at least know your name?" I ask, standing up straighter.

She looks up at me, her eyes still narrowed before moving her right hand around with two fingers up almost like a peace sign. Then holds up her pinky. Next, an "o" shape. Then maybe an "L". Then an almost open fist, and finally a fist with her thumb pressed between her index and middle finger.

"I'm Trent." I smile once she drops her hand.

She doesn't say anything else or move her hands around. She just rolls her eyes, and pushes past me out the door.

My eyes don't leave her retreating form as she walks away without looking back. I can't help but be confused by the entire interaction. I have never had a woman write me off this quickly. And without saying a word to me at all? I don't understand what just happened.

As she continues down the hallway to the common area of the house someone else walks toward me. They look young, like they could be one of the teens that live here, but I don't care, I need to know who that woman was.

"Hey kid, who's that?" I ask, nodding my head toward the blonde as she turns the corner and leaves my view.

The kid looks at me wide-eyed before answering. "Uh, who? Ms. Violet?" he stutters like he's nervous to say anything. I can only imagine how crazed I look right now between the confusion from my interaction with Violet, and my need to know more about her.

"What does she do here?" I question.

"She...uh...teaches sign language or something." The kid backs away from me to continue walking where he was going before I stopped him.

I nod in response before he turns around, and quickly walks the way he was headed. *Sign language.* That's probably what she was doing with her hands, she was saying things to me in sign language. From the look that was on her face as she signed to me, I can't help but think she was cussing me out.

Too bad, she intrigued me, and now I'm determined to get to know her more. Maybe this shitty community service assignment won't be as bad as I thought if I can focus on getting to know her instead.

4

Present

What an ass.

If I had worn my hearing aids today, I might have known he was standing there, but I chose to leave them at home. I shake off the weird interaction I had with that guy back in the classroom. I didn't expect to see someone standing there just staring at me. Then, he spoke and it's obvious he had tried to get my attention while my back was turned considering, he said something about working for my attention...*all night long.* Gross.

I told him to fuck off, and he's wasting his time trying to talk to me if he's going to think like that. Of course, he didn't know what I was saying, but I don't care. He looks like an arrogant ass, and I don't even know what he would be doing here. He also looked decently older than me, mid-thirties probably.

He was pretty good looking, if I'm being honest with myself.

He's got that typical "bad boy" look with the tattoos and muscles. Plus, his almost black, dark brown hair, and the light brown eyes.

However, I'm not interested in the slightest. I'm too busy to date, and I don't do hook ups. I've slept with one guy; one time and it wasn't that great.

It wasn't good at all.

So bad actually, that I haven't done it again in three years.

It was my first year in college, I figured I should lose my virginity. It hurt; it was uncomfortable. I didn't have a connection with the guy. Plus, I didn't even finish. I tried dating a bit more, went on some first dates, but they never progressed past that. I failed to find a connection with anyone, and as college progressed, I've only gotten busier. Dating has fallen off my radar almost completely.

So yeah, *Trent* doesn't interest me, and I doubt he had any interest in me beyond my body anyway.

I head into the manager's office to let him know I'm headed out for the day. I don't need to, but I know Travis prefers when staff let him know when they come and go from the house. Same with those that live here. Since it's a transition home it isn't locked down, except at night. So, I know Travis likes to know who is in the house and who isn't at all times.

When I knock on the door, I wait a beat before opening it to step inside. Travis looks up, and once he sees it's me, he waves his hand, "*Hi*" with a smile.

I smile back. "*Hi.*"

Travis is nice, but his knowledge of ASL is limited at best, though he does try. He knows simple phrases, but anything more in depth I usually use my voice or write it down.

"*How did it go today?*" he signs because that's one of the phrases he knows since he uses it every day.

"*Fine, who's the new guy?*" I see him look confused beyond "fine" since he knows that one. I chuckle, and say with my voice, "Who's the new guy?"

I see Travis about to say something, but then his eyes move to look behind me, and he stands up. "This new guy?" he asks.

With a silent groan I glance over my shoulder, and sure enough, Trent is waltzing into the office with a smirk on his face. I watch as he moves to stand next to me.

"So, you can speak," he says, and I grimace.

Of course I can, you ignorant piece of shit.

I know I could sign that, and he wouldn't know, but instead I sign, "*Yes, just not to you.*"

His smirk turns into a sinister smile, and I watch his annoyingly full lips as he says, "I like a challenge."

I don't hide the scoff I let out before turning back to Travis. "*See you later.*"

I don't want to be around Trent anymore, and I don't care enough to get answers about who he is or why he's here.

Pulling out my phone I see Jenson replied while I was teaching.

> Jenson: I feel judgment.
>
> Violet: Probably because I was judging. Want to get lunch?
>
> Jenson: Always. Café on fifth.
>
> Violet: On my way.

~

WALKING up to our favorite café, I already see Jenson sitting at a table on the patio. He waves at me, and I give a small wave back before walking around the gate to join him.

"How was work?" he signs.

I take a sip of the water that was already waiting for me before answering. *"Fine. There's some new guy."*

Jenson's eyebrows raise dramatically, and I know he wants me to share every detail. He's going to be sorely disappointed at my assessment of said new guy.

"Don't get excited." I tell him with an eye roll.

"Give me all the details and I'll decide if I can be excited or not."

"His name is Trent and he's a twat waffle."

He looks at me, confused, finger spelling back to me what I just said. *"Twat waffle?"*

"Yes."

He opens his mouth like he wants to say something, but settles on signing back, *"I don't want to know how or why that's the insult you chose."*

I just shrug. I could come up with a million and one insults for the obnoxious man I met, but my hands would get tired from signing that much so I settled on the first thing I thought of.

"Okay, but most importantly, is he good looking?"

I grimace, of course Jenson would ask that. I do love my best friend, but he has this flaw of letting pretty people get away with too many things. At least, that's been my opinion with him. His last two boyfriends were extremely good looking, but assholes. Yet, he continued to stick around for way too long and put up with way too much.

Reluctantly, I answer, but only because I know he can tell when I'm lying, and he won't drop this.

"He's okay looking."

Jenson's eyes narrow at me.

"Yes, he's hot, but he's older and annoying and an asshole."

"Older? Like daddy older?"

"I don't know what you mean, and I don't want to." I roll my eyes.

"Fine, I'll drop this for now, but don't hold back on me."

"You already know I will." I give him a knowing smile because I will never talk about more than I need to when it comes to guys in my life.

Not that there is any.

And not that Trent will be.

My official goal for the rest of the summer is to stay as far away from Trent as possible.

5

Trent

25 Years Ago (Age 10)

My mom is taking me over to her friend, Tasha's house again. I don't mind because she has a son my age named Ken, and I like hanging out with him.

Tasha greets us at the front door with a smile. She's always nice to me so I never have a problem coming over here with my mom.

"Trent, nice to see you. Ken is in his room," she tells me, opening the door wide enough for my mom and I to walk inside.

"Thanks," I say before walking down the hallway I know leads to Ken's room.

He's already playing a first-person shooter game, and barely glances at me once I walk into his room.

"Hey Trent, grab the other controller," he instructs, and I do just that.

We play a few more rounds before deciding to put on a movie, a new horror one I know my mom wouldn't normally let me watch. My dad wouldn't care, but he usually lets me do a lot of things my mom won't.

Ken grabs some popcorn from the kitchen before we turn off the lights and watch the gory movie. Blood doesn't really bother me, but the jump scares do, and I can kind of see why my mom wouldn't want me to watch this because I might end up with nightmares tonight. Not that I'll tell either of my parents if I do. My mom might be mad I watched this in the first place, and my dad expects me to be strong at all times. Just like he is.

By the time the movie is over I feel my eyelids getting heavy, and I wonder why my mom hasn't come to get me so we can go home. There are times we are here until late, but I feel like it's later than usual.

Ken fell asleep at some point and is laying on the floor next to where I'm sitting. I make my way to the living room to tell my mom I want to go home, but neither her nor Tasha are there.

That's weird.

The house isn't very big, and I check the kitchen and dining room, but they aren't in there either. *My mom wouldn't go home without me, would she?*

I'm walking around the house when I hear some noise

coming from one of the closed doors, it's not talking, it's like...*moaning*. It's probably a TV or something. Maybe my mom just fell asleep like Ken did.

The noise gets louder as I approach the door, and it's not locked. I open it slowly.

"Mom?" I call just above a whisper.

There's no TV on, and the noises are much louder. The lights are off, but I make out movement under the blankets on the bed.

"Mom?" I ask, louder this time.

"Trent? Oh my god, go back to Ken's room," she says frantically.

I can't see much in the darkness, but I have the overwhelming feeling that I don't want to.

"Trent please," my mom tries again, but I'm frozen.

After a moment I turn and run down the hallway back to Ken's room, slamming the door behind me. I lean my back against it trying to wrap my head around what just happened.

What were they doing?

I have a feeling I don't want to know.

Ken sits up and looks at me with wide eyes. Clearly, the door slamming woke him up.

"What's going on?" he asks, rubbing his eyes.

"I don't know," I shake my head, trying to get the sounds and images out of my head.

It doesn't take long before Ken's door is opening, and I see my mom's blonde head peeking in. Her eyes look scared as they meet mine, but her voice is calm. "You ready to go home, Trent?"

I look away from her, quickly, and nod once. She walks out of the room, and Ken looks at me confused.

"You okay?" he asks with a yawn.

I shake my head.

"See you later?"

"I don't know if I will," I tell him because I don't think I will be able to come back here again. Or at least I don't think I will want to.

Ken doesn't say anything else as I walk out to meet my mom.

I refuse to look up from the ground as we walk to her car. Even after we've both closed the doors, she doesn't turn on the car yet. I still won't look at her.

"Trent?" she says softly, and I don't acknowledge her. She continues anyway, "I don't know what you saw or..." she sighs. "Please don't tell your dad."

I can't say anything in response. She waits to see if I will, but she must realize I'm not going to. With a deep sigh, she turns on the car and drives away.

There's nothing I can say at this moment, I feel like everything just flipped upside down. Looking out the window the scenery becomes nicer the closer we get to our house. My dad works hard to give us the life we have, I know this.

We have a big house. We go to the country club every Sunday with their friends. My parents golf at the golf course we live on, at least once a week. I know why my mom doesn't want me to tell my dad anything from tonight. She doesn't want to lose any of this. She has the "perfect" life with the "perfect" family. What happened tonight would ruin all of this and take it all away.

I look up at my mom for the first time and see her focusing on the road. I can't help but think about how hurt I am by her, that she would do this to my dad. To me. To her family. The world feels like it's crashing down around me, and there's nothing I can do about it. Everything is completely out of my control.

I look away from her because I know I'll never be able to look at her again.

6

Trent

Present

My day at the Wright House is finally over, and now I can get back to *real* business.

My first task is to connect with the contacts I kept while I was in prison to get caught up on everything. I know the feds are sniffing around everything and have been for a couple years. I also know the busts that were made a few years ago when I was first locked up had more to deal with my dad's side of things than mine.

I've been trying to separate my shit from his for a long time, but it hasn't been so simple. He likes to piggyback off the contacts I make in order to further his business since I won't touch the skin trade like he does. I prefer to sell product rather than people. Drugs, guns, fake bills, shit like that.

My dad getting involved in my shit got really bad when I started acquiring strip clubs around Portland. Especially those along what's considered the "track". Prostitution doesn't bug me, do what you gotta do, but I prefer my girls to be legal. And willing. My dad doesn't care either way.

To think I used to look up to him is hard to wrap my head around now.

He started using my clubs for his own uses, especially when I got locked up. Which, of course, was his biggest disappointment when it comes to me. I had some of my people keep me updated, but some got pulled into my dad's side under false promises of more money and power. Like this guy, Cap, he was good for my business, and look where he ended up once he decided to align with Chris Moore instead of me. Now he's in for ten years minimum.

I was in for five, and the only reason I didn't get more time is because I was able to get the best lawyers possible. They were able to cut me a deal that is unheard of. Plus, "good behavior" goes a long way apparently.

That's the problem for people like Cap that fall under my dad's spell, once there's trouble, he leaves you out to dry. Money is pulled, and help isn't given.

It's kill or be killed in this life.

And I stopped relying on him or anyone a long time ago.

I call one of my guys, Jason. That is one good thing Zander actually did for me was bring him into our business. He's good at getting information and keeping pretty quiet. He continued to slip me info while I was in lock up and was the first to tell me the feds are involved now. I had a thought a while ago that he might be a snitch, so he hasn't been privy to much info *from* me, but he's been helpful at gaining info *for* me.

"Sup?" he answers.

"Jason, it's Trent." I swing my leg over my bike to sit while I figure out where I need to go.

"Damn, you really are out?" He laughs which leads into a cough, I assume he's smoking something. Jason may be helpful, but I don't think I've ever seen him sober.

"Why do you sound surprised, are people talking about me?"

"People are always talking, but it will probably be good for you to show your face."

I sigh, rubbing my jaw. He's right, I know as soon as I do the word is going to get back to my dad. I haven't talked to him in five years, and I don't know if I'm ready to yet.

"Yeah, tell me where," I say since I know some of the clubs got shut down when Cap was arrested, and I don't know the places people are going now. I'm having to play catch up with everything.

"Your club on eighty-second and Stark," he says, and I take a second to remember which one that is. I'm a little surprised it wasn't one that got shut down in the raids, but I'm not about to question it.

"I'll be there in an hour."

I hang up, put my helmet on before revving the engine, and taking off toward my house. It's been so long since I've had to show people on the outside of the power I hold. I'm going to make sure I remind all these fuckers who I am, and not just Chris Moore's son.

This is about me, and I'm about to ensure everyone else knows that.

I REALLY NEED to get a car in addition to having my Ducati because wearing slacks on a motorcycle isn't practical. I've always liked to present as official as possible. I'm someone to be taken seriously. It's only half the battle, my attitude being the other half, but I truly believe it helps.

Since my bike is my only means of transportation for now, I settled on jeans and a dark button up shirt with the sleeves rolled up to my elbows. It isn't exactly how I'm used to presenting myself, but it will have to work for today.

The club has music playing so loud I can hear it from the outside as I pull up, and park. Security lets me through without any issue, and I'm in the dark club. The main lights are lighting up a stage in the center with a pole leading up to the ceiling. There's a little brunette dancing up there, and yet again I'm reminded of the fact that I haven't fucked anyone in five years. The sight of her bare tits makes me instantly hard like a fucking teenager.

I need to get through business first, then I need to let off some fucking steam and stick my dick somewhere warm and wet.

Looking around I scope out the people in attendance tonight. I see some familiar faces, but more strangers than not. Toward the back there's a booth where the biggest group is congregated, and I see Jason standing off to the side, looking at the ground.

I walk over, everyone in the group almost instantly changes their facial expression as soon as they see me. The girls giving dances don't stop, but they do look at me in question, clearly not aware of who I am.

I take a seat in one of the chairs quickly vacated by a small guy I don't recognize. A girl is instantly in my lap. I know the deal; I was the one who implemented it. The girls have a job to check everyone that comes in for wires. I'm glad this hasn't changed, but it does show that I really did need to show my face since they think I need to be checked.

Of course, I let it happen because I'm not about to turn away this hot girl in lingerie running her hands all over my body. The way this is done is disguised as a dance because it's rare someone will turn down or question a free dance from one of the girls.

She gives a subtle nod to one of the other guys I don't recognize before leaving my lap.

"Trent Moore," he says, which makes me furrow my brows at him considering he knows me, but I don't know him. "I've heard good things from your dad, well, except the lock up."

"Can't say the same since I don't know who you are." I signal a waitress over so I can order whiskey.

He chuckles. "I'm Dagger, I took over for Cap after he got his ass locked up like you."

I scowl at the second mention of my arrest. I'm sure my dad has gone around telling his guys about how disappointed he is, but if this nobody thinks I'm going to take it from him, he's sorely mistaken.

"You work for my dad?" I ask as the waitress hands me my drink.

"Yup, he put me in charge of this side of the track," he says proudly.

I take a long sip of the whiskey, letting the familiar burn linger for a moment as I savor the smokey flavor I've missed before I respond. Especially since this is about to turn into an issue I wasn't wanting to deal with yet.

"Funny," I begin, setting down my empty glass. "Considering he doesn't have any say in that. You're in my club."

I watch Dagger's face closely. First, there's confusion, then there's an uneasy smirk. "Maybe it was before, but a lot of things have changed."

I sigh, I really didn't want to throw around my weight on my first day back, but apparently, he's going to force my hand. I stand up, my six-foot-one frame towering over him while he sits. I consider him for a second, but then I let my fist fly into the right side of his face so hard he's knocked out of his seat.

A few of the people around us look unsure of what to do.

Some move like they want to grab me, but then change their mind quickly. I stand above Dagger while he groans on the floor, screaming every cuss word in the book at me.

"Looks like they haven't changed that much," I look at the people standing around, still not stopping me. I know they can see who is in charge here, and it's me.

Dagger is finally able to look up where he sees no one is backing him up. I fold my arms across my chest.

"Go run and cry to my dad if you want, but get the fuck out of my club."

I wait for him as he takes his time getting up. I see him make eye contact with several of the men around us, clearly expecting them to do something. They don't.

"Leave." I tell him sternly. I don't raise my voice; I don't need to.

Reluctantly, he listens, and eventually makes his way out the door.

I sit back down in the seat I was previously occupying, signaling for another drink. I lean back with my legs spread, silently challenging anyone else to question my authority before I speak once again.

"Now, who is going to catch me up on business because I'm done fucking waiting."

7

7 Years Ago (Age 14)

We had to move to Portland. I wasn't excited about leaving my school, my friends, or my life, but my parents didn't give us a choice. My dad was laid off from his job, and this is where he was able to find a new one. Mila was even more upset than I was. She's about to start her junior year, and the last thing she wanted was to leave all her friends behind.

My parents offered to enroll me in another deaf school, but the closest one is almost an hour away, and it would make things really complicated. I would have to live there during the week, and since I just had to leave everything I've ever known, the last thing I want to do is leave my family. So, I said I'm okay with going to a hearing school, which is true. I'm okay with it, but they are making me have an interpreter which I am not okay with.

The best way to draw attention to yourself is to be a new kid on the first day of high school. The second-best way is to have some adult following you around all day. I wonder if I could outrun them and hide.

I actually consider it.

I know I could handle a hearing classroom, I can read lips really well, and I will just speak without signs, and it'll be fine...

It's not fine.

Teachers should really focus on talking to the classroom facing us instead of turning to write on the board as they talk. Everything is fine, I'm able to read the teacher's lips, then in the middle of a sentence they turn around, and I have no idea what's being said.

Reluctantly, I turn to acknowledge my interpreter who has been really understanding and hasn't been suffocating me with his presence, though I know he is there. So does everyone else. I see the looks being thrown my way and I can read their lips as they whisper about me.

The worst part is no one tries talking to me or asking *me* anything. They will ask the interpreter, "what's wrong with her?" like deafness is contagious or something. My interpreter, Jonathan, tells them to speak to me directly. Which then leads to a look and walking away.

Or worse, they exaggerate their words, speak slowly, and assumably loud when they attempt to speak to me. It used to make me want to scream.

Now, I don't even care because I know the people treating

me like this and acting like this aren't people I want to be around anyway. It still stings, but I had to learn to be tough when I was young. I had to learn a whole new language, learn how to react to hearing people out in the community not understanding how to communicate with me. I had to be strong, and accept that this is my life, and honestly, I don't give a shit if anyone has a problem with it.

My third class is wrapping up, and it's lunch time. I tell Jonathan I don't need him for lunch, and to meet me in class afterwards. He looks unsure, but I wave him off. If I have any shot of making any friends, I need some time on my own.

Scoping out the large cafeteria, I debate on where to sit. None of the options seem great for me. I don't know anyone, and my backup plan was to find Mila to sit with her, even if she hates it. Unfortunately for me, I can't find her anywhere.

I wring my hands together tightly to prevent them from shaking as my anxiety gets worse each second, I'm just standing here staring at the tables. Finally, I see a boy who looks around my age with brown hair hanging in his face like he's trying to hide as well.

Taking a risk, I approach the table, and he glances up at me through his hair. I don't say anything, I just point to the chair with my eyebrow raised in a question. He seems to hesitate for a moment before nodding slowly.

With a sigh of relief, I sit down, and pull out the lunch my mom packed for me. It's just a turkey and cheese sandwich with some chips. I look up at the boy I'm sharing the table with, he has a school lunch, but doesn't look like he's eaten any of it. In fact, he's just pushing it around with his spork.

"I'm Violet," I blurt suddenly. He jumps at my voice; I may have said that louder than I intended.

He looks at me, still seeming unsure of my presence, but finally I see his mouth move. "I'm Jenson."

We are both quiet for a few moments until I decide to try talking to him again. I don't sign while I speak, and I don't like the feeling, like I'm hiding a part of myself. "Are you a freshman too?"

He seems to hesitate again before answering. "Yeah."

I nod because I'm not sure what to say. He seems more nervous than me, and I wonder why. Without thinking too much I speak again and say the one thing that pops into my head. "I'm deaf."

Jenson looks at me, meeting my eyes for the first time, they are a dark blue and he has a cute face; I wonder why he hides it behind his hair. He seems to study me for a second, and the longer he takes to say anything makes me worried. I'm not sure what his response will be, but I'm really taken aback when his mouth opens again.

"So, you speak sign language?" he asks. I can tell from his lip movement he's speaking normally, and I sigh in relief.

I nod, and sign, *"Yes."*

"That's so cool, will you teach me?"

I smile, wide. *"Yes."*

Just like that, I know I've made a friend. Maybe Portland won't be so bad after all.

THAT DAY when I come home I'm excited to tell my parents that I made a friend. We are all sitting at the table eating dinner when my mom instructs us to share something positive about our day. I'm excited to share so I go first.

"*I made a friend,*" I sign proudly.

"*That's amazing, Vi, who is she?*" Mom asks.

"*It's a boy, his name is Jenson.*"

I catch Mila clearly taunting me with her face as she signs, "*Violet has a boyfriend.*"

"*He's just a friend.*"

"*Mila, why don't you share.*" My dad tries to take the attention away from me, which I'm thankful for since I feel my cheeks getting hot.

"*I signed up to try for the dance team.*"

"*That's great, you'll make it.*" Mom smiles at Mila in encouragement. She's always so positive, and always has been. "*I managed to unpack most of the boxes.*"

I can't help but chuckle at her exaggerated motion of

putting her hands on her hips like she just accomplished something much greater than just unpacking some boxes.

"And I'm here with my three favorite girls," Dad says. He always does this, and when he can't think of something to share from his day he says something about us being his favorite girls.

"*That shouldn't count,*" I tell him with an eye roll.

"*It's the best part of my day, though. It's the best part of all my days.*"

My mom puts her hand on her heart like she's touched by what he's saying before leaning over to kiss him. I shake my head, though I want to be grossed out by them I can't help but enjoy when they are so loving toward each other, or to us. It makes me happy. And thankful.

I've met other kids that are deaf, and not all of them are as lucky as I am to have a family that learned ASL for them. When I lost my hearing when I was five from several severe ear infections, my mom ensured our entire family learned the language together.

As I watch my parents smile at each other, I can feel the love between them. I can only hope someone will look at me like that one day.

8

Present

I'm really hoping I can avoid Trent yet another day. I haven't had to see him since our first interaction, and I'm hoping to never see him again.

It's not that I can't handle his arrogant attitude or anything. I totally can, I just don't want to spend any of my energy on it. I stopped wasting my energy on people I don't give a fuck about a long time ago.

Part of my avoidance technique is as soon as I'm done teaching, I pop into Travis' office for a quick, "see ya." Then, I'm gone.

Today, I get caught up talking to Kylee, one of the kids that lives at Wright House. The program is co-ed, but girls and boys have separate wings of the house, and only have interaction during the time designated for specific activities at the home, such as my class.

Kylee approaches me once everyone else has walked out of the room.

"*Ms. Violet, can I talk to you?*" she signs, and I'm impressed with how well she does. She's a little slow, and I can see the look on her face that seems unsure if she's using the correct signs.

"*Of course.*" I smile because she seems nervous about something, and I want to make her feel at ease.

"*I...*" she starts, and I can see she's struggling to find the words, whether it's because she doesn't know the sign or it's hard for her to talk about, I'm not sure.

"*You can use your voice if you aren't sure of the signs or ask.*"

She worries her lip for a second, and I'm not sure if she understood what I said, but she doesn't look confused, just contemplative.

"Some of the other girls have been really nasty to me lately, and I don't know what to do." Kylee shakes her head, and I can tell she's worried about telling me this.

"*What do you mean?*" I ask.

She sighs. "I'm not like the rest of them, not really. I'm only here because I had some small drug charges, and my case worker didn't have anywhere to put me because I run from all my foster homes."

"*What are they doing to you?*"

"Just a bunch of shit. It was petty, just talking behind my back, but now they are getting worse. This morning I woke up and all my clothes were thrown in the shower area completely covered in shaving cream."

I'm a little speechless. I'm not great at giving advice. Actually, I'm not great at giving any advice.

"Have you told Travis?"

"I can't snitch to him, it'll only make it worse," she shakes her head. "I just…you're my favorite staff here and I just wanted to feel like I have someone on my side."

I think about how I should respond to her. Obviously, I should tell her to talk to Travis and that he will make sure nothing happens to her.

On the other hand, I'm not naïve enough to believe that. I know that in life, more often than not, you have to handle shit yourself.

"Okay, look…" I start to tell her, both with my voice and signing as I speak. "Growing up, I had my fair share of bullies, and it might sound cliché, but the best thing I learned was to ignore them. Act better than them because you *are* and let it all roll off your back. Don't let it show that it affects you because that's all they want. A reaction. And you should probably tell Travis, but I'm not going to make you."

Kylee smiles. "Thank you, Ms. Violet. This is why you're my favorite. You understand."

She gives me a smile before waving goodbye. I sigh once I see her leave the doorway, turning back toward the desk, I finish grabbing my things. Once I face the doorway again, I see a deceptively good looking figure leaning against the doorframe.

Rolling my eyes, I start toward him because I will push my way out of this room if I have to.

"That was cute." Trent says as he smiles slowly, showing his perfect teeth, and it makes me even more annoyed at his presence.

"Fuck off."

"I really hope that was something dirty." He winks, and I grimace.

"Who do you think you are?"

"When do you think you'll give into this crazy sexual tension, Flower?"

Flower? Is that because of my name? Barf.

"What sexual tension, I don't even know you!" I sign aggressively because I'm beyond irritated by him alone, and when he opens his mouth, it just gets worse.

"Now, I know that was something dirty." He pushes off the doorframe, holding my gaze as he slowly approaches me.

I should probably be a little uneasy by the way he's slowly

stalking toward me like a predator approaching its prey. I can't find it in me to be scared of him though.

He's big, over six feet and clearly strong, indicated by fabric clinging to his torso and straining from his muscles. Plus, there's the way he's looking at me. His gaze, it's.... *hungry*, and I don't think I've ever experienced this level of intensity from anyone looking at me before.

"You wish."

I don't dare back away, even as he gets closer. I won't show any weakness, not to him. I'm doing exactly what I told Kylee to do, which I'm sure he heard. I'm not giving him the reaction he so badly wants.

He's less than a foot away from me now. I have to lean my head back slightly to be able to watch his face. I refuse to acknowledge the thoughts about how attractive he is now that he's standing so close. His short hair is dark brown, almost black, but his eyes are a light brown, almost amber, and seem like they practically glow. His tan skin has tattoos running along his exposed forearms up past his biceps covered by his shirt sleeve and up onto the sides of his neck. I can't help but wonder how much of his body is covered in ink, but I shake away the thoughts just as quickly.

"What's your deal, Flower?" He tilts his head, and I watch his eyes scan my face.

My deal?

"First, I don't like self-assured, arrogant, assholes who have no

boundaries or patience. Next, you're clearly way too old for me. Lastly, I will never ever fuck you, so stop trying."

With that, I walk past him, bumping my shoulder with his arm as I stomp out of the room.

As soon as I'm in the hallway I take a deep breath. I didn't realize how the air in the room felt so heavy and charged until I'm out of it. I know I should let Travis know I'm leaving, but I can't stand the thought of being in this building anymore.

Before I'm able to move again, my phone vibrates in my pocket. I pull it out to see a text from Jenson that makes me smile because it's exactly what I need.

Jenson: Tomorrow. You. Me. Riot. No arguments.

Riot is my favorite club because I feel like they play the music the loudest, and they play heavy music I can practically feel down to my bones. It's one of my favorite feelings. When things have been tough, I always turned to music, even though I can't hear it or listen to lyrics I can *feel* everything about it. Which is, arguably, a deeper experience. It's less surface level, it's like the music is embedded in my soul.

Violet: I'm in.

I walk out of the house with my head held high, and the whole interaction with Trent a distant memory already.

As I enter the kitchen, I see Mila eating some sort of mush, and I'm sure it's yogurt with fruit or granola or something in it.

I silently gag as I look in the fridge for something actually edible to eat.

I am pretty particular when it comes to textures of food. I'm sensitive with texture period. If fabric on a piece of clothing or blanket is too rough, it will send me into a panic until it's off me. Same goes with food. I will gag and get sick with certain textures.

Yogurt is a no go. Same with milkshakes, melted ice cream, cottage cheese, smoothies. Really anything I consider *mushy*. I can't take it.

There's nothing in the fridge that sounds good, so I end up grabbing an apple from the counter and turning to walk to my room. I notice Mila in my peripheral waving me down. I turn toward her, my eyebrows raised.

"We are going to see dad later," she signs like it's not a big deal.

"Were you even going to ask me?"

"If I did, would you say yes?"

"No."

"Then no."

I roll my eyes, of course she wasn't, and I know she will end up dragging me along kicking and screaming because it's happened before.

"Whatever." I wave her off, turning to go into my room.

I'll probably just find a corner or go to my old bedroom at my dad's house and read until I can leave. It's not like my dad actually notices if I'm there or not since he refuses to talk to me.

Mila and I walk into our dad's house a few hours later, and just like always he greets us with his head down, and I'm sure he says something to Mila, but no use of any sign for me.

I don't even try anymore. I used to try and sign to him to see if it would make a difference. It never did, and then for a while I spoke to him, and he would reply. At least I like to think he did since he couldn't even look at me when he did, so I wasn't able to read his lips. Then eventually I just stopped trying altogether.

"*Hi dad,*" Mila says and signs because for some reason she does still try. I don't know why, we don't talk about how this affects me, but she continues to sign while she speaks to our dad.

He turns around, facing away from us and acts like he's focusing on something in the kitchen. I'm sure he's talking, but I have no idea what he's saying. And just like it always is, I use this as my cue to leave.

Clutching my purse tightly like a security blanket, I head upstairs to the room with skylights that used to be a sort of "hang out" when Mila and I were younger. I think it might have been intended to be a playroom for kids when it was built, but since Mila and I were in high school when we moved here it became more of an activity room. We used to fight over who got to use it when we would have friends over.

Well, she would have friends over I would mostly only have Jenson, but still.

Then, our mom died, and Mila left, and it was no longer a happy room. I would come in here when my thoughts became too overwhelming. Sometimes, I couldn't handle being in my room because I felt suffocated by the memories of my mom kissing my forehead goodnight and telling me she loves me.

This room was where I came to escape. I don't know why, it's only down the hall from my bedroom, but maybe it's the skylights, or how there's the perfect corner to sit in. I truly don't know. It just made me feel calm.

Settling in a dark corner since I don't bother turning the lights on, I pull out my e-reader and continue on with the thriller I'm reading. I feel like I know what's going to happen, and the love interest isn't who he says he is, but I have to know for sure.

The faint light streaming through the sunlight fades as the sun sets, casting the room in a blanket of darkness. I barely look up as I fall into my book. I have always been able to become so immersed in the stories I read. They used to take me away from my reality when things were really bad, and I liked being able to live through someone else's eyes.

I don't realize how long I've been up here until Mila nudges my foot with her own. I can't see her so I shine the light from my device, and she signs to me that we should leave.

Good.

I nod, and we leave the house. I hope that as we are leaving my dad will acknowledge me. Stop me from leaving and say something to me. *Anything.*

I'm disappointed as always when I don't even see him as we walk out the front door, and to Mila's car. I don't say anything to her as she drives us the short distance back to our apartment. I used to ask if he talked about me. Asked about me.

Yet another thing I stopped doing when it comes to my dad. If he's not going to make an effort, then neither am I.

THE NEXT DAY I don't have to work, but I realized I forgot my binder I use to lesson plan at work. I don't necessarily need to get it, but I like to feel prepared before I go in or else, I feel anxious. Jenson is already on his way over because he wanted to spend the day together before going to Riot tonight. I'll just ask if we can swing by Wright House before doing whatever else he wants to do today.

After a significant amount of complaining, Jenson drove me to work. I quickly grabbed my binder from the classroom and avoided any further interactions with the asshole who feels the need to bother me every chance he can.

Jenson is leaning against the driver's side as I approach, heading toward the passenger door.

"Got what you need?" he asks, and I just hold up the binder in response.

As I'm opening the door I feel a slight rumble under my feet, and I can't help but think what asshole is overcompensating with what is probably an overly obnoxious souped-up Honda Civic.

Suddenly the source of the rumble appears, parking next to Jenson's car and it turns out I was half right. It is some overcompensating asshole, but he drives a motorcycle and wears a cocky smirk as soon as he removes his helmet. His amber eyes staring right at me. My face involuntarily pulls into a scowl.

The car shakes under my hand before I flick my eyes to Jenson who is giving me a pointed look after hitting the top to get my attention.

"Who's that?" Jenson asks with a raised eyebrow.

My scowl deepens as I slowly fingerspell Trent's name, hoping he will recognize it and know we are talking about him. Though, I know it isn't the case since he doesn't know a single sign.

"That's Trent?" Jenson signs enthusiastically, before glancing back at the asshole who is still looking right at me as he swings his leg over the bike. "*You said he was hot, but you didn't say he looks like some sort of god.*"

"More like the Devil," I say, scowling even more.

Trent approaches us, and I can see Jenson's face remains a lot more interested than mine. Especially once Trent opens his mouth to speak, I watch his annoyingly full lips as he forms the words.

"You leaving already, Flower?"

9

Trent

Present

When I pulled up, I saw Violet talking to some guy outside a car. I watched their interaction longer than I care to admit as the misplaced jealousy burned in my chest at the thought this could be her boyfriend.

That jealousy intensified when I saw them signing to each other because he is clearly able to communicate with her in a way I can't. I gauge his reaction as I approach them. Violet has kept her adorable scowl on her face since she first saw me, and I'm sure it would only deepen if she realized how that face made my cock hard for her.

"You leaving already, Flower?" I ask, as they both continue to look at me.

"Flower?" the guy questions after a beat of silence. He also moves his hands as he speaks, assumingely signing for Violet.

That's when an idea pops into my head.

Ignoring his question because I don't need to give him the reason for the nickname. I turn my head slightly to him but keep my head forward enough that Violet can read my lips.

"I'm Trent. Who are you?"

The guy looks a little taken aback by my tone, glancing at Violet quickly before looking back at me. I see her eyes narrow even more.

"Um, I'm Jenson."

I nod once in acknowledgment. "Jenson, are you Violet's boyfriend?"

He snorts a laugh. "No, just a friend."

"Good, I would hate to have to hurt you." Jenson's face blanches, and Violet bangs her hand on the roof of the car before signing something to Jenson.

He turns his head back to me before saying, "We gotta go."

"Translate for me." I say to stop him from getting in the car.

Violet bangs her hand on the roof again before signing something clearly directed at me, but she knows I don't understand. I give a pointed look to Jenson to signal him to tell me what she said.

He looks over to her, then back at me with a sigh. "She said it's 'interpret', not translate, you ignorant piece of shit."

I can see his shoulders scrunch at the insult, but it only makes me smile since it came from my feisty little flower.

That's what they don't know. Neither of them knows why I decided to call her that, probably assuming it's due to her name. It's not, though. She reminds me of other types of flowers, ones with thorns or an oleander.

Beautiful, but dangerous to man, especially if they have a taste. Too bad for her, I'm always drawn to danger, and it only makes me want her more.

"Interpret for me then," I correct, my eyes not leaving Violet's.

She brings her pointer finger, and middle finger together, snapping them down to meet her thumb quickly.

"Any chance that means 'yes'?" I question, though with the look on her face I know the chances are low.

Violet just does the same motion again, so I look at Jenson. He just shakes his head.

"Does it mean 'shut up'?" I feel like this is more likely.

She repeats the motion once again, so I raise my eyebrow to Jenson. He sighs again before answering.

"No, it means 'no'."

I raise my eyes to meet hers again over the top of the car. "You don't want to have a conversation with me, Flower?"

She rolls her eyes before signing more.

Once she's done, I glance at Jenson waiting for him to tell me what she said. He seems conflicted on being in the middle of this with Violet clearly signaling him not to interpret.

He sounds exasperated before finally telling me what she said. "No, I don't want to talk to you. If you want to have a conversation with me, you'll learn sign, and until then you can go back to the hell you came from."

My smile widens at her obvious anger toward me. "Oh, pretty Flower, I spent the last five years in hell, and now that I'm free I intend to take full advantage. You both have a good day."

I turn to walk into the building before seeing her reaction. Violet may talk a big game, with her clear hatred toward me, but what she doesn't realize is that I don't stop until I get what I want.

My eyes are set on her, and whether she realizes it or not, she's already mine.

My day at the Wright House is boring as always. I mostly just sit and make sure none of the kids fight or fuck each other. I'm supposed to be interacting and shit, but if anyone actually believes that's going to happen, they are delusional.

Once I leave, I have one goal in mind for tonight, and that's to go where I know Violet is going to be. I want an interaction with her that isn't at work, though I'm sure the outcome will be the same, I don't care. I just want more of her. I've never been so drawn to anyone. I would blame the five years of celibacy, but I know that isn't the only reason.

I was surrounded by half naked girls at the club the other night, and if my track record is anything to go off of, I know I could bring home anyone I want. I really can't explain why I haven't at this point, five years of just my hand has made me crave pussy like crazy. Though every time I think of fucking someone, it's Violet's face I see.

Maybe it's the appeal, and the thought that I have to work for it. Maybe it's because she fights me, and I've always enjoyed the fight because it's so much more satisfying when they finally give in. Either way, I want to fuck her and find out. Then she can be out of my system, and we can both move on with our lives.

I don't do more than a one-night stand anyway. I don't get attached to anyone because I've seen how that turns out and that is not the life for me. My dad taught me no woman is worth it, and I've seen with my own eyes what can happen when you think things might be different.

I park my bike outside the club, Riot, the music so loud and the bass so strong I hear it in the parking lot. After Violet walked out of the room yesterday, I watched her, and looked over her shoulder to see the text about coming here tonight.

There are a million other things I know I should be doing

other than this, but I push those thoughts to the back of my mind. I'll deal with more shit tomorrow, tonight I want to see if I can get my flower to let me have a taste.

The music inside is so loud I feel the vibrations in my chest. I really am not a fan of places like this, but I'm going to make this night worth it.

There's an upstairs that has a view of the entire first floor of the club, I make my way up where I'm informed it's the VIP section. I expected that, and pay off the bouncer to let me in. There's a separate bar up here where I grab a glass of whiskey before taking my place at the railing so I can look for Violet.

The first floor is full of people dancing so close together they all are practically grinding against each other purely because they don't have the room not to. I scan the crowd for the familiar blonde head of hair. The lights are low, but I'll know once I see her.

After a few minutes I spot her. The glow of the lights illuminating her like that's their sole purpose. She's dancing with her arms above her head, body swaying in the crowd like she doesn't care about all the people around.

I spot her friend, Jenson, dancing close to her, and even though they said they are friends it makes my hackles rise. This possessiveness is new for me, and I don't particularly enjoy it. But I don't want anyone else touching her.

That's when I see a different guy approach her from behind. I watch him slide his hands tentatively around her waist. She doesn't seem to mind as she continues to dance and doesn't push him away.

I continue to watch the scene unfold in front of me, waiting to see if she will push him away. She doesn't. Instead, she turns around to face him and continues to dance, pressing her body against his.

I'm squeezing the glass in my hand tightly, if the music wasn't so loud, I might have heard a crack. Downing the rest of my drink I storm down to the first floor.

Both Violet and this guy are going to regret the second his hands touched her as soon as I reach them. The area is packed, but I make a determined beeline toward them. Jenson notices me first and looks at me wide eyed in recognition. I narrow my eyes at him in a signal to not say anything. For a moment I'm not sure if he will listen, but he does.

I press my body close to Violet's back and wrap my arm around her waist to pull her back against me. And away from the douchebag at her front. I feel her tense in my arms slightly but she continues to dance.

I give a hard glare at the man in front of her signaling him to leave without saying anything. He seems to take a moment, debating what he's going to do before deciding to walk away. As he turns to walk away Violet's movements slow even more as I feel the tension in her body increases.

Pressing her tightly against me I breathe her in before allowing her to turn around and ruin this because I know once she sees it's me, she's going to run for the hills. The top of her head is right under my nose, allowing me to become overwhelmed by her coconut and floral scent. What a perfect combination for my flower.

Violet's movements stop completely, and she pushes against the hold I have on her. I turn her around, keeping a tight grip on her hips so she can't instantly run away. As soon as she is facing me, I watch her mouth open slightly in shock, and her eyes flare with anger.

"Hey, Flower," I say without raising my voice since there's no need to yell over the music, she knows what I said.

She shakes her head, planting her hands on my chest, trying to push me away. I don't let her go, tightening my hold on her.

"Aren't you happy to see me?" I smile while she continues to try and get away from me.

She stops pushing at me for a second, and signs something I can only assume is telling me to let her go. I shake my head.

"I just want one dance, Flower."

She scowls. *"No."*

I smile since that's the one sign I know for sure now.

I squeeze her hips. "Just one."

She winces, and I see the indecision in her eyes burning along with her hatred. Without saying anything else she presses her chest against mine, her eyes not leaving mine. My cock throbs at the feeling of her tits pressed against me, and I band my arm around her.

Just when I think she's going to start fighting me again she starts swaying her hips slightly, brushing my quickly hardening cock with every movement. I can't help the low groan that escapes my throat.

Violet's eyes haven't left mine as her movements become more purposeful and she's fully dancing against me. She looks like she's challenging me in this moment, and it just makes me want her more. I press her hard against my pelvis so she can see how hard I am, and almost miss the slight gasp she lets out.

Our hips move against each other, neither of us saying anything, purely communicating with our eyes. Hers full of distaste and mine full of lust. I move one of my hands up her back until it's tangled in her hair, pulling her head back so I can get a full look at her face.

She scowls even harder at my movement, and I smile, but she doesn't push me away. Her movements against me continue, as I lean down, running my nose along her jaw, then her neck just taking her all in. She allows it to happen with her hands tightening against my shoulders.

I run my lips lightly over the sensitive skin of her throat as I move my mouth back up to her jaw, peeking my tongue out to lick her skin for a second just to get the smallest taste of her. My lips hover over hers, so close our breath is mingling in the small space between us. Her nails dig into my shoulders as I hold her tighter against me, dying to close the minimal distance between our lips.

She peeks her tongue out to lick her lips, and it grazes

against mine briefly, and I snap, needing to taste her. My lips crash against hers, and I bite her bottom lip quickly before she's pushing me away as hard as she can, and I unwillingly let her. The disdain on her face is obvious along with confusion. Her chest is heaving as she stares at me before turning to push her way through the crowd, away from me.

10

Violet

Present

What the fuck is wrong with me?

I was just trying to taunt him. I liked feeling his desire for me, knowing nothing would ever happen. I wanted to tease him. I could feel that he wanted me, it's not like he's hidden it. Then he kissed me, and I freaked out.

That was why I had to get away because I don't know if I wanted him to kiss me, or not and I can't deal with feeling conflicted.

I can't stand him.

I *do not want him.*

At least that's what I'm telling myself.

Pushing my way through the crowd I get to the hallway that

leads to the bathroom, fully intending to go in there, splash some water on my face and maybe convince Jenson to leave. I don't want my night to be ruined by this asshole, but I clearly can't trust myself to be around him with the alcohol running through my bloodstream. It might have something to do with how unnaturally attractive that man is, and my body likes what it sees, even if my brain doesn't.

He's an asshole who only wants you for one thing, Violet.

The more space I get from him the more my rational brain begins to work again. I know nothing will happen with Trent. I won't let it. He's too much of everything I want nothing to do with.

Suddenly, I feel a hand clamp around my arm, pulling me back. My back is slammed against the wall before I'm able to reach the bathroom. Breath escapes my lungs, and I almost scream as the hard body traps me against the wall, and I see it's the man I have been trying to get away from.

"Why'd you run? Things were just getting good."

"Let me go," I sign, and I know he doesn't know what I'm saying. I know I could easily tell him off in a way he *will* understand, and yet I continue to sign instead.

"Come on Flower, I know you want this. Why continue to fight?"

The lighting in this hallway is dark, and he's so close it's hard to read his lips, but I get the gist of what he's saying, and it makes me scoff.

"I don't want this." And I don't know how he knows I actually do. Not that I'll admit that to him.

Trent smirks, adjusting his body so his thigh is forced between my own, and I suck in a sharp intake of breath.

"I bet if I reached in your little panties, I would find you soaked for me, wouldn't I?"

I try to wiggle away from his hold, but it only results in me rubbing myself on his thigh slightly, the friction sending a wave of electricity through me. I bite my lip to stop the gasp from the delicious feeling. I fight back the urge to rub myself harder against him because I'm still trying to convince myself that *I don't want this.*

"*No.*" I lie.

If I were to speak the word right now, I know it would come out weak, but my sign is much more confident.

He smiles, and it's almost sinister. Everything about him screams dangerous, and I know there's something about him that should make me afraid. I know his cocky persona is because he's used to getting what he wants and it doesn't matter who he has to hurt in the process. I know at this moment what he wants is me, despite my constant denial. But he's never going to get me.

"Should I find out?" He presses closer to me, his thigh rubbing against my throbbing clit again, and this time I can't stop the squeak I let out. I know he heard it by the way his eyes darken.

I shake my head in response, because now I don't even trust my hand not to shake around a single sign.

"Seems like I might not need to. I could make you come by just rubbing my thigh on your little clit, couldn't I?" He presses again, and I can't help the way my hips rub against him. The friction feels too good, and I hate that he's right. I could come like this. It wouldn't take much either.

I shake my head again, but I'm also slightly aware that I'm pulling him against me more. Trent drops his head against my neck, trailing his lips. I feel his hot breath and soft lips as they trail along my throat. I lean my head back, my head hitting the wall behind me as I give him better access.

My subconscious is screaming at me to push him away again. The arguments are dulled by the drinks in my system, and the overpowering feeling of an impending orgasm from the perfect way his leg is rubbing against me. I refuse to let him know how desperately I want this. Or want him at this moment.

Trent's lips become harder against my neck, and jaw until I feel his teeth scrape where his lips were, and my hips increase their movement. I know I should stop. I don't want him. I don't want this, but I'm blinded by how good everything feels. I'm blinded by the way my body becomes pliant in his arms so easily.

No, I need to stop this. I need to get away from him and *stay away*. I need to –

I feel the wall shake slightly behind my back, differently than how it was a dull vibration from the music. I look to the side to see Jenson is now in the hallway and is banging his hand on the wall giving me a confused look.

That's all it takes to snap me out of this insane lust filled moment with Trent, and I push him away, panting from how close I was to release. My mind is coming back into focus, and I realize I was about to give in. For a moment I would've given him whatever he wanted. That would've been the dumbest decision I'd ever made, and I know I would regret it instantly.

Shit, I regret this whole thing already.

I need to keep my distance from him. I clearly can't trust myself.

Pushing my hair into place, I walk toward Jenson who is looking at me with both curiosity, and concern. I don't say anything as I walk past him, knowing he will follow. I really don't want to go home yet, but I know if I'm in proximity to Trent any longer I might continue what we started, and I just can't do that.

I don't dare look behind me to see Trent again. I don't know if he and Jenson say anything to each other, and I don't want to. If I can help it, I'll never see his stupidly handsome face again.

Jenson finally catches up to me. *"What was that?"*

I wave him off, I really don't want to talk about it. I don't know what I can even say.

Once we are outside, and I'm hit with the still warm summer air I take a deep breath, finally feeling like my mind isn't completely clouded.

Jenson steps in front of me with a raised eyebrow. *"I thought we didn't want the too-sexy-for-his-own-good jerk in there."*

"I don't."

"That's not what I saw."

"What you saw was me drunk in a weak moment and him taking advantage of that."

"You don't seem that drunk to me."

He's not completely wrong. I'm exaggerating slightly. I'm not drunk. Slightly buzzed, but aware that I am capable of controlling my own actions. And was Trent taking advantage of me? *Not completely.* He took advantage of a moment, but in a way, so did I. I'm questioning everything that just happened now that I'm able to be somewhat rational. I refuse to take any of the blame for what just happened. That was all him…*right?*

"Let's go home." I ignore his comment about me being drunk as I call for an Uber on my phone.

"You know, it's okay to want a little fun sometimes," Jenson signs slowly, almost like he's nervous to say that to me.

"I do have fun. I was having plenty of it before Trent tried to shove his tongue in my mouth and accost me in the hallway."

The side of Jenson's lip tugs up in a slight smile.

"You looked pretty willing for all of it, just saying."

I ignore him again, refusing to justify him with any sort of response.

Mostly because I don't have one to give since I don't even know how I'm feeling about what just happened. I refuse to accept that I may have been more willing than I want to admit.

11

Trent

25 Years Ago (Age 10)

I haven't told my dad about what I found out about Mom, but I haven't been talking to her much. She will try to have normal conversations at dinner, and I just shrug or give one-word answers. I know my dad can tell something is up with me, but he doesn't push it.

I've heard them talking at night when they think I've gone to bed. Dad asks if Mom knows what's going on with me, and she just denies knowing anything. It only makes me more pissed at her. Lie after lie after lie.

It's like she doesn't even care.

"Don't forget you have piano tomorrow," my mom says at dinner after a particularly awkward amount of silence.

"Not going."

"What? Why not? You love piano." She sounds surprised.

I do like piano, and I'm pretty good at it, but it's something she wanted me to try, and something she always takes me to. That alone makes me not want to do it anymore.

I shrug, "I want to go with Dad tomorrow."

"Go with Dad, where?" she questions, looking over at him.

"The guys and I are going to the country club for some poker tomorrow, you sure you want to come with, champ?"

"Yeah, I want you to keep teaching me how to play."

My dad nods, while Mom looks between us a little shocked like she didn't know about any of this. It makes me want to laugh. She can't act surprised with the number of secrets she's holding herself.

"Chris, isn't he a little young to learn to play poker with you and your friends?" she asks through gritted teeth, and I can't help the smile that I hide when I look down.

"Of course not. He likes it, and it's good to learn how to perfect a poker face young, isn't it, son?"

I nod. "It's more useful than piano."

My mom looks shocked, and a little hurt, but I don't particularly care.

"Fine, you can skip tomorrow, but you should practice some

tonight then." She looks down at her plate, clearly upset at this conversation.

"Nope, I don't want to." I push back from the table. "Can I be excused?"

"No."

"Yes."

My parents answer at the same time with differing answers, my mom clearly wanting me to stay.

"Thanks Dad." I ignore her completely as I take my plate to the sink before walking back to my room.

Their voices are quiet. I can hear my mom asking my dad what is going on with me, and something about them needing to be a united front with me. I don't hide my laugh before I get to my room. I shut the door behind me, cutting off their voices before I can hear more and reveal my mom's big secret.

It's always bubbling at the surface, and it's already been a month without her telling him. I don't know if I'll be able to keep it in any longer, my dad thinks everything is normal with our family, and it's not fair to him.

It's not fair to me.

The keyboard in my room is tempting to play right now. In all honesty, I do like playing. It is a way to get out my emotions when all I want to do is hit something. Both my parents have said I've always been an emotional kid, especially angry.

They tried to put me into different activities to get out the "emotions". Piano stuck because of the way I have to focus on the music, and the way the notes flow together. It's enough to silence the anger simmering inside, but it was always something I did with my mom.

It makes the anger so much worse, and instead of trying to calm it by playing the keyboard it makes me want to smash it. I kick the stand over, so it goes toppling to the floor before I throw myself onto my bed and scream into the pillow.

I just want everything to go back to how it was. I wish I didn't know what my mom was doing behind my dad's back, and I wish I could just tell him.

I hate her. I hate what she's done to us. All of us.

12

Trent

Present

I decided not to follow Violet after the situation in the hallway. If anything, that whole interaction makes me want to reevaluate my priorities when it comes to her. Or forget about her entirely.

I'm clearly wasting time, and don't usually need to work this hard to get a woman to fuck me, so I really should just move on from her.

But I can't.

I'm fucking addicted.

Everything she does just makes me want her more. Forbidden fruit and all that shit. The fact that she clearly can't stand me makes the thought of being with her all the more appealing. There's nothing better than hate sex. Nothing.

As I'm walking out of the club my phone rings. I see the blocked number, and I know exactly who it is.

"Dad," I answer once I'm outside.

"Trent, I hear you're out of the shit hole."

"Obviously."

I make my way over to my bike, hoping to get off this call in less than thirty seconds.

"Good. Meet me at Whiskey's in an hour."

Whiskey's is a member only bar that requires a hefty payment every month to keep your membership active. It's known as a safe place for certain businessmen to do their business without eavesdroppers or potential snitches. If anyone is suspected of being a rat, they are taken care of.

"Nah, I'm good," I finally respond.

"I didn't ask if you were good, son. We need to talk, and get some shit figured out. I'll see you there." He hangs up before I even have the chance to say anything else.

As much as I want to defy my dad, and not show up, I know it'll just make our inevitable meeting worse. That's what I tell myself as I make my way to Whiskey's early, so I have a drink or seven before I see him.

Once I'm at the exclusive bar I decide seven drinks isn't the best, but I still have two before I see my father, Chris Moore, walk into the bar. I've always been told I look like him, but I've never seen it. Now that I'm thirty-five, I see some resemblance and I hate it. He's in his late fifties but doesn't look like it. His brown hair has grayed, but he's still larger than life, just like he's been my entire life.

Downing the rest of my old fashioned before standing to greet him.

"Son," he nods in my direction.

"Dad," I do the same.

No handshake. No hug. Nothing that would indicate any sort of close relationship, and that's because there isn't one. Not anymore.

He looks me over, no doubt assessing my slacks and button up with the sleeves rolled to my elbows. He's probably wondering why I'm not in a suit like him, but I don't care. He can judge me all he wants; I wasn't planning on this meeting.

With a silent command, he gestures me to one of the back booths. I consider not following him because I know this power dynamic, but I also know we do have things to talk about. First and foremost, him getting his shit out of my business. I don't want to deal in women, and he's known that. Drugs and willing sex, sure. Selling women who have been forced is not my area of interest.

As soon as my dad sits in the booth, he waves down a waitress. I'm slower to slide into the booth, leaning back while crossing my ankle over my knee to show how unaffected I am by this meeting. By him.

I order another old fashioned with the intention to drink it slowly, so I don't end up drunk. The waitress leaves, and I purposely look around, trying my best to ignore the man in front of me, and hoping we can get this over with quickly.

"So," he begins, "how was your time locked up? You look…different."

I chuckle. "Different is one way to put it, old man."

Five years of working out daily and adding tattoos to my collection on my body. I look significantly *different* from the last time I saw him.

"Careful, boy, you may look like a man, but I'm still your father."

Now, that earns a full laugh from me.

"I don't know what being a father means to you, but you haven't been one in a long time."

His eyes narrow, and I can tell this conversation isn't over, but talking about our shit relationship is not something he does so willingly, and today is certainly not the time to do so.

"I guess now that you're back you should be caught up on what has been going on with our businesses."

"Mine," I snap.

"What?"

"My businesses you mean. And I had them handled from the inside."

"I'm sure you did, son. I made them better, so you'd come back to success rather than struggle."

"Do you expect me to thank you?"

He folds his arms across his chest, regarding me.

"I think it deserves a thank you, but I'm not naïve enough to think I'll get it."

"I'm glad you realize that. Now, you can go back to Arizona and don't worry about what I'm doing."

Now it's his turn to chuckle.

"I don't think so, I quite like it here. I think I'm going to stay a little longer, maybe plant some roots here."

As much as I hate that idea, and want to convince him otherwise, I know if I give a bigger reaction, it will only spur him on. So, I don't fight against what he's saying. I just give a subtle nod.

"That's up to you, but you can take your women with you, I don't need them in my clubs."

Before he has a chance to respond the waitress returns with our drinks. She walks away, but our conversation doesn't continue right away. I see the calculating look on his face. I know what he looks like when he's trying to have a poker face, I mean, he's the man who taught me how to have one in the first place.

The irony of him teaching me every trick and skill he has up his sleeve has only increased as I've gotten older. He wants to stay ahead of me, wants to always be better, but I was able to learn, adapt, and adjust. Clearly, the stint in prison was not ideal, but even that taught me shit he will never know.

"Something wrong with my women in your clubs?" he finally asks.

"The ones you bought, yeah. I don't want them there unless they are willing."

"Trust me, son, they are willing. You don't know what their lives were like before. I'm saving them."

I laugh. "I'm glad to see your God complex hasn't gone anywhere."

"Not a God complex when I truly am doing good."

I really can't tell if he's grown more delusional or just wants me to believe him.

"Get them out of my clubs by the end of the week." I take a large sip from my drink.

"Or else what, son? You can't give half threats; I've taught you better than that."

"You're right, you did. But you also taught me not to show

my hand, and that's exactly what I'm doing. Get out of my business. I have it handled."

I stand up from the table, done with this conversation, and done with him. As I'm walking away, I hear his voice behind me, but I don't stop to acknowledge his words.

"You need me, son. And I'll prove that to you."

13

6 Years Ago (Age 15)

I've never thought much about death. Never had any experience with it other than my goldfish when I was seven.

But death just slapped me across the face while pulling the floor out from underneath me and I feel like I've been free falling since my mom first told us she was sick.

I didn't understand. I still don't understand. She was only forty. How is it even possible? Why did this happen? I've wanted to scream. I've wanted to cry. I've wanted to break everything around me, but also be held by her for as long as I could.

And now I'll never get the chance to be in her arms again.

She's gone.

It was only a month ago she sat Mila and I down and told us

she was sick. She said she was going to fight. She did, but apparently the cancer had taken over too much of her body.

It's just not fair.

It's not. Fucking. Fair.

Now here I am in the cemetery. The weather is crying with us, as Mila and I stand huddled under the same umbrella staring at the stone that has our mom's name on it.

Joanna Susan Pederson.
Beloved mother and wife.

My dad hasn't spoken to me since she died.

He talks to Mila, but that's just it. He talks. He doesn't sign.

My mom signed to me until her body was too weak to raise her hands anymore, and I understood. She apologized. She told me she wished I wouldn't remember her like this, and that she wanted to continue to sign to me.

I wasn't upset with her when she couldn't sign anymore. I just wanted her here. I would give up everything to just have her back.

Mila nudges me, and I look up at her. Our eyes look similarly red rimmed and swollen from crying constantly over this past month.

"Dad said it's time to go," she says.

I sigh. I've never felt like I missed out on conversations in my family because they always sign for me. But now that my dad has stopped, I feel like an outsider with Mila needing to interpret constantly.

Plus, our dad won't even really look at us which makes it impossible to read his lips. And he won't look at me to see what I'm trying to tell him.

I just want things to be back to how they were before.

I want my family back.

14

Present

"Seriously, tell me how it was. He looks like a good kisser. He looks like he's good at everything." Jenson has been harping me about the other night *constantly* and I won't tell him anything because I'm trying to forget it even happened.

"*You're a shitty friend, you know that?*" I tell him with an eye roll, as I walk out of frame from the Facetime we are on so I can change into my sleeping t-shirt and shorts.

I can still see Jenson as he says, "*If you don't want him then I will gladly take him off your hands.*"

After I'm dressed again, I reply, "*Be my guest.*"

"*You don't want to compete with me.*"

I chuckle which turns into a yawn. *"I'm going to bed, feel free to find Trent to spend your night with."*

Jenson smiles. "*Don't tempt me. Goodnight.*"

I end the call with a wave. As I'm scrolling through my ebook library trying to decide what book to download next, I get a notification from the only social media I use, though I rarely get on it anyway. It's an Instagram message, and I cringe when I see who it's from.

Trent: Hello Flower.

Ignoring the message, I take my phone with me into the kitchen to grab some water before I go to bed. I see there's two men I don't recognize in the kitchen. Hesitating for a moment, I debate going back into my room and calling the police, but then I see Mila is there talking to them.

I approach slowly, trying to keep myself hidden until I can read their lips to at least try and figure out who these guys are. Luckily, I'm wearing my hearing aids which helps me lipread properly.

"I'm trying," Mila says to them.

One of the guys is extremely good-looking. He's the one that replies to Mila. "We aren't saying you're not. There's just a lot more going on that we need to figure out and need you to dig around."

"I said I'm trying." Mila looks annoyed.

The other guy, who is also handsome, but doesn't look as

loaded with muscle as the other man says, "You're good Mila, we know you are. This isn't an attack on you, we just wanted to let you know."

I have no idea what they are talking about, and what is going on. What is Mila good at? What is she trying? *What is happening?*

Without meaning to, I must have made a noise because their heads swing in my direction.

Oops.

"*I thought you were sleeping.*" Mila looks scared, looking toward the men then back to me as I walk toward them.

"*Who are these guys?*" I ignore her comment about me sleeping. It's not even that late, and I'm not a child.

I see her hesitance, and I know my sister well enough to know she doesn't want me to know them. Too bad I don't care about what she wants. So instead of waiting for her to make a decision I place my phone on the counter and stretch my hand out to the really good looking one. He has brown hair, hazel eyes and a body rivaling a body builder. He could crush me if he wanted to.

"I'm Violet," I say, mostly just to piss off Mila.

He smiles, and it only made him even better looking. "Nate," he replies.

I reach over to the other guy, who is also good looking. Dark hair, his skin is darker than Nate's, which only makes his gray eyes practically glow. "Mitch." He smiles.

"How do you know my sister and why are you here?" I ask, still ignoring Mila. I can feel her eyes on me, burning holes in my back.

Nate and Mitch look at each other, and it seems like they aren't sure of what to say. They look behind me, and that's when I acknowledge Mila for the first time, but only because she's looking at my phone on the counter. I grab it, holding it against my chest, but she saw something.

"Who's that?" she asks.

"You answer me first, who are they?"

"I'll tell you when you tell me who's calling you Flower."

I groan, turning back toward the unnaturally attractive men in my kitchen. "Do either of you have siblings?"

They both laugh, and Nate answers first, "Nope."

Lucky.

"I have three brothers," Mitch says

"Gross," I mumble. "So, who are you?"

"We are detectives," Mitch answers for them.

I turn back to Mila. "*Are you in trouble?*"

"No. I work with them, kind of."

"You're a bartender."

"I said kind of."

Narrowing my eyes at her I feel like there is a lot to get into with this, but not right now apparently. I try to turn back toward the men, but Mila stops me with a hand on my arm.

"Who was that on your phone?"

Rolling my eyes, I reluctantly answer. "Just some guy, Trent, at Wright House, who won't leave me alone."

Her eyes go wide as she looks over me to Nate and Mitch. "Trent?" she asks me with sign and says to them at the same time. "Trent what?"

"I don't know. Don't care." I shrug. "So, which one of you is dating my sister?" I ask, purely to embarrass her. She smacks me on the back.

"Not me, I have a girl at home and an eleven-year-old daughter," Nate answers with a smile on his face.

Mitch just gives me a small smile when he says, "I'm happily single."

"Interesting…" I begin, but I'm yanked back again by Mila.

"You're done with this. But you need to tell me who this Trent is."

Mila has never been protective of me and has definitely

never asked about any guys that I've talked to before. Not that I'm talking to Trent. We just kissed a little, and it'll never happen again.

"No, I don't." I shrug her hand off me and choose to remove myself from this kitchen now.

Before I can leave, Nate waves his hand, signaling me to look at him. He has his phone in his hand, and he pushes it toward me on the counter. "Is that the Trent you know?"

Glancing down at his phone, I see a mugshot. It's of a handsome man with dark hair, amber eyes, and a face I recognize. He doesn't have the tattoos on his neck like he does now, and he looks a few years younger. But it's him, there's no doubt about that.

Looking back up at Nate, I nod. Then, I feel like I'm invisible in my own house. Nate and Mitch are talking, not looking toward me so I can't really read their lips. I try to look back at Mila to see if she is interpreting for me. She's not, and she's talking to them as well, but she clearly doesn't want me to know what is being said.

I try to follow the conversation, but Mila is purposely hiding her mouth from me, and I'm not able to keep up with the back and forth. She knows how much this pisses me off, and that it's not okay to do. As I grow more frustrated by the lack of including me, I slam my hand down on the counter to get their attention.

"Don't talk like I'm not here when clearly, what you're talking about, has something to do with me."

Nate takes a moment before speaking, "I was trying to see if your sister would be okay with you helping us with our investigation."

Now, I'm intrigued.

"Good thing I'm a consenting adult, and don't need my sister's permission. Lay it on me." I tell him confidently, but then Mila forces me to look back at her.

"You don't know what this is about, it's not safe. Trent isn't a good dude, and you need to stay out of it."

I scoff. *"You don't think I can do it. Well guess what? I can. And I'm going to."*

"It's not that I don't think you can it's the fact that this is dangerous. These people are dangerous. Criminals, Vi, you could get hurt."

"I'm doing it."

I don't give her a chance to respond before I turn back to Mitch and Nate. "Tell me everything."

They hesitate again, and it makes me think they don't believe in me either. It causes my frustration to ramp up once again. I'm about to say something to them when Nate speaks, looking straight at me.

"I don't know about telling you everything yet. Short version is, Trent is involved in some serious stuff and has been for a while which is why he spent five years in prison. When he was away the businesses and connections kept growing so we knew it wasn't just him. We finally have a name, and it's believed to be Trent's father, Chris Moore. We don't know who is doing what exactly, but if you have a connection to Trent, and a way to get close to him you may be able to find out how he's involved. Then, maybe we could get enough information to get Chris behind bars."

It was hard to follow everything he was saying, but I appreciated him not speaking too fast. Now, I'm processing, and I knew Trent was a shitty guy. I could feel it even though I didn't have any hard evidence.

"So, you want me to...get close to him?" I ask hesitantly.

"And get information, yeah," Nate says.

I know this is probably going to be something I'll regret. I know I'm going to be putting myself in the middle of a shit storm. I know getting close to Trent is going to kill me inside. Despite all of that, I find myself answering anyway.

"I'm in."

15

Trent

19 Years Ago (Age 16)

I slam the cards down in front of me, announcing my win to the other guys at the table. The smell of smoke and booze is thick in the air, and it fuels me, though I don't take part in either.

The guys groan at my hand as I pull the pile of money toward me.

"Trent," I hear my dad's voice call from behind me.

"Well, this has been fun, we will do it again soon." I tell the men at the table as I collect the money.

Walking out with my dad, he asks how I did tonight.

"Pretty good, though I think some of them still have some money in their pockets, so not good enough."

"That's my boy," he nods his head in my direction before we climb into his car.

"Where are we going now?" I ask as he starts driving.

"Meeting with some suppliers."

I've been going with my dad on some of his business ventures to learn more about what he does since my parents divorced five years ago. I used to go to my mom's every other weekend, but over the last couple years I've made excuses to get out of most of my visits with her.

She tried...at first. Tried to make up for being a shitty mother. Tried to make up for ruining our family. I just couldn't get past it. I don't even know how my dad found out about her affair, all I know is that he did and then they were divorced.

My dad hasn't gotten remarried. I know he never will again. He sees women, I guess dates them at least for a short period of time. I only know because sometimes they are around when we are out doing things, but he never brings them home. And I've learned I never want to get married or have any serious relationship. At least I can thank mommy dearest for that.

My phone pings in my hand, I glance at who texted me before shoving the phone in my pocket without replying.

"Who's that?" Dad asks.

I shrug. "Just some girl I've seen a couple times."

And by seen, I mean fucked.

Dad grunts in response. "What's her name?"

"Doesn't matter, she's no one."

"You're smart, son. Smarter than I was at your age."

"Learned from the best."

"Speaking of no one. Have you heard from your mom lately?"

I shift in my seat before answering him. "Yeah, she tries to call at least once a week."

"When was the last time you answered?"

I shrug. "Not since I saw her a couple weeks ago."

It was her birthday, and I was guilted into spending some time with her, though I hated every single second of it. She tried to get me to talk about what I enjoy doing. She asked about piano. I wouldn't admit to her I still play sometimes. I haven't taken any lessons since the divorce, but I hate that I do enjoy playing. That's the only reason I haven't given it up completely yet.

Though, I'll never tell her that.

"She's so selfish, I'm glad you see it now. Glad you see how she ruined our family."

I nod. "It's bullshit."

"That's why you're not going to make the same mistakes I

did. That's why I'm teaching you about all of this so you can be successful, make a fuck ton of money, and not worry about some bitch coming in trying to take it."

"I like learning from you, Pops."

"As you should, now let me tell you what I'm going to need you to do when we go into this meeting."

16

Present

Since meeting with my dad, I put a few of my guys in charge of getting his dealings out of my clubs. The people, the drugs from *his* suppliers. Anything and anyone having to do with Chris Moore is gone.

I want things to go back to how they were before. I facilitate a lot of the business behind the scenes, and have other people deal with the bullshit I don't want to. Unfortunately, due to my absence I'm having to deal with a shit ton more than I would like.

Which is the only reason I'm here now. I meet Jason at the table in the back where I punched Dagger last time I was here. I glance around to look over the girls, making sure they all look legal and sober.

The biggest difference this time is none of them come over to check me for a wire.

"Hey boss," Jason greets, and I appreciate that he knows the score.

"Jason," I nod at him, gesturing around. "Has the trash been dealt with?"

He nods. "Yeah, Chris' guys haven't been around in a few days, and any of the girls that came with them haven't been welcome back. Your usual suppliers for the other stuff is a little higher than what you were paying."

"I don't care about that. Quality is worth it. I don't need that fake fentanyl shit coming in here and killing people left and right."

"Got it. And you need more guys, a lot of them went to your dad after you got locked up. Some stuck around, and recently left, but you need more."

I nod. I've known that, but it's hard to find people you can trust enough in this line of business. People willing to do illegal things usually aren't loyal to anyone. And I don't trust anyone so it's a dangerous combination.

Right as I'm about to start coming up with solutions to give Jason my phone goes off. I look to make sure it's not an emergency, and I'm pleasantly surprised at what I find.

> Violet: Took you long enough to stalk me on social media.

I hadn't expected Violet to message me back since it has been days since I sent the initial message. I'd found her profile the day I met her, but I didn't want to utilize it. I wanted to get her to want me the old-fashioned way, and not use messaging.

Since that hasn't worked out well for me, I decided to message her anyway, anticipating she would ignore it.

> Trent: I wouldn't need to if you gave me your phone number.

Her reply comes right away, which surprises me. Though, I guess it shouldn't since my little flower has been anything other than predictable.

> Violet: And give you another way to bother me? No thanks.

I practically forget where I am and what I was doing because I'm so focused on actually being able to talk to her. I've been infatuated for reasons I can't even explain, but this is an actual *conversation*. Or at least the start to one, and I can't help but appreciate that.

> Trent: Trust me, Flower, I can always find more ways to bother you.
>
> Trent: I do need to know something... How many times have you thought about our kiss? Imagined what could have happened next? Touched yourself to the thought of it?

> Violet: Why do you call me Flower?

She ignores my other message just like I assume she would.

> Trent: Answer me first.

> Violet: I haven't thought about anything from that night. Not once. Your turn.

So, she's a liar.

> Trent: Because you remind me of a flower.
>
> Violet: Seems a little cliché, even for you.
>
> Trent: You don't even know me. I can be anything you want. Except gentle.

She doesn't respond right away this time, and I ignore the irritation I'm feeling, blaming it on how much I like this game we are playing. It has nothing to do with her, it could be anyone. I just like to play.

Putting my phone away, I focus back on Jason so we can continue to come up with a plan to get everything back to where it needs to be.

17

Present

I hate to admit that I googled Trent after that interaction in the kitchen. After I agreed to something I shouldn't have agreed to. I mostly did it to piss off my sister, and I have yet to talk to her about it since. I learned that Trent went to prison for attempted murder. He took a reduced sentence on a plea deal and has several more years of parole now.

I also haven't seen him recently. However, I did reply to his message. Eventually, anyway. That interaction, like all the previous ones, was short lived. This is going to be harder than I thought, but I have to do this. If only to prove everyone, especially Mila, wrong.

I can do this.

> Violet: Heard I should stay away from you, but you're making that pretty impossible.

Choosing to taunt him because as much as I have wanted

him to leave me alone, and have actively pushed him away, it only seems to make him want me more. I'm no psychologist, but I would love for someone to explain that shit to me.

Without looking at my phone after I press send, I get back to putting myself together for the concert Jenson and I are going to. I love concerts. The music filling the entire space, the speakers making the beat vibrate through my entire body. There's nothing like it, and it's one of the only times I feel completely free. I'm able to feel like nothing else matters.

The concert tonight isn't at a big venue, it's a more intimate bar setting. But I don't mind because a concert is a concert. Music is music to me as long as it's loud. I never wear my hearing aids to concerts because the music can cause feedback, and I prefer to feel the songs.

With a final touch on my red lipstick, I look in the mirror, and hardly recognize myself. I almost never wear makeup like this, but I feel like I need to stand out. I don't want to be in the shadows. I don't want to be underestimated. My dark brown eyes are extenuated by the dark makeup around them. Blonde hair falling in waves around my shoulders. Lips a dark red.

The dress I'm wearing is tight on top, and loose around my hips. I have my black lace up boots on my feet that I know I'll regret after hours of dancing.

I look badass.

Confident.

It helps me feel that way, even just slightly. I know I'll be able to handle everything with Trent. I know I can do this.

Picking up my phone I see he replied, and I can't help but roll my eyes.

> Trent: Doesn't seem like you're trying too hard. Maybe you don't want to.
>
> Trent: Also, not sure who you're talking to about me, but they are probably right, and you should stay away. Though, I know you won't.
>
> Violet: It's true, I don't usually do what people tell me to do.
>
> Trent: You just haven't had the right person telling you to do the right things.
>
> Violet: What would those be?
>
> Trent: Maybe you'll find out.

I leave him on read, not justifying an answer to that. Plus, I know Jenson will be waiting. We agreed to take separate Ubers there since neither of us will be able to drive by the end of the night.

AFTER THE CONCERT Jenson and I make our way to a smaller bar because neither of us are ready to go home yet. My skin is still buzzing from the adrenaline. My feet hurt from my boots, but the alcohol buzzing in my system is helping to numb it.

I down another shot that magically appears in front of me thanks to my best friend who is determined to get me drunk enough that I forget about all the bullshit going on.

"*No more.*" I tell Jenson, who just laughs.

My phone vibrates on the table, and I scowl when I see who it is that is messaging me. I really shouldn't be surprised, but I would rather it be my sister than him. Even though I'm supposed to be getting close to him, I still don't like *actually* dealing with him. Plus, I assume he isn't too happy about being left on read earlier.

Trent: Where are you?

Violet: Not your business.

Trent: Who are you with?

Violet: Still not your business.

Jenson slyly pushes another shot over to me. I take it just as the next message comes through.

Trent: Tell me.

It might be the alcohol over inflating my confidence right now, or just the mischievous need to play with this man. I'm not sure, but it's the only excuse I have for typing what I do next.

Violet: Find me.

Trent: Don't move. I'm on my way.

The butterflies erupt in my stomach and I can't tell if they are good or bad.

Violet: Portland is a big place, good luck.

And just because I don't think there's any chance he is going to find me I send an obscure picture of the bar we are at. The picture shows some of the back wall and a sliver of the front window. I check, and there's nothing in the picture that gives away the name of where we are.

I don't let Jenson hand me any more shots. Instead, I opt for one of their specialty vodka cocktails.

Time goes by, and it's probably only been about ten minutes since I sent Trent the picture, but I feel my anxiety increasing by the second. I know he won't find me.

"He gets five more minutes before we leave," Jenson says. I just nod. I want to leave now.

Taking a sip of my drink, I'm trying to finish so we can leave. I see movement in my peripheral vision, and my heart rate increases before I fully see who it is, but I already knew.

He found me.

18

Present

There she is.

I almost wish she turned this into more of a chase, but I can appreciate the fact that she didn't just send me the picture and then leave. Because I know a part of her wants to be caught by me, even if she continues to deny it. My little flower wants this just as much as I do.

A slow smile spreads across my face at the sight of her flustered, and by the look in her eyes, a little tipsy. The music in here is extremely loud, and the first thought I have is that if I take Violet somewhere hidden in the shadows, I bet I could make her scream without even alerting anyone. Let her feel the music through her whole body while I drown her in pleasure.

It's almost like she can hear my thoughts because the look on her face has now turned from flustered to panic as she takes me in. I approach her slowly.

She looks toward her friend who is too busy flirting with the bartender to notice what is happening. I approach her, the look in her eyes clearly showing indecision on if she should run or face me. I make the decision for her as I cage her in with my arms on either side of where she's sitting. Nodding to her almost empty drink, I finally speak.

"What are you drinking?"

Her eyes track my face while I speak, and I see when she settles back into her usual annoyance with me. Then, it morphs into a look of mischief. She moves her hands to sign something and says the words too quietly for me to hear, but I think she said, *"find out."*

Violet stands up from her chair, putting our chests so close together we are practically touching, and I refuse to back away from her. Our eyes remain locked, her dark eyes glassy from the drinks she consumed so far. Her hands move up to my chest, sliding up until they rest on my shoulders, and I'm rooted in place wondering what she's about to do.

Suddenly, she's pushing me down so I'm on my knees in front of her, the movement taking me off guard, which is the only reason I fall so easily, especially in this crowded bar. The thought of the sticky floor under my knees makes me grimace, but I'm too intrigued at what my little flower is about to do for me to care.

I watch her lips as she takes the final sip from her drink, but she doesn't swallow it. Instead, she looks back down at me, still on my knees for her, something I would never do for anyone. Her fingers find the back of my neck as she tilts my head back, eyes remaining locked on mine. I ignore the way my heart picks up speed in my chest like I've never been this close to a woman before.

Before I can question what she's doing, her face is coming close to mine as her fingers holding the back of my neck tighten. She hovers her mouth just barely above mine, and I part my lips slightly before hers are ghosting over mine, not enough to be considered a kiss, and the liquid that's warm from her mouth slides into mine.

I swallow the drink eagerly, I can't even tell what it was. I'm too focused on the way her taste infused it, and now the fact that she's pulling away from me. Then, without a word she turns around and heads toward the back of the crowded bar.

Standing quickly, I follow, keeping my eyes on her blonde head as she walks away from me. I watch as she rushes into the bathroom, catching the door before it closes fully. I push my way inside, Violet watching me in the mirror as I close and lock the door behind me.

She turns around to face me, her skin flushed as she breathes heavily.

"What was that?" I ask.

She just shrugs.

"Well, I found you."

"Now what?" she whispers as she signs. I can tell how badly her hands are shaking.

Instead of answering I stalk toward her, closing the distance quickly, pushing her body against the sink with my hips. Her hands come up to my chest, but she doesn't push me away. She fists my shirt, not pulling or pushing. I see the war going through her mind, and I'm about to make her admit that at least some part of her wants me.

"Now I get my prize." I dip my head down to graze my lips against her throat.

Violet's hands grip my shirt even tighter, and I feel her internal war rage even hotter, especially when she whispers weakly, "I'm not your prize." I don't even know if she means to speak it, but she did. And I'm about to prove how wrong she is about that.

I'm done talking. Plus, I couldn't pull my lips from her neck right now even if the building was falling down around us. I'm kissing, licking, and biting up her throat and jaw until I reach her lips. Hovering for a second, I wait to see what she will do because I'm going to make her be the one to decide this. She's going to drown with me in this moment, even if it means she's going to hate herself for it.

Our breath mingles between our parted lips. It feels instantaneous and also like a lifetime before Violet pulls me into her, crashing our lips together. She instantly releases a breathless moan into my mouth. I press my hips against hers roughly, completely pinning her to the sink. My hands fall to the back of her thighs before I pick her up. Violet's legs wrap around my waist like they were made to be there.

Slamming her back against the wall by the sink, our mouths staying fused together. I force my tongue inside, and she tangles hers with mine as we fight for dominance in the kiss. One of my hands fists her hair, angling her head back so I can properly fuck her mouth with my tongue. Her little whimpers of pleasure increase as my hips grind against her.

I want to feel how wet she is for me.

I need to feel her clench around me.

I need to fucking *feel* her.

Slipping my hand between us, I thank whatever being there is that she's wearing a dress. I'm able to easily feel her drenched lace between her thighs, pulling it to the side, and running my fingers through her wetness.

I can't help the growl that comes from my throat, and I so badly want to tease her into this, but as soon as her soft wet pussy is in my hand, I lose it. Plunging a finger inside her while she gasps in my mouth. I kiss her harder. Fucking her with my finger and claiming her mouth with my tongue. I'm consuming her and making sure she feels completely overwhelmed by me.

I swallow down every single noise she gives me. They aren't rehearsed, they aren't fake like so many girls do to try and convince us guys they are enjoying themselves. Her noises are raw. *Real.*

Adding another finger while pressing my palm against her clit and pushing hard with my hips to add even more pressure. I bite down on Violet's bottom lip while she lets out a particularly loud moan. I don't even care if anyone can hear her. I hope they do. I hope they know that I'm the one making her fall apart like this.

I move my hips to press my hand harder and deeper, wishing it was my cock that was buried deep inside her, but not yet. When I fuck her, it's not going to be in a fucking bar bathroom out of desperation. I'm going to tear her apart and put her back together around me and only me.

Violet's panting is increasing, she's clenching tightly around my fingers, and I know she's close. Her eyes close, head falling back against the wall. Taking my free hand, I grab her jaw, forcing her to look at me so she can see what I'm going to say to her.

"Come on my fucking hand, Flower. Soak the both of us so I can lick you clean."

I don't even know if she's coherent enough to recognize what I'm saying because she's clenching so hard around me, I know she's coming with a silent scream. Her jaw dropped, eyes rolled back, and I have never seen something so fucking perfect.

My movements continue to push her through her climax. Her hips buck against my own. I want to free myself so badly and push inside her. I won't. Not yet.

Her breathing is hard as she comes down. I ease my hand away as she opens her eyes. She's staring at me, and the look on her face is hard to decipher. She almost looks like she's in awe, but quickly it changes to narrowed eyes.

I place her down on the floor carefully, not daring to break our eye contact. I continue to hold her waist, so she stays standing.

"Leave with me," I tell her. It's not a question, but she shakes her head while raising her hand to sign the one word I'm extremely familiar with.

"No."

"Come on, just go for a ride with me."

This time she takes longer to reply, but when she does it's the same answer. *"No."*

"Well Flower, I didn't exactly ask."

She starts to move her hands, but I don't let her. I know I'm about to cause a scene. I don't care. Anyone can try and stop me; they won't get far.

Without another word, I scoop Violet up in my arms, throwing her over my shoulder, and holding her by the back of her thighs. She screeches and begins pounding her fists against my back.

I storm out of the bar with a purpose, not even stopping to let her friend know, she can text him or something. I don't care, I have one focus and it's her.

Placing Violet on her feet, I keep one arm banded around her waist so she doesn't immediately run. Looking up to my face I see she wants to say something mean to me, or escape. Either way she wants to fight.

"Get on my bike. Hold onto me tightly. And just enjoy the

ride," I tell her, watching her dark eyes as they track every word I'm saying.

I expect more resistance from her, but when I loosen my hold on her, instead of fighting like I know she wants to, she climbs on my bike. What I also didn't expect was the jolt of...*something* seeing her straddling my bike like that. Looking at me like she wants to gouge my eyes out. My dick is rock hard in my jeans, but really, it has been since she forced me to my knees in front of her. Then, it only became more obvious when I felt her legs wrapped around me, then my fingers buried in her pussy. Now, I feel like I could come from this sight alone.

Since I didn't actually anticipate any of this when I came here, I only have one helmet with me. I put it over her head, and smile. I climb on in front of her, starting the engine, and kick it into gear. I haven't felt her arms, so I reach back, and pull them tight around my torso, pulling her completely flush against my back. I feel her everywhere. Her legs and arms hugging mine. That hot cunt of hers against my ass. Her chest against my back.

Before I do something right here in this parking lot, I'm driving us into the darkness.

19

Present

I feel like I'm being driven to my murder. At least it's a nice view as Trent weaves through traffic, leaving the lights of downtown and heading onto roads that lead deeper into the forest. The wind is whipping around us due to the speed. My arms are going to be frozen by the time he stops, and I don't know if I'll be able to let go of him.

Feeling him in my arms is different like this. Different than the various assaults he subjected me to during our last few interactions. I don't know why I keep letting it happen, but it's escalating, and I know next time it will likely be more than his fingers inside me…and that thought terrifies me more than I'll actually admit.

And not for the reasons I originally thought.

What if I'm not what he expects, and I've failed my commitment to help because he won't give me the time of day anymore.

I'm too young, too inexperienced for him, and I'd be naïve enough to think he will want to stick around for long after he finally gets what he wants from me.

I shake the negative thoughts from my mind. Confidence. I need to be confident to get through this, and I can keep teasing him. I'm good at that. He seems to be into it. I can do this.

Trent drives us deeper into the forest, there's no streetlights, the road barely illuminated by the light from his motorcycle, and I'm terrified some animal is going to jump out causing us to crash. I'll be found dead on the road with a felon. If my dad wasn't disappointed in me as a human already, that would just seal the deal. Plus, the gloating Mila would do to my grave.

Squeezing Trent's torso tighter, I feel him reach back to touch the skin on my leg, and I panic a bit more. I try to tell him to use both hands to drive, but I doubt he could hear me through the helmet, and I'm sure the bike is loud based on how it vibrates under us.

Finally, we pull up to an A-frame home with giant windows nestled in the forest. The inside is illuminated by some lights, making it easy to see the living room furniture. It looks like a nice normal home, and not the dwelling of a demon, so I can't imagine this is where Trent lives.

Cutting the engine, he unhooks my arms from around him before stepping off the bike, taking the helmet off my head and helping me stand. My legs wobble for a second from clenching so tightly the entire ride. Not at all having to do with what happened in the bathroom. Not. At. All.

Trent walks ahead of me up to the front door, and the panic truly sets in. I'm about to go into his house. He's going to try and fuck me, I know it. How will I get out of this? I can't say I'm on my period, he already felt everything and it wasn't bloody.

Shit.

I'm an idiot. Oh my god, and Jenson? Yeah, Jenson! He doesn't know where I went, maybe he thinks I was kidnapped, but I can use him as an excuse to leave.

Before following him through the front door I blurt, "I have to go."

Trent turns around to look at me, an amused look on his face. "No, you don't."

Folding my arms across my chest, I stand my ground, still not crossing the threshold. "You don't know anything about me. I have to get back to Jenson."

He approaches me, getting so close we are practically chest to chest. I continue to stand tall and refuse to take a step back.

"No. You. Don't." He clearly enunciates each word, which pisses me off. He knows I read lips just fine, and don't need him dumbing it down for me.

Thinking about what I need to do, how I'm getting access to his home. A home that could have a plethora of information the cops need, I decide to push away my nervousness, but my pettiness remains. He wants to talk to me like I'm stupid, I'm going back to just signing.

"Fine."

He shuts the door once I'm inside, and I take in my surroundings. There's the living room I could see through the window that leads into the modern kitchen. I choose to explore what I couldn't see through the window, and go into another room with a fireplace, and something I wouldn't have ever thought I would see here. A piano.

I'm not a piano expert, but I think it's a baby grand. The black and shiny instrument clearly being the centerpiece of this room. I feel Trent's presence behind me. He doesn't touch me, but I know he's there.

"You play?" I ask, knowing he can see my hand movements from over my shoulder. I don't know if he says anything because he remains behind me.

Instead of turning around to look at him I walk toward the piano, reaching out to touch the smooth surface. There isn't a speck of dust on it which leads me to believe it does get played. Or at least, taken care of.

I run my hand along the keys, but not pressing down, just feeling them. There isn't any sheet music, so I wonder if he plays by memory. Or has a stash of it somewhere.

Finally, I look up to see Trent is still standing where I was before, but he's leaning against the wall, hands in his pocket looking way more attractive than he should. His jeans hug his muscular legs. Button up shirt with the sleeves rolled up to his elbows. His dark hair just barely long enough to grab onto.

There's more to his physical appeal other than his looks. It's his presence. The way he holds himself. The air of maturity that I'm not used to with guys my age. There's also the air of danger that is just screaming at me to run in the other direction because I know this man is not a good man. He's dangerous. And yet I keep provoking him for some asinine reason.

"What are you staring at?" I finally say when he doesn't move or open his mouth. He just stares.

Tilting his head to the side, he seems to be assessing me, and I feel my confidence weakening under his gaze. I don't like it. So, I act out like the mature adult that I am.

"You forget what it's like to be close to a woman after five years being surrounded by only men?" Even though I know he doesn't understand me, my heart rate increases at the thought of what he might do to me if he knew what I was saying.

"You done using your voice with me again, Flower? I thought we were making progress." His smile is so sinister. I don't even know if he knows it's supposed to be something that depicts happiness because he seems to do it to inflict anything but.

I shrug. "You spoke to me like I'm stupid, so I'll speak to you how I want."

Rounding the piano again so I'm standing in front of him, looking up into those practically golden eyes, I wonder what he's thinking.

"Come on, Flower, I thought we were past this."

I rear back at that comment. *"Past this?"* I scoff before speaking and signing at the same time. "Past what exactly? Me being deaf and using my preferred language? What exactly are we supposed to be *past,* Trent?"

He groans, I think, while running his hand over his face before closing the distance between us.

"No, but you know I don't understand *your preferred language,* so I thought we were past you making it difficult for me."

My jaw drops at the audacity of this man.

"Difficult for *you?* God forbid, anything be difficult for *you,* right?" My hands are slapping together at the aggressiveness of my signs as I speak.

"I'm just saying, you know how to read lips and I don't know sign, so it just makes sense if you – "

"If I *what?!"*

"If you just keep speaking to me. Like this."

I laugh.

But there's no humor behind it.

No, I laugh at how fucking ridiculous this is.

I laugh that I thought I could handle his brand of asshole for long enough to actually help those detectives. I didn't underestimate myself, and my ability to do this. I did overestimate him, and his ability to be a decent human being.

"You know what, Trent?" I press my chest against his, no longer having the room to sign while I speak. "How about you learn to sign, then I won't be making anything difficult for *you* anymore. Until then you can fuck right off."

I go to walk away, but his hand lands on my bicep, stopping me from moving away from him, but I'm seething, and I don't know how I'm going to get out of here. I don't know if Ubers even come out this far, but I will take my chances in the fucking woods before I stay here any longer.

"You are the definition of difficult, Flower, and not just because of the signing. I don't do attitude; I get what I want and then everyone goes on their way." I can feel his own anger rising to the surface.

"Then, I'm not the girl for you." I try to pull away again, but he doesn't let me. In fact, he takes me by complete surprise because instead of letting me go, he pulls me against him, slamming his mouth against mine.

This kiss is angry. This kiss is a fight. This kiss is like a fucking fire threatening to take us both down, and yet I continue to let it happen. Trent's tongue pushes into my mouth and for some reason I let him. For some other reason, I tangle that tongue with my own, and then I'm lifted in his arms.

I want to stop this. I know I need to stop this, just like every time before the warning bells are going off everywhere around me, but I'm ignoring them. I ignore them as Trent moves us up the stairs, never once breaking the kiss.

I continue to ignore them when we are in a bedroom, and I'm thrown onto the soft bed. This is about to be pushed past a point of no return, but I don't even care because all this anger and hatred I'm feeling is going to come out one way or another.

Trent's strong body comes down on top of mine, pressing me into the mattress. Mouths fused together, and the fire inside me beginning to burn hotter, especially when the bulge in his jeans pushes against my barely covered center. Without even meaning to, my hips begin to move against him, seeking more of the brief friction he teased me with.

I'm panting, and I feel the familiar buzz of release beginning to take over when Trent lifts himself up, ripping his lips from mine, he hovers over me so I can't continue to rub against him. I wiggle with discomfort as I try to smother the frustrated noise I know I make.

He smiles down at me, and for some reason the urge to bite his lip takes over, but then he speaks. "You going to come for me again?"

I smile back before raising my hands to sign in response. *"Again?"*

Trent looks at me, confused and he says, "Yes?"

"How would it be again? I haven't come yet." I say with a smirk, signing as well.

"You did earlier."

"No, I didn't." I'm still smiling. Maybe this will ruin the moment after all. Which is good, I was becoming a little too unfocused on what I'm here to do.

His gaze hardens on me. "Yes, you did. I felt it."

My smile widens. "I faked it."

Trent drops his hips to press against me, hard, and I squeak out in surprise.

"You couldn't fake that any better than you could fake how close you were just by rubbing that little pussy against me."

"Fake. All of it. I just wanted it over, and it's easy for girls to do. You're just not as great as you think you are."

He watches me, looking into my eyes, trying to detect the lie. Which it is. I totally came, but he doesn't need that ego boost right now. Or ever.

His smile returns, and it makes my hackles rise because I can tell this taunting didn't have my desired effect, and I might regret what I just brought onto myself.

"Fine. First, I'm going to make you come on my fingers, next my tongue and then my cock."

I gasp softly. Definitely did not expect that to be the reaction.

"Then," he continues, "I'm going to do it all again just to

make extra sure this time. I won't let you leave this bed until you have been thoroughly fucked."

My jaw drops, a protest on my tongue, but he doesn't allow it to come out because his mouth is on mine again. I'm pinned beneath him, unable to do anything other than to see this through, and hope he was just exaggerating. No human can come that much, there's just no way. I'm either about to experience the greatest unwanted pleasure I've ever experienced.

Or I'm going to die.

Those are the only options.

20

Present

I let her comments fuel me as I'm ripping her dress over her head, revealing her soft barely covered body beneath me. Violet squirms for a second, her discomfort obvious. I don't let it take over to ruin this as my mouth descends on her again. I lick down her throat down to her perfect tits.

I faked it.

Growling, I pull her bra cups down roughly before biting the rosy buds of her nipple beneath. She didn't fake shit, and I'm going to prove that two times over. She gasps at the pressure of my teeth before I pull back to suck instead and soothe the burn.

Her hands are in my short hair trying to find purchase, and I want her to rip the strands out of my scalp once my head is between her legs. I want her to be so out of control with need she can't control herself. I want her so sated she stops fighting me, at least for a moment. Because to be honest, I like the fight. But only with her. What I said before is true. I don't normally do attitude. I get what I want. She gets what she wants. That's it.

Violet is the first one in a long time I've had to put this much effort into. And also, for the first time I don't hate it.

Making my way down her body, licking and biting her pale skin until I'm at her panties. One touch between her thighs, and she is fucking soaked.

She faked it my ass.

I roughly tear the flimsy lace away from her body. Her words fill my head again, fueling the lust filled angry fire burning inside me.

Fake.

All of it.

I just wanted it over.

You're just not as great as you think you are.

She's right. I'm better, and I'm going to prove it.

I run my tongue along her entire seam roughly. She gasps while trying to tighten her grip on my hair, and it makes me smile. I bet I can pull the first orgasm from her in less than a minute. She's so responsive.

With that goal in mind, I start to devour her like a starving man. Which is exactly what I am. I'm starving for her. Sucking on her clit roughly, her hips buck up to try and grind against my mouth. My hand reaches up to push down to keep her from moving. She's at my mercy right now, and she's going to take everything I give her. She questioned my ability, so she's going to accept my control.

I vary between sucking on her clit, and flicking it with my tongue, then moving down to her entrance. I test every movement to figure out what makes her gasp and struggle the most. I'm so fucking hard, this is my own brand of torture not to just slam into her so hard we both see stars, but I'm proving a point.

With another suck onto her swollen bud, I can tell she's close. I groan against her so she can feel the vibration, and that sends her over the edge. Her grip on my head tightens painfully as she holds me against her cunt. While she's in the middle of her pleasure I push my finger inside, feeling her clench around me so tightly my cock jumps at the thought of being inside her.

She's so wet, soft, and tight. I can barely pump my finger. When I curl it inside her to hit that sensitive spot inside of her, she goes off again, almost instantly. I doubt she even finished her other orgasm before being sent off the edge of another one.

The noises she's making now do make the ones she made earlier pale in comparison. And I'm soaking all of them in because I know none of this is fake. None of this is a show, if anything I feel like she's holding back because I know my Flower doesn't want me to know how much she likes this.

I lift up to watch Violet, as I continue to pump my finger

while she falls apart. She looks almost angry as she comes, and it's the greatest sight I've ever witnessed. She's grabbing the sheets trying to find purchase on anything to hold onto as I force every second of pleasure from her body with my hand.

Finally, I think the wave has subsided, she's breathing heavily, tits bouncing with each breath as her eyes open slightly, but remain hooded, and tired. It makes me smile because that was just the warmup, and we're not even close to done.

Removing my hand, I bring my finger covered in her release to her lips at the same time I bring my other hand to her throat, wrapping around it, but not applying pressure. She looks up at me, so many emotions in those dark eyes. I still see the fighter, and that she wants to keep fighting.

"Open." I command, not even sure if she is focused enough to see what I'm saying. Or if she will listen.

Violet's eyes narrow, and I think I'm going to have to force my finger into her mouth. She decides to listen. I smile, sliding the digit onto her waiting tongue, "Good girl."

She bites down on me, and the last minuscule shred of control I had before is gone. My hand around her throat tightens so she releases my finger in her attempt to suck in the air I'm currently cutting her off from.

"My flower has thorns. Just for that, I'm going to make this hurt."

She looks like she's about to say something else, but before she gets the chance, I flip her onto her stomach. With my hand on her back, I straddle her legs, holding her in place as I work my clothes off. Violet fights underneath me, bucking her hips to throw me off. When she tries to lift her torso up, I move my hand holding her down to her hair, tangling in her blonde locks tightly to keep her still.

Normally, I would be telling her exactly what I want her to do and threaten a slew of things if she didn't stop fighting me. With her face down in the mattress it would all be for nothing. So, she can continue to fight and I'm going to do what I want anyway.

With that in mind I bring my hand down, slapping her ass sharply three times. Violet cries out, and it renews her fight. I bear down on her, holding her down harder with my hips and my grip on her hair.

I throw my shirt onto the floor, then start working my belt off roughly. I let her feel the cool buckle on her red ass, my handprints beginning to take form on her. I didn't think I could be harder, but my dick is almost painfully hard at this point.

Testing her, I ease off her to take my pants off. She turns her head to the side, but to my surprise she doesn't get up. Her eyes watch me as I undress completely. She doesn't stop watching, and I see her panic once my cock is free from the confines of my boxers.

I run my hand over her cheek, pushing the hair that has fallen in her face behind her ear. "Don't worry, it'll fit."

Her face scrunches up in annoyance, and then the fight is back in her eyes. "I was more worried about you lasting longer than ten seconds, old man."

Leaning over to my nightstand, I pull out a condom with a chuckle. "Oh Flower, yet another thing you don't need to worry about. You'll be begging me to stop soon. But remember," I put the condom on, watching her gaze as it's fixated on me the whole time, "I won't stop."

She tries to rise up on her hands, but I'm back behind her, grabbing her hips roughly, yanking her up onto her knees before she can get up and run. Lining up at her entrance I feel her tense beneath me. It only spurs me on, and I push in slightly, but she's clenching so tight I can barely get more than an inch in.

"Come on, Flower, let me in." I know she can't hear me, but I don't care.

Running my hand up her spine I grab the back of her neck, pulling her up so her back is against my chest. Her chest is heaving as she pants. My hand moves to the front of her throat again as I trail my lips and tongue along the skin of her shoulder, still just teasing her entrance with shallow thrusts with just my tip.

When she finally relaxes enough, I bite down on her shoulder at the same time I slam her body onto mine with a sharp thrust of my hips, fully seating myself in her tight channel. She screams with the intrusion, and I take a second just feeling her around me, clenching like she's trying to pull me even deeper.

I soothe the bite on her shoulder with my tongue, and trail my lips up to her jaw, using my hold on her throat to turn her head toward me. She's flushed and panting. Her pink lips are wet from her tongue, and I need to taste her again. Pulling her mouth against mine roughly, I groan as I still taste the faint sweetness from her pussy on her tongue.

The sensation makes my hips start to move, pulling back, then slamming inside of her again. Violet whimpers against my lips, but she's meeting me thrust for thrust. I need more. I need deeper. I need her coming again. I need her covering my cock with her release and then I need to make her do it again and again.

Releasing her mouth, quickly. I flip her around so she's on her back. She looks up at me, eyes wide in shock. I don't give her a second to move before I'm on her again, pushing inside as she gasps, nails digging into my back.

I reach down to guide her legs around my hips, once she's secured her ankles behind me, I tilt my hips, and pound relentlessly into the spot that has her writhing beneath me. I take one of her nipples in my mouth, stimulating the extended bud with my tongue as her nails dig into me harder.

She's getting wetter, clenching harder and I know she's going to come again. Her breathing picks up, and I move to her other nipple to give it the same treatment. The pace I've set with my hips doesn't let up as she begins to fall apart beneath me. As soon as I hear the sharp gasp that signals the beginning of her orgasm, I rise up to watch her fall apart.

My Flower is so fucking beautiful with her mouth open in a silent scream, eyes pinched shut completely while she shakes under me. She's probably drawn blood on my back with how hard she's digging into my skin, but I don't even care. I just fuck her through her pleasure.

Her thighs tighten even more, and I can't hold myself back anymore. It's too much, I groan my own release, spilling inside the condom I wish wasn't there. What I wouldn't give to fuck her bare. Feel her like this with nothing between us. I doubt she will let me, but I'm going to fucking try.

Our sweat slick skin sticks together as we both come down. Her eyes open slowly, and it's hard to decipher what she's thinking in this moment. Does she still hate me? Probably, and that's okay. I like the fire. I'd like it to stick around.

I get up, pulling the condom off, tying it and throwing it away. Violet has barely moved when I come back, but I made her a promise. I was going to do everything twice, just to make sure. Though, if she tried to tell me she faked any of that then she must think I'm a complete idiot.

When I crawl back onto the bed, sliding my shoulders under her legs, she reaches down to stop me.

"No more," she whispers.

I lick my lips with a smile. "I told you I was going to make extra sure you came this time, and that's what I'm doing."

"I did," she huffs, and I can tell she doesn't want to admit it.

I tsk my tongue, "I gotta make sure, Flower."

With that I dip down to tongue fuck her to another orgasm. She might have a lot of opinions on the type of man I am, but I want to make one thing clear to her. I'm a man of my fucking word.

When I say I'm going to do something, I follow through.

No matter what.

21

6 Years Ago (Age 15)

The floor underneath me vibrates with the music. I'm lying on the floor of my room, eyes closed, hearing aids out, just focusing on the beat as it flows through my entire body. This is the only time I feel kind of okay.

When I'm lost in the music.

When I feel it all around me, encompassing me and overtaking my body.

I feel calm.

Free.

Suddenly, the thumping bass beneath me is gone, and my eyes shoot open to see what caused my music to stop.

Mila is standing by the speakers with her hands on her

hips. I narrow my eyes at her, ready for the fight that's about to commence. She's been so much worse since mom died. So much angrier and mean. She's also withdrawn, but I guess I have too. That's what happens when your dad doesn't care about you anymore.

"You need to turn this shit down; you're going to get the cops called on us."

I roll my eyes. "Let them come, maybe dad will say something to me then."

"Considering he sent me in here to tell you to turn this off, probably not."

My chest stings at her comment, but I know it's true.

"Find something else to do. Something quiet."

I scowl at her back as she walks away. Something quiet my ass. I like music. I like how it makes me feel. I like how it makes me forget, even for a minute, that my world is falling down around me.

Jenson and I are going to a local music festival this weekend, and I've been going through the various artists to see which ones I like the best, and want to make sure we see, but apparently that isn't allowed in this house anymore.

Sometimes I feel like my entire existence isn't allowed in this house anymore.

∼

THE CROWD IS BORDERLINE OVERWHELMING, but I love it. The amount of people making the already warm summer day feel even hotter out here. Jenson and I have been scoping out the various stages to see who is playing where so we can figure out the best place to be.

As we are making our way to the next stage, I see there is an ASL interpreter by it. I rush over to get a spot as close as I can to them. I'm not sure what band is playing, but I'm pulled in by the interpreter, and the way they are signing along to the music. It's almost like a choreographed dance the way the woman moves. She looks like she's having the time of her life as she signs the words the singer is currently singing.

For the first time, I feel the beat through my body and know what the song is about. It's an angry song, and about taking your life back. I relate to every single lyric, and barely notice when the song leads into another one, and another one until that particular band is done.

Jenson and I continue to jump from stage to stage experiencing different bands. A couple more of them have ASL interpreters, but not all of them. The day turns into night, and even though my body is exhausted from the sun and the dancing I refuse to leave yet.

In a perfect world, I would never have to leave.

I hate that my own family doesn't care about me anymore, and that I'm an outsider in my own home. But here in this field, surrounded by thousands of strangers, I start to feel like I belong somewhere, and that for the first time since my mom died everything might be okay.

22

Present

I can't believe I actually fell asleep here. That's the first thought I have when my consciousness starts to return. After Trent fulfilled his promise of making me come more times that I even thought possible, I passed out into the deepest sleep I've ever experienced.

As I begin to wake up a bit more, I feel how warm I am, and the weight that's around my waist. When I open my eyes, I look down to see Trent's tattooed muscular forearm banded around my naked waist and cringe.

Which leads to the second thought I have which is, *what is wrong with me?* I'm pretty sure when you're helping take down criminals you aren't supposed to sleep with said criminals.

Everything felt different in the dark. Now that the light of day is streaming in through the window I'm struggling with my decisions from last night and hating myself more and more. I need to leave. I can't face him after what happened.

The memories assault me from all angles. His face between my legs, the pressure of his hands on me. The feeling of being so full of him. So consumed by him.

My sexual experiences have been limited, and by limited… this was only the second time I've had sex, and I know that I can never go back. He's ruined me with just one night and that just adds to my need to get away from him as fast as I can.

Carefully, I extradite myself from Trent's hold, trying my hardest not to wake him up. Once I'm free from his warm hold, I collect my clothes from the floor and try to remember where my phone is.

Pulling my dress on I go downstairs to find my bag which holds my phone, and I hold my breath that it's not dead. When I see how many times Jenson has texted and Facetimed me, I wince. I know I'm going to hear about this from him. He's probably going to be mad at my lack of communication, but he will also probably be so happy I slept with Trent that he won't stay mad long.

I'm scrolling through all my texts from Jenson and can't help the slight pang in my chest that my own sister, who knows I'm potentially with a convicted criminal, didn't even reach out to check on me when I didn't come home.

While I'm in the middle of typing a text back to Jenson to tell him I'm alive, I feel large warm hands slide around my waist. My entire body stiffens at his touch because I can't help the thoughts racing through my mind at how big of a mistake last night was.

Trent's lips skate up my neck, and I tilt my head to try and push him away. His grip on me tightens to turn me around to face him. He's shirtless, wearing only sweatpants that sit low on his hips. His tattooed muscled torso is on full display, but I look away because I can't get sucked into bed with him again. Not now, and not ever. I'll tell Nate and Mitch I'm sorry, but I can't do this.

Trent takes my chin between his fingers and forces me to look at his face again. I want to close my eyes, so I don't have to look at him like this either. Because of course, not only is his body amazing, but his face is deceptively beautiful. And I hate it.

"Were you trying to sneak out, Flower?" he asks.

I shake my head. Technically, I wasn't. I mean I was just standing in his living room texting. My text may have been planning my escape route, but I wasn't necessarily trying to sneak out. Not really.

"Then what were you doing?"

I so badly want to go back to purely signing to him but decide to save the fight for right now. "I'm getting an Uber back home."

"I'll take you home," his tone leaves no room for arguments.

"No."

"Uber doesn't come out this far, and you don't know my address to tell anyone to pick you up. I'm taking you home."

I hate that he's technically right. I want to tell him that my sister can't see him drop me off, but I don't want to open that door for him knowing about Mila. I also don't want to hear whatever my sister has to say about this. Most importantly though, I can't stay here any longer.

"Fine." I roll my eyes at his satisfied smirk. "Put clothes on."

His palm lands on my ass with a single smack as he heads back to his bedroom. As I'm making sure I have everything in my purse, I debate making a run for it anyway, but before I get the chance Trent is back. I don't think a basic black t-shirt and jeans has ever looked better on any man. I also hate it. And despite what happened between us last night I still hate him. Pulling my eyes away from him, I make my way to the front door so I can leave and never look back.

Trent comes out holding another helmet while I wait by his bike. I don't like the thought of needing to be wrapped around him again. He puts the helmet on my head and secures it for me without saying a word. It's like he can tell I don't want to talk, despite the fact that it hasn't stopped him before.

Once he's straddling the bike, I get on behind him. Just like last night I attempt to keep my distance, but he pulls my legs forward so I am completely against him. Before he has the chance to grab my hands to put around him, I reluctantly do it myself so I'm hugging him from behind.

I ignore the feeling that settles low in my stomach as Trent takes off. It feels like an eternity until we are pulling up to my apartment complex. At this moment I realize I never told Trent where I live, and an uneasy feeling settles over me. I hop off the bike and shove the helmet at him.

"How did you know where I live?" I snap, crossing my arms over my chest.

Trent removes the helmet to answer me, "I have connections."

"That doesn't answer my question."

"Don't worry too much about it, Flower." He winks and it makes my frown deepen.

"I don't need you stalking me."

"You like it," he smirks.

I really don't, but I'm done with this conversation.

I'm done with *him*.

With that, I turn to walk away, but he catches my arm to stop me. I turn around, and before I'm able to say anything his mouth is on mine in a surprisingly soft kiss. I let it happen for a moment before I come to my senses and pull away.

"I'll see you again soon," he says confidently.

"Nope. I'm going to go inside and forget any of this happened." I insist.

Trent just smiles. That infuriatingly cocky smile when he

speaks again. "You'll want to forget me, but I'm going to make sure you never can."

Before I respond, he is walking back to his motorcycle and has his helmet on before taking off.

I hate that he's probably right about that.

Once I'm inside I'm relieved that Mila isn't greeting me with a confrontation. Immediately, I go to the bathroom to take a shower. I need to wash the smell and feeling of Trent off me right away. I even debate throwing away the dress I was wearing because I know I can't look at it ever again without thinking about him.

The hot water falls over me, I close my eyes enjoying the burn, and am instantly assaulted by the memories once again. Despite being sore, the dull ache begins between my legs, and I groan at the need to do something about it. As soon as my fingers graze my clit, I pull them back. I can't do this. I meant it, I want to try and forget him so touching myself to the thought of him is not forgetting him.

Frustrated, I turn off the water, wrap myself in a towel and go to my room. I throw the dress on the floor of my closet hoping I'll forget about it there before pulling on some cotton shorts and a t-shirt.

The light from my phone starts lighting up, signaling a call, and I see Jenson is Facetiming me. For just a moment I debate not answering. With a groan I give in, and his glaring face greets me.

"Bitch," he signs, and I know he's not going to let me get out of this without an explanation.

"What do you know already?" I ask reluctantly.

"Nothing except you disappeared with the Adonis for a bit, then got carried out of the bar by him."

I groan again before falling face down onto my bed. I really hoped at least part of that was some nightmare, or something I just conjured up in my intoxicated mind.

Raising my head back into the frame of the phone Jenson is giving me a pointed look, clearly waiting for me to explain.

"He took me back to his house."

"And?"

I shrug.

"Violet."

"Jenson."

"Did you sleep with him?"

I scrunch up my face, not wanting to answer that particular question.

"You did." He confirms by my lack of response.

"I hate you, you're supposed to be my friend, which means you aren't allowed to let me do stupid shit."

"I was too busy with that cute bartender, I knew you were in good hands," he winks, and I grimace. I wouldn't describe Trent as being in "good hands" considering he's a convicted felon, but I'm not bringing that up to Jenson.

"So, where do you go from here?" he questions.

"I forget about the whole thing and avoid him for the rest of my life."

"I don't think that's one of your better plans."

"Maybe not, but it's the only one I have. It's never happening again, and that's it."

The look on Jenson's face lets me know that he doesn't believe me, and I hate to admit that no matter how adamant I am about this, I don't believe me either.

23

Trent

Present

"You know, son, something I've learned in life is that everything is possible with enough money. You want power? With enough money you gain power and the control of more people. You want sex? Buy it. You want access to anything, buy it. Everything can be bought. Everything."

I wish I could say this is the first time I've heard this speech from my dad, but it's not. I learned from a young age that money is everything to him, and it became everything to me. Power came later, and that was what mattered most to me. The high I got from being in control was heady, and better than holding a wad of cash in my hands.

Now, here I am sitting across from my dad once again, when I want to be anywhere but here. Ideally, I'd like to be back inside my Flower, but she is actively avoiding me, and has been for the last three days. I get it, but that's about to end.

"Is there a point to this useless lecture?" I ask, my tone is bored.

"You are losing out on a lot of money cutting me out of your businesses, you know this, Trent. I've raised you better than this, and I want you to realize what a mistake this is."

I don't know why I thought he would just accept getting cut out of my shit, but for a second I did. And now he's trying to entice me with some supplier exclusive and waving the potential money I can make in my face. Oh, and demeaning me because that's what he always does when things aren't going his way.

"I have more money than I need, and enough to buy anything I want and more. You're wasting your time, Pops, just quit while you're ahead." I down the rest of my whiskey, preparing to leave this impromptu meeting.

"You're going to realize your mistake, son, just know that."

"That's fine, I don't hide from my failures, I learn from them and get better."

With that, I walk away from the man I used to idolize. Jason catches up to me, leaving the building at the same time as me.

"He's trying to sneak his drugs back in here, and just trying to cover his ass," Jason tells me, even though I already know about that. I may not be around all that much, but I always know what's happening in my clubs.

"I know, that's why I have guys like you to help me out, right?" I raise my eyebrow at him.

Jason nods, "I got a couple new guys working security and they seem good, they're the ones that caught the shit coming in."

I acknowledge what he's saying, though I'm half listening. I have plans I have to get moving on, these have a deadline.

"Anything else I should know about?" I ask, getting on my motorcycle and pulling the helmet over my head.

"Don't think so, boss."

"Keep me informed," I tell him before kicking on the engine, and taking off.

I WISH I could say I have been able to go about my day-to-day life like normal after that night with Violet, but that would be a lie. She's consumed my thoughts, and the main one being, when I can see her again. I searched through her social media when the idea came to me.

She had posts from a couple years ago at a few music festivals. There were a few other concerts for bands I haven't heard of, but when I looked them up, I was a bit surprised that was the type of music she's interested in. It's a lot of metal, screaming, loud pounding beats.

Then, during my research I saw one of the bands she posted about, Oblivion, was coming to Portland. The normal tickets were sold out, but I was able to get a suite. Which I prefer anyway, a way to have her all to myself while she also gets to see the concert. It's a perfect plan.

Too bad I haven't been able to tell her since she's been avoiding me. The concert is tonight, so that is about to end. I'm waiting outside her apartment building, leaning against my bike as I text her.

> Trent: Come outside.

She doesn't respond right away, and for a few moments I think she's not going to respond at all.

> Violet: No.

> Trent: Don't make me come up and get you.

I don't actually know which apartment is hers. I only know her building because I followed her back home after work one day. I needed to know where she lived, but I couldn't follow her inside without being obvious. Though, now that I think about it, I should figure that out soon.

> Violet: I don't want to see you. Leave.

> Trent: We have plans. If you don't come down, we are going to be late.

> Violet: I would remember making plans with you, and I didn't. So, leave. Bye.

> Trent: Coming up now.

> Violet: No!

> Violet: Give me 10.

> Trent: You have 5.

I can practically feel her fuming from here, but I don't care. I also don't necessarily know why I'm doing this in the first place. I half expected to be done with her after getting a taste, but my obsession has only grown, and that's a dangerous spot to be in for me. I'm not capable of a relationship or giving her what she probably wants from a guy.

I'm going to break her, one way or another, she's not getting out of this unscathed.

And neither am I.

After exactly five minutes the doors open, and Violet is walking out with a scowl on her face. She's in jeans, and a dark tank top, showing every one of her curves. My hands itch to touch her again now that I know what those curves feel like underneath those clothes while she's writhing beneath me.

She approaches me, hands folded until she speaks, accompanying her words with signs. "What are these plans?"

I smile. "Hop on and find out."

She looks back at her apartment, and I sense her hesitation. I hold out the helmet for her in a silent command.

With a sigh she puts it on before climbing on behind me. I don't even need to guide her to hold onto me this time, she does it all herself. Before she has a chance to second guess her decision, we are peeling out of the parking lot, and speeding off.

24

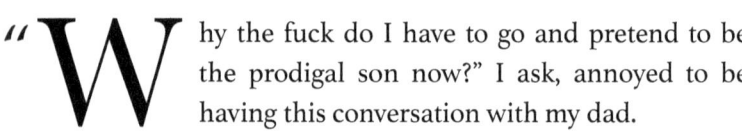

15 Years Ago (Age 20)

"Why the fuck do I have to go and pretend to be the prodigal son now?" I ask, annoyed to be having this conversation with my dad.

"Because you never know when you're going to need certain people to have your back, and they might be useful for us."

I scoff, "Doubt it."

"Trust me, son."

He's making me go see my mom and her soon-to-be new husband. I've barely talked to her since I turned eighteen, and my dad is expecting me to make nice with her now for her wedding. It's stupid.

I think this guy she's marrying has a kid, a son, a couple years younger than me. I also know she moved really fucking fast with this guy. I don't think they've been together longer than six months. If that.

Reluctantly, I leave my dad's and head to my mom's house about twenty minutes away. Well, I guess it's her fiancé's house, but same shit.

She called wanting me involved in the wedding, and I turned her down at first. I was not going to be involved at all, then my dad convinced me I should. I've been fighting it ever since, but now tonight is the rehearsal dinner bullshit, and tomorrow is the wedding. I'm dreading it all.

I get to the house and am greeted by my mom running out to throw her arms around me in a tight hug. She struggles to reach my shoulders since she's so short.

"You're so grown, Trent," she beams at me. I grimace because of course I would be grown in the last couple years, she hasn't really seen me.

I don't get a chance to respond to ask what the fuck she's getting at when a man walks out behind her. He looks around the same age as her, mid-forties, and he greets me with a firm handshake.

"Scott Wells," he introduces himself so formally, last name and all. Which is fair since I didn't know what my mom's new last name was going to be until this moment.

"Come on, you need to meet Zander," she beams like there isn't a thick layer of tension covering all of us.

I assume Zander is Scott's son, or some other child or friend she's had that she hasn't told me about since secrets seem to be her way of life.

We all head inside. The house is nice, it looks like a cookie cutter typical suburban home in a typical Phoenix, Arizona neighborhood.

"Trent, this is Zander," she says, gesturing to the kid standing in the kitchen. He's tall as shit, has to be at least six-foot-four. He just nods at me, so I do the same. "Zander is only three years younger than you, but I feel like you guys might have some things in common."

I want to ask her what we might possibly have in common considering she doesn't know me at all. I open my mouth to say just that, when Scott speaks instead.

"Dinner starts at seven, you both need to be ready by then, Zander can you show Trent where the guest room he will be staying is?"

This guy, Zander, seems annoyed at his dad speaking to him, and I want to laugh since he seems to have a problem with his dad like I have with my mom. Maybe that's what we have in common.

I follow him down a hallway, away from the kitchen. He opens a door on the right. "Here ya go," he says simply.

"Thanks," I nod at him.

I half expect him to just walk away, but he doesn't. Instead, he leans against the door frame while I toss my backpack on the bed.

"I hate this too, just so you know," he finally says.

"What? My mom?"

"Not really, she hasn't done anything to me, I just hate this situation. My dad moving us here and marrying your mom. Especially so quickly. It's bullshit."

Maybe this kid isn't so bad.

"Yeah well, tell your dad to run while he can. She's a lying bitch, and whatever act she's putting on for him will go away at some point," I tell him, folding my arms across my chest.

Zander runs his hand through his hair. "Yeah, bitch seems to be his type though I guess."

"Your mom suck too?" I didn't plan on actually learning anything about this guy, but I can't help it.

"Yeah, I guess." He doesn't seem like he wants to tell me anything else, and I don't want to press him about it. "Don't think we are going to be brothers or friends or whatever. As soon as I'm done with this school year I'm out of here. I have shit for me in Oregon, and I'm not sticking around here any longer than I need to."

I scoff, "Wasn't planning on it. I have my own reasons to be here, and none of them include you, I'm out of here as soon as this stupid fucking wedding is over."

"Good." Then he's gone. What an asshole.

The rehearsal dinner fucking sucks.

I had to meet more of Scott and Zander's family, including Scott's mom who apparently also lives at the house with them. She's old, and I feel like a couple times throughout dinner she starts to nod off.

The worst part of this whole charade is how my mom is talking up Zander to everyone at the table.

Not me.

Not her son.

Zander.

She says how smart he is. How promising of a future he has. What an amazing artist he is, and how he's sure to go places.

What does she say about me? Her only son? Her only fucking child?

Nothing.

Not that she knows anything about me anymore, but she could at least try to act like a decent mother, and pretend, but nope. Everything is about Zander.

It makes me seethe throughout the entire dinner. I know that kid isn't as perfect as she makes him out to be. I know he would turn on everyone at this fucking table given the chance.

I've had one conversation with him, and I know he's not this sweet kid my mom is making him out to be.

I choke down the food and manage to get alcohol from the bar despite not being twenty-one yet. The brown liquid burns my throat as I drink it, but I don't care. I just need something, anything to get through this night.

The more she talks the more irritated I get. The entire table is fawning over Zander, and I just endure it until it's finally over. When we leave, I don't say anything to anyone. A few people try to say goodbye to me. I brush them all off and storm off.

My mom thinks she can just replace our family with this one, and it makes everything better. She gets a new husband she can manipulate into loving her. She gets a new son, one that doesn't hate her yet. One she can manipulate into thinking she's a good mother.

Fuck her old family, right? She's got a new one. New house. New money. New husband. New son. I'm nothing to her anymore. And she's nothing to me either.

As soon as the wedding is over the following day I grab my shit, and leave. I never want to look back. I refuse to be involved in anything having to do with my mom's new family. The fucking Wells. Have a good fucking life because I'm not going to be in it.

25

Present

I recognize where we are going before Trent pulls into the parking garage. I know Oblivion has a concert here today, but I wasn't able to afford tickets. As much as I would like to deny the excitement I'm feeling, it's there.

Before we start to walk toward the venue I turn to Trent. "How'd you know I like this band?"

He just smiles. "Give me some credit, Flower."

I narrow my eyes at him, not completely sure if that's what he just said, or what he means. I decide that maybe I don't necessarily want to. But I'll take a free concert, especially because I haven't been able to go to many since starting college. Money is obviously harder to free up when you have bills, and it sucks.

We enter the venue a different way than I've ever been in

before and take an elevator up. I don't say anything, but I'm confused as to what is happening.

I understand that maybe he wasn't able to get tickets in the pit, or anything, but when he presses the button for the top floor, I can't help but feel disappointment. I know I'll still be able to feel the music, but any chance of me being able to see the interpreter well is slim to none, depending on where we are.

Stepping off the elevator I'm even more confused. This isn't where seats are. These are...boxes. Like the suites at the very top of the venue. I've never been up here, and never really wanted to if I'm being honest.

Trent leads me to one of the doors before opening it to reveal the inside. It's fancy, that's for sure. There are seats in front of the glass that looks out onto the entire venue. There's a bar along the back wall with a rounded counter that wraps around with bar stools. There are also several TVs on the walls, like even when you aren't looking out the glass, you'll be able to have a view of what is happening.

I'm taking it all in, looking around, and I know I would never have been able to experience this on my own, but I can't help the thought that this isn't what concerts are for me. They aren't just watching a performance. They are a full body experience I feel down to my bones, and I'm not going to get that sitting up here.

Trent is leaning against the counter; his muscled arms are crossed in front of his chest as he watches me. Thick muscles strain the fabric covering his body and there's no denying this man is a work of art. The tattoos that decorate his skin, the way his clothes hug him. His eyes that have seen more than he will let on, and the slight stubble on his jaw that creates a perfect friction between my thighs.

There's also the authority he seems to have, and not just because he's so much older than me, those fourteen years aren't what gives him the authority. It's the way he holds himself, and I can't deny the way it makes my knees weak, but I can't let it. I can't let him affect me in this way. I have to remember to keep my head around him, especially since I know how easy it is to lose it.

"What do you think?" he asks with a smirk on that mouth I know is capable of doing wicked things.

Shaking the thoughts away, I sign, *"It's okay."*

I turn back around to look out onto the venue to people watch, and to avoid looking at Trent anymore.

It doesn't take long before I feel him close in on me. He's close to my back, his warmth breaking the barrier of my clothes, but he isn't touching me. Not yet. He gets closer, and I feel his breath on my neck, just slightly.

When I turn around my chest grazes his, and our faces are only a couple inches apart. My breath hitches at his proximity. I back up a step so I can breathe, but my back hits the glass so I know I can't go further. I raise my hands between us to speak, and to put space between us.

"Tell me how you found out I liked this band."

"You used to post a lot about concerts on your social media."

I honestly forgot about that. I barely post now, and even back then it was more for attention than anything since I wasn't getting any at home, I just wanted any I could get.

"*Right.*" I sign, then continue while speaking as well. "So, why did you do all of this?"

I see the indecision on his face for a split second before it's gone, and the typical cocky asshole is back. "I wanted to impress you."

"Why?"

"Was that 'why'?"

I nod.

He moves closer, crowding me against the glass. I take in a sharp intake of breath as I start to become overwhelmed by him once again. His scent, that hint of whiskey and leather always present along with his cologne. He's almost too close for me to read his lips, but I catch what he says right before they are against mine.

"I don't know."

Then he's kissing me, and yet again, I'm letting him. His lips move over mine, but when his tongue touches the seam of my mouth I pull away and push past him before sinking into one of the giant leather chairs.

He gives me a skeptical look, probably noting how heavily I'm breathing while I focus on lowering my heart rate. He settles into the chair right beside me.

"Tell me something about yourself since you stalked me." I manage to keep my voice and hands level while I speak.

"It's not stalking when it's out there for the public." I give him a pointed look. "But fine, what do you want to know?"

I think for a moment then blurt the first thing I think of. "Tell me about your family."

"Typical. Two parents. Next question."

"No siblings?"

"Nope. One stepbrother, we aren't close."

"What's his name?"

Trent's face scrunches up, and I can tell he doesn't want to answer, then he finally does, and I don't recognize the name he says.

"Spell it." I tell him.

He looks at me, curiously before pulling out his phone, and holding up what he wrote on the notes app.

ZANDER

"Interesting name."

Trent grunts in acknowledgment. I can tell this guy is some sort of sore spot for him, and it makes me want to keep asking about him.

"Where does he live? What does he do?"

I can feel the reluctance coming from Trent as he answers. "The coast, and he's a tattoo artist."

"And your parents?"

I can tell Trent hates this entire conversation, and it's only egging me on to dig deeper. I want to find every little thing that makes him tick and use it against him.

"Mom is in Arizona, we aren't close. My dad is here, also not close."

I want to ask more about his dad since I know that is who the cops are really looking at, but before I get the chance the lights are dimming around the venue as the opening act is about to start.

Once they do, I'm disappointed to find out I was right. The box is cool, but it takes away from the experience for me, and I can't feel the music penetrating my entire body, surrounding me. It's more like how it feels to listen to music in the car. There's a slight bump of bass, but that's it. Plus, I don't have my hearing aids in because I knew wearing them while wearing a helmet would be a feedback nightmare.

I'm disappointed. And I hate that I don't want to seem ungrateful that Trent did this for me. Though, I usually enjoy pissing him off, at least a little.

After the opening band is done, Trent looks over at me, and clearly, he can see that I'm not too thrilled.

"What's wrong?"

I shrug before standing to go back and grab a water bottle from the bar. When I turn back around, he's leaning over the counter in front of me.

"You okay?"

I take a long sip from the water with a nod.

He studies me, and I start to become uncomfortable from the extended intense eye contact, so I walk around him to stand in front of the window again. I like watching the people, I'm too far away to try and read anyone's lips, but that's one of my favorite pastimes.

It doesn't take long before Trent is turning me around with a hand on my shoulder.

"Talk to me, Flower, I did this for you, and you seem miserable."

I roll my eyes. "You did this to get in my pants again, don't try and act like it was anything more than that."

His eyes narrow, and I swear I see a glimpse of another side of him. One that is scarier than how he normally presents.

"I did it to have an excuse to see you again, sure."

"And then you didn't give me much of a chance to say no."

"I take what I want, Flower. I always have, and always will."

"And you think you want me?" I scoff.

"I – " he stops himself, seeming to consider what he's going to say next for a moment. "I know that I want you, and this is different for me."

"What is?"

"Liking someone I guess." He looks almost unsure after the words leave his mouth, and it just spurs me on more.

There's no way I saw that correctly. Sometimes I misread lips, especially without my hearing aids in, but that is what it looked like he said, I just refuse to believe it.

"You think you like me?" I laugh, and not because it's funny.

"Well, I don't do shit like this for anyone, so yeah clearly I fucking like you."

I continue to laugh. "No, you don't. You like a hearing version of me. Which is a version of me that doesn't exist and never fucking will, Trent."

"That's what you think? I like…what? The idea of you?" That smile of his returns. The one that makes him look borderline sinister in the hottest way.

"Yup. You do this without thinking about the fact that I can barely feel the music being played, which is, by the way, how I listen to music. You refuse to learn any sort of signs and expect me to keep speaking to you all the time. You don't like me. You like someone who doesn't exist."

I barely register the fact that the lights are dimming down again because Trent has crowded me against the glass. This time without leaving an inch of space between our bodies, his face looming close to mine.

"If I didn't like you, I wouldn't have tried at all. I wouldn't have thought about you for a single second after you left my house. I would've fucked you and been done, Flower, I don't know why, but you're invading my fucking mind. Every time you fight me, I want to yank you closer to me. I wish I didn't like you. I fucking *wish* I wasn't tempted by you in every single way. What the fuck are you doing to me?"

"I don't know, but I'll make it easier for you, and I'll get out of your life for good, then you can stop obsessing over some fake version of me and I can forget about the narcissistic asshole you are."

He leans so close his breath is against my mouth, and I can barely see the words he says, but it looks like he says, "I fucking wish I could."

Then he crashes his lips to mine, and just like last time we were in a similar position at his house the kiss is angry, and it's like we are letting out every single thing we want to say to each other into the kiss. Trying to rip each other apart by our mouths. Trent's hands slide to the back of my thighs as he lifts me up. My legs wrap around his waist involuntarily as he presses me back against the glass.

His erection presses against me in the perfect spot, sending a gasp flying out of my mouth into his. I barely register the feeling of the music playing behind me. Trent has successfully invaded my thoughts and made me almost forget where we are. He thrusts his hips against me, and I moan.

He's moving us back, and I don't realize where until I'm brought down onto his lap. He sat in one of the large chairs, with me straddling his hips. Our mouths haven't separated from each other, and I know we should. I shouldn't give in to him again. I can't let this happen again. I can't.

Finally, I'm able to break free from his mouth, but all he does is move his lips down to my jaw, my neck. His teeth nibble on the sensitive skin and I find myself moving against his lap, and I know I need to stop this.

I gasp out a weak, "Stop."

Trent raises his head from the spot on my neck he was in the middle of licking. His chest is moving with heavy breaths. His barely contained erection is rock hard beneath me.

"We can't do this again." I don't believe the words I'm saying, but they need to be said.

"Why not?" He tries to kiss my mouth again, but I pull away, and don't let him.

"Because we can't. And especially not in public like this." I shake my head, the lust fog clearing slightly.

"Yes, we can. You want this, I know you do, Flower. I know

you're soaked for me. I know you've thought of me every time you've touched yourself since our night together."

I bite my tongue and squeeze my hands tighter on his shoulders because I know if I say anything it will be to tell him he's right.

"No one can see us. Just pretend all those people down there aren't there. Close your eyes and focus on me. Focus on the fact that none of them will ever get to have you like this, see you like this. You're. Mine."

In a swift move, Trent has lifted me up and turned me around so I'm back on his lap, facing out toward the concert again. The lights are flashing, but I can barely focus on that when I have Trent hard beneath me, my back pressed tightly against his front. His arm is banded around my chest, holding me to him. His hot breath hitting my neck right before he presses open mouth kisses all along my skin. He pulls the strap of my shirt off my shoulder so he can continue his assault.

I want to pull away again, but I feel myself melting against him, and my hips rolling against my will, seeking any sort of friction.

The band is playing down below us. The room we are in is dim, but lit up by the lights shining on stage. I don't believe we are invisible here, but at the same time I don't particularly care as the heat is creeping up and taking over my body.

I throw my head back against Trent's shoulder when he bites down on mine. While keeping his left arm banded around me, his right hand begins its descent down my stomach to the waistline of my pants. I barely register the button being flicked open on my jeans, and Trent's hand sliding inside my underwear and when I feel his finger make contact with my clit, I can't stop the moan that escapes.

My hips lift up to try and gain the pressure of his hand as he lightly teases me, running his finger up and down lightly, just barely grazing the spot I need it most with each pass. It doesn't take long before I'm growing frustrated with the lack of contact. I'm shamelessly bucking my hips to get him to touch me more fully.

Reaching one hand back, I grab onto the back of his head, gripping the short hair as I try to gain leverage, but it doesn't help. I turn my head, seeking his mouth and angle my head so our lips meet in a clash of tongues and teeth, at the same time Trent presses his finger hard, right where I want it.

Then it's like the band has broken, and he's rubbing me with purpose before dipping his hand further and pushing inside me while keeping the palm of his hand against my clit. He's not teasing anymore, and I feel the release building inside me quickly. I don't know if it's the fight, or the raw chemistry we have that I want to keep denying.

I'm so close, I feel myself racing toward the orgasm, and I want to capture it so bad. My hips continue to move. Trent's fingers doing amazing things even confined by my pants, and just when I feel myself about to tip over the edge, he removes his hand quickly. I cry out at the loss.

It isn't long until my pants are being ripped down my legs, my panties going with them. I feel Trent quickly push down his own pants just to his thighs before I'm being pulled back on top of him. My mind clears for a single moment to gasp out, "condom."

Trent pauses for a moment before grabbing his wallet from his bunched-up pants, pulling out a condom and slipping it on in record time.

With me straddling his thighs backwards, facing out to the arena I sink down on him, groaning at the feel of him filling me so fully. I take a second to adjust to him. I feel his hands move to my hips, holding me there before I lift up, and drop back down roughly. His grip tightens on me.

I dig my nails into his forearms while I lift up again. Before I can drop down on my own, Trent is yanking me down and guiding my movements, taking control. And I let him. He's lifting his own hips underneath me so our skin slaps together over and over. I'm moaning, begging for more as he continues to drive into me.

I'm lost in the feeling of him.

Lost in this moment.

Lost in everything going on around us, but unable to focus on anything other than the way he fills me, and the orgasm threatening to take over my entire body in an intensity I know I'll never have felt before.

The feeling continues to build with each movement as I grind down each time he's buried to the hilt, and the release I was so close to from just his fingers is stronger than before.

Trent's face is buried in my shoulder, and I feel his lips

move, I'm sure he's saying dirty things. I wish I was facing him to know what he was saying, but there's a different intensity of watching the concert go on in front of us. Knowing all those people are surrounding us, without them having a single clue as to what we are doing up here.

It's like our own world, where it is just him and me, where I am really his. And maybe in some weird way, he is mine.

That's the thought I have when I finally explode. The feeling takes over my body as my release barrels through me. I clench around him, squeezing my thighs against his legs, but I remain open and full because he won't allow me to shut them completely.

A scream is ripped from my throat from the power of my orgasm. I'm bucking and sweating and swearing. I feel like I'm not even in my body anymore. I'm brought back when Trent's arms tighten around me, and his body stills beneath mine with his own release.

We stay pressed together while we both catch our breaths. Finally, when I feel like my legs won't give out beneath me, I peel myself off his lap. Pulling my pants back up over my hips I refuse to look at him again.

I suddenly want to leave. I know one of my favorite bands is playing, but I can't even focus on that since I can barely even feel the music.

All I feel is Trent.

How he held me against him.

How he felt inside me.

How he made me come.

He's all I feel.

And I feel suffocated by it.

By him.

    I feel his hands on my hips from behind, slowly pulling me back. I want to fight, but I purely don't have the energy. So, I allow him to pull me back into his lap sideways. I won't look at him, instead I watch the rest of the concert. Trent doesn't try to talk to me, and just…holds me. It feels odd to be held like this by him. I feel like this isn't something he does. He doesn't seem like the type.

    He also doesn't seem like the type to date, and like someone, which he basically told me before. And goddammit if I don't like how it feels to be in his arms like this.

    I barely register the rest of the concert and before I know it, it's over. And when he's moving me off him so we can leave I ignore the way I feel like I've lost something as soon as his arms aren't around me anymore.

    As we leave, I remind myself to keep the fire of hatred burning inside me for this man, but I feel it weakening, and I don't know what I'll do if it goes out completely.

26

Trent

Present

After the concert I want to bring Violet back home with me. I want to spend another night with her. I want to consume her, so she forgets everything that isn't me. And that's exactly why I don't, and why I fight every single urge I have, and bring her back to her apartment instead.

Just like the last time I brought her home she tries to run away as soon as she's off my bike, but I stop her, pulling her back to me to kiss her deeply.

By the time I pull away I see the glazed look in her eyes, but she obviously decides to fight it as well because she walks away, and into her apartment building.

I need a distraction, so I don't end up breaking into her apartment to take her to my house anyway. The best distraction I can think of is to deal with work. Nothing will get my dick softer than dealing with bullshit.

So, before I pull away from Violet's apartment, I call Jason and tell him to meet me at one of the warehouses that is used to hold extra product. We graduated from out-of-town storage units and invested in out-of-town warehouses instead.

One of them was compromised when that dumb fuck Cap decided to use it to kidnap a cop's girlfriend when they found out he was undercover. While I can appreciate the thought, it took away a good place from me.

By the time I pull up I see Jason is already there, leaning against his shitty car while smoke flows from his mouth.

"Sup boss," he nods at me after I've cut the engine on my bike.

"You gone in yet?" I ask. Part of why I wanted to meet here is to check out the inventory. I don't trust my dad, and I wouldn't doubt if he tried to clear me out of my supplies just to piss me off.

"No, I was waiting for you to get here." He throws down the butt of whatever he was just smoking as we walk up to the entrance.

I had locks with codes put on, and the code changes weekly. We head inside, the walls lined with shelves of different product including various drugs, and then hung up on the wall rows of weapons. I may not deal in the skin trade, but I'm not a good person. That thought alone should tempt me to keep my distance from Violet, but I can't bring myself to do that.

I mentally track the supply of everything. Nothing looks

like it's too low since I like to keep a consistent supply of the popular items, so we don't run the risk of running out and losing business. Especially to my father.

At the back of the building, there's another locked room where money is deposited. I like to keep a decent amount of cash here for emergencies. I'm the only one with the code, and it changes daily. There's a drop box so my guys can drop off the cash, but they aren't able to get into the room. No one is.

Opening the door, I know something is off before I even look inside, and when I am able to see inside, I know why. It's all gone.

I have several bank accounts with healthy amounts in all of them, so I'm not broke, but it doesn't change the fact that someone stole from me. I turn to Jason and see the shocked look on his face. While I want to instantly blame him since he has the closest thing to trust that I'm capable of, I don't think he's a good actor. And the look on his face seems genuine.

"Who did it?" I ask him anyway; in case he's heard things.

It's different being on the ground with people, running in circles and not being the boss. They tend to talk more freely when they don't know exactly who you are or what you do.

"Dunno, boss, everyone who has a problem with you went to work with Chris."

"Chances of it being my dad?" I snap. I know the answer, but I want him to say it.

"Probably pretty high."

"Fuck!"

While I wanted a distraction away from Violet this is not exactly what I wanted. It's like my dad wants a war against me. He wants us to work together or me to not be around at all. But that's not going to happen.

"Get everyone together to meet here tomorrow. There has to be someone still working with my dad in my ranks. And I need to make it known who the fuck is in charge around here."

I don't bother locking the door to the now empty room as I storm out. I leave Jason to deal with locking up the whole building while I leave the area to go back home. I'm so mad I want to track down my dad and kill him, but I know that can't happen. Not yet anyway.

What started out as a distraction from my Flower, has now made it so I need her to consume my thoughts again. So, once I get home, I send her a text because she's the only thing that is going to calm me, and I don't want to delve too deep into what that actually means for me.

> Trent: Still thinking about me?

As I head to my room my eyes linger on the piano in the living room. My hands itch to play, to use it to let out some of the anger I'm feeling.

Instead, I walk away and strip off my clothes, the clothes that still smell like her and remind me of what we did only hours before. It feels like it's been days since I've felt her in my arms, felt her wet heat wrapped around me. I need it again. Right now.

Reluctantly, I strip down to get in the shower, though I want to keep the scent of her on me forever but it feels tainted by what I just discovered in my warehouse. I check my phone before turning on the water, slightly surprised she replied so quickly.

> Violet: Seems like you were since you texted first.

I smile. Of course I was. I still can't believe I told her any of that stuff, I know it wasn't much sharing the bare minimum about my parents, but it's more than I would normally share with anyone. Especially mentioning Zander, what the fuck is wrong with me? It's like I couldn't stop myself, and any filter I would normally have just evaporated.

And then I think of that argument we had. How she thinks I like a hearing version of her. Clearly, I can't learn sign language overnight, so I don't think it's that unreasonable for her to speak to me. And despite what she thinks, I do like her. Exactly how she is.

And I don't like anyone, never have, so this is untouched territory for me.

Something tells me it's somewhat new for her too.

> Trent: I'm always thinking about you, Flower.

I send the text, then get into the shower. The hot water pelts my skin as I try to wipe the bullshit in my life away and think of what Violet could be doing right now.

Instantly, I think of her in some tiny fucking panties and a tight tank top without a bra. I can imagine how perfect her pink nipples would show, practically begging for my mouth.

My dick hardens at the very thought of her, and I'm lost in the fantasy. The thought of her being in my room like that, ready for me to join her. She'd already be touching herself, the only sound in the room being her little whimpers and the wet slide of her fingers as she fucks herself.

My hand wraps around myself as I continue to picture my little Flower spread out on my bed for me. As soon as she sees me come into the room, naked except the towel around my waist she stops what she's doing to come over to me. Immediately dropping down to her knees in front of me. The look in her dark brown eyes almost pleading.

"Take it off," I tell her.

She watches me too intensely all the time, the pure focus in her eyes whenever she looks at me is the thing of dreams and nightmares all at once because I find myself becoming addicted to every piece of her. She tugs at the towel softly, so it falls from my waist easily, and she looks up at me waiting for my next command.

I groan thinking of her being so submissive for me. I've felt her become pliant for me, but never like this, the fantasy continues to consume me while I work myself in my fist.

Violet takes me into her mouth, the wet warm perfection surrounding me as she sucks, then runs her tongue along my length. I push deeper into her throat while my hand squeezes myself tighter.

Suddenly, my phone dings with a text and it pulls me out of the fantasy. My cock is painfully hard, but if it's Violet that texts me, maybe my Flower could join the fantasy, or even better, make it a reality.

I'm out of the shower quickly, and instantly grabbing my phone, smiling at the response. Seems like she might want to play.

Violet: What exactly are you thinking?

Trent: You really want to know?

Violet: Tell me.

Trent: Well, I was just thinking about what it would be like to have your mouth wrapped around my cock.

She doesn't respond right away, and I wonder if maybe she wasn't as prepared for my response as she thought. I toss my phone on my bed while I pull on some boxers before climbing into bed, my dick straining the fabric.

Violet: You like the thought of me on my knees for you?

Trent: You have no idea.

Pulling my waistband to my boxers down, my hand is around myself again as the fantasy takes over right where it left off, except now Violet is bobbing her head up and down on me with my hands buried in her hair.

When I look at my phone she sent a picture with her next text, and I groan when I see what the picture is. She's posed on the floor, on her knees with the phone angled above her so she has to look up into it. Giving me the exact view I'm dying for.

> Violet: Like this?

> Trent: Flower…don't tempt me to come over and make this a reality.

> Violet: You wouldn't.

> Trent: I really would. I can be there in less than 15 minutes.

> Violet: That's probably not a great idea since my sister is home.

> Trent: Too bad. Tell me what you're thinking about then.

> Violet: Other than you leaving me alone?

I don't know why her attitude makes me stroke my dick even harder, it's the equivalent to dirty talk to me when it's coming from her.

> Trent: I know you want my mouth on you again. Or my hands. Or my cock. Tell me, Flower, when you're alone in your room like this what is it you think about?

> Violet: I think of tying you to the bed, shutting you up, and making it so you can't see or hear anything. Seeing how cocky you are when you're at my mercy.

My strokes continue to get rougher and faster at the thought of her doing exactly that. I like control through and through. I don't trust anyone, and I don't give it up, ever. But for some reason I consider making that a reality.

> Trent: I'd be willing to do that for you, only you.

Violet: Now that's something I'd like to see.

> Trent: Maybe if you beg. I'd love to see you beg for me.

Violet: You'll never see me beg.

> Trent: Never say never, Flower.

Violet: Goodnight Trent.

> Trent: Dream dirty dreams about me.

I know I will as I continue to beat my dick faster and harder until I'm spilling into my hand picturing it's on Violet's tongue instead. Grabbing tissues to clean myself up I can't help but think about how fucked I am for this girl.

There's a reason I don't have attachments to anyone, but for some reason she's making that impossible, and yet I don't plan on letting her go.

THE NEXT DAY I'm in the warehouse staring at the group of men in front of me. The men that claim to work for me. Be loyal to me, and my business. Supposedly. Clearly one or more of them is betraying me, and I can't have that.

This group is a lot smaller than I remember it being before. I felt like everything was growing so well until I went to prison, and it all got fucked.

"Does anyone know why I called you all here?" I ask the group. I'm standing tall, arms folded across my chest, the silent intimidation.

I scan the room, looking at everyone to see who looks suspicious, shifty. There are a few guys not looking directly at me, and I make note of who.

"Someone in here is a fucking rat, and I need to figure out who it is."

There's murmurs and movement around the room, but no one is speaking up about anything yet.

"If you come forward now, I may make it less painful." I try to tempt them out. I didn't think it would work, no one wants to be caught.

"Someone knew about our drop spot and stole all the money in it. They could've taken product, but they didn't. Just the cash. Does anyone know who would want to do that?"

"Your dad?" Some quiet guy toward the back guesses.

"Exactly. My dad. Christopher Moore. He's mad I turned him down to combine our businesses because I want no part of his. He wanted revenge. He wants a war. Does anyone here want a war?"

More murmurs, but no one steps forward.

"Didn't think so. Consider this your warning. I'll be watching and if you're caught, I won't be easy on you."

I wave them all off to go back to their business. They all seem to hesitate, obviously not wanting to piss me off more than I already am. As everyone starts filing out, Jason approaches me.

"What do you know?" I ask him because I can see the look on his face, and it's clear there's something he wants to share.

"I heard this guy, Jax, on the phone when I got here. I thought he was talking to you because it sounded like he was agreeing to some orders, but when I got closer, he was quick to hang up." Jason says quietly so no one else still in the building can hear him.

"Wasn't on the phone with me, I haven't talked to any of these fuckers. Bring him back in once everyone is gone."

Jason nods, and I wait.

We have him in a chair in the middle of the room. I've asked some soft questions, he is sweating bullets though, and I know he's not going to be hard to break.

"When did you first meet my dad?" I ask, finally starting to get to the more important questions.

"I – I haven't. Well, maybe once while you were still in lockup."

"So, which is it? You haven't or once?"

More sweat. He looks over to Jason like he's going to help.

"Once, I guess."

"And how long have you been working for him?"

"I – I'm not. No, I work for you."

I hum in agreement. "Right. You do. And you also are double crossing me by working for him too. What does he have on you?"

"Nothing."

I pick up a knife from the wall, it's a butterfly knife. I haven't used one of these in a while, but it's like riding a bike the way I flick it open with ease.

"Did he threaten your family? Have some sort of blackmail against you?" I flip the knife around a couple times, getting used to the feeling in my hand again.

"N – no. There's nothing," he says again, but it's much weaker this time.

I shrug before bringing the knife down, slashing it across his chest. Only deep enough to rip the fabric of his shirt, and leave a small cut, one that will feel like a paper cut. It'll barely bleed but will burn like a bitch.

"I'll give you one more chance before I start cutting deeper," I threaten.

Jax seems to start shaking a bit more. "I mean it, Trent, he doesn't have anything on me. I don't know what you're talking about."

"So, you're calling me stupid?" I snap.

"No! No, I'm just – "

I slam the knife down into his right hand that is white knuckling the chair he's currently sitting in. His scream bounces off the walls as I pull my knife from his hand. He starts to try and stand up, but Jason slams him back down with two hands on his shoulders.

"Don't fucking lie to me again."

"I mean it, I'm not working for him," he sobs.

I see Jason pressing harder on his shoulders while I shrug, about to bring the knife down on his thigh this time.

"Wait!" he calls out before the knife makes contact. "He wanted something on you. Something to get you to agree to work with him."

My interest is piqued. "And stealing all my cash was that thing?"

"No, I don't know. I don't know about that. He just wanted info on you. I told him about this place, he said he just wanted you guys to work together."

I scoff, yeah, he wants to continue to control me, but I won't tell this asshole that.

"You're going to send him a message from me. In exchange, I won't kill you, but if you don't give him the message and if I ever see your ugly fucking face again, you're dead."

To accentuate my point, I drive my knife into his other hand anyway. Once his screaming quiets again I tell him what I want my dad to know, which is to stay the fuck out of my way.

Jason deals with kicking the guy out because I wanted to keep hitting him. I wanted to kill him. No one gets to cross me. It makes me look fucking weak, and I'm not weak.

I have blood on my hands, my entire life has been living on the wrong side of the law. I don't deny the fact that I've hurt people, won't lie that there's some bodies on my conscience from when I've gotten too carried away. I even tried to kill my stepbrother for betraying me.

This is why, if I was a better person, I should stay away from Violet. I shouldn't drag her down into this life and expose her to the dangers that come with being around me. I wouldn't hurt her, but I know people that would.

Having someone you care about is a weakness, especially to someone like my dad. He would never understand caring about anyone. He never has.

Violet can never see my real life; I can't let her. I also can't stay away, and I know this. I'll keep all of this away from her, I know it's the only option because no one can know she exists. No one can know she's potentially a weakness for me. I'll protect her, but she can never know about this. She wouldn't accept it, she's too good. She might have thorns. She might be strong. But underneath it all she's a good person, I can tell. And this would destroy her.

Plus, she already thinks I'm a piece of shit, and this would prove her right. And then I'd lose all progress I've made with her. I have to keep convincing her to give me a chance.

I have to keep her.

27

Present

I'm not necessarily proud of what I'm doing right now, but I need to do something to remind myself of the reason I'm putting up with Trent. I need some sort of reality check so I can stop falling into his traps that lead to orgasms.

It's scary how quickly he's pushed me out of my comfort zone when it comes to sex. I would never consider doing anything remotely sexual in public, and then the concert happened a few days ago. Plus, there's the texts afterwards.

I'm losing my mind, and I need to get it together because this has blurred the lines too much for me.

This is why I did some research, and found a tattoo artist named Zander in Newport, Oregon, and I'm driving there to meet him. Luckily, he has a unique name because that made things significantly easier since I didn't have a last name for him. Or a specific city.

Maybe I should be a detective or a private investigator or something instead of a teacher. Lip reading is probably a great skill to have in being a P.I.

I booked a tattoo appointment with Zander, because I didn't want to show up without a plan. I have considered getting a tattoo for my mom anyway, so this works out in a weird way. It pushes me to finally do it, even though I secretly wished it was something Mila and I could do together. Plus, I can try and see if Zander will share any information about his stepbrother.

It's a win-win.

Even if I have no idea how I will possibly bring up Trent to him since it doesn't sound like they have a great relationship. I don't want this guy to know I know his stepbrother.

I also had to borrow Mila's car to drive out here. I feel like mine is going to break down at any point, so I don't want to end up stranded. It took some convincing for her to let me use it. When I explained it had to do with the investigation she is also a part of, she reluctantly agreed.

This is the first time I've gone to the coast since I was little. Sometimes my mom would randomly want to go on an adventure somewhere, and sometimes that would be to the coast. Of course, like a lot of things in my life, after my mom passed, we stopped doing things like that. I guess in a way it's fitting to come here for the tattoo for her.

Pulling up to the little shop, it's in the downtown area where the ocean breeze hits me as soon as I am out of the car. Despite it being summer, it's colder than I thought it would be and I regret not bringing a light jacket.

It's much warmer inside the shop, and I'm greeted by warm lighting and lots of artwork on the walls. The entryway is small, and there's a hallway I assume leads back to the artist's stations. I look around, admiring all the various art on the wall which is everything ranging from landscapes to portraits to abstract pieces.

I turn around and see a man standing near the entrance of the hallway, he's extremely tall, his big arms covered in tattoos. The t-shirt he's wearing shows the clear bulk of muscles beneath and holy hell is he attractive. Brown hair falls over his forehead, and bright turquoise eyes. Zander doesn't have any pictures of himself on his social media aside from an obscure, small profile picture, and for a moment I think there's no way this is him.

Until he opens his mouth to speak.

"Are you Violet?"

I nod.

"Nice to meet you, I'm Zander."

Well damn, okay. I would blame the genetics as to how he's so attractive, and so is Trent, but they aren't even related by blood. So, I have nothing to blame.

"Hi, I don't know if you were trying to talk to me before. I couldn't hear you, I'm deaf." I tell him, along with signing. I didn't tell him that before, I usually don't preface that with anyone, either they figure it out or I'll tell them, so they don't think I'm being a bitch and ignoring them.

"Thanks for letting me know, come on back we can talk about your tattoo." I follow him back down the hallway and this guy seems nice. Maybe that's why Trent has such an issue with him because he can't stand nice people. I'd believe it.

Zander leads me to a small room off the hallway where there's a chair, and a table with the supplies out. The walls in here are also covered in artwork, I can't help but examine all of it. One picture in particular draws my attention the most. It's a painting of a beach, there's a swing set on the sand and above the ocean is a night sky filled with stars. Some are brighter than others, they seem to outline what looks like a key.

I continue to examine the picture when I notice Zander stand next to me, looking at it as well.

"Did you do this?" I ask.

He nods, turning toward me with a small smile. "Yeah, I use my free time around here to work on it, but I just finished it recently, it's going to be a present for my wife."

"It's beautiful. Are the stars in the shape of a key?"

His smile grows a little more, he keeps looking at the picture with so much happiness in his eyes I can almost feel it.

"They are. Keys are an important symbol for her."

"Why?"

It looks like he chuckles. "Let's get your tattoo started and maybe I'll tell you."

Fair enough, I don't know if I would be okay sharing something that is clearly special with a complete stranger.

I told Zander what I wanted in my original message, or at least the idea of what I wanted, which was a simple outline of the sign for "I love you" since it was the last sign my mom was able to sign to me. It was shaky, and not perfect, but it was there.

I also don't care if it's cliché, it's what I've wanted for a while. Zander told me he was going to draw a couple different designs for me, and I could pick the one I like the most.

He pulls up the drawings on his iPad to show me. My favorite is one that is a single line that forms the sign, then below it spells out "I love you". It's simple, and exactly what I want. I point to it.

"Cool, I'll get the stencil ready," he tells me.

As I continue to examine other art on the walls of the room, I see there are a lot of keys in various forms, colors, shapes and sizes.

"I need to know the deal with all these keys," I tell him as he pulls a piece of paper off a printer.

He smiles wider this time while he's cutting out the outline for the tattoo and putting it into another printer looking thing.

"My wife, Mel, and her best friend, Aylin, came up with it in college. They say there are keys to your life, and when things get hard that's the motivation to keep going."

I think back on times from my own life, and what keys that would be for me. Music obviously, is a big one for me. I smile back at him.

"I like that." I tell him.

"Good, now where are we putting this?"

I decide to get the tattoo on my forearm. Once Zander has prepped my arm, placed the stencil in its location, I settle in the chair, ready for him to get started. I watch as he prepares the tattoo gun, looks at me and asks if I'm ready. I nod, and he gets started.

To be honest, I expected it to hurt a bit more than it does. It just feels like a dull scratch, and even though Zander is looking down I decide to try and see if I can get some information from him since that was the reason I came here to begin with.

"So, how long have you and your wife lived around here?"

Zander leans back to get more ink in the gun. "Around five years."

"You like it?"

He nods before focusing back on my arm.

"Do either of you have family around here?" I know it's a risky question, and I'm not even sure if he will answer it.

It seems like he's almost too focused on what he is doing to think twice about what I'm asking, and just naturally answers without thinking about it. He leans back to refill the tattoo gun with ink, so I'm able to see when he answers.

"Not really, her dad is in Portland and my family is all out of state."

"That's cool."

I think about how I want to try and bring up anything having to do with Trent. Maybe he doesn't even realize he's out of prison. Or doesn't consider him family, which I guess would make sense.

Maybe if I start to share something about myself, it won't seem as weird to keep asking him questions.

"My sister and I were supposed to get tattoos like this together." I tell him.

He pauses again to wipe off the area on my arm. "Will she be mad you got it without her?"

"No, I doubt she will care. We don't really get along. Do you have siblings?"

"Nope," he answers before looking down again.

"Not even step or half sibling?" I try.

He doesn't answer right away and pauses again before looking up and replying. "I technically have a stepbrother, but I don't talk to him."

I chew on my lip, wondering if I should continue to push this with him. It doesn't sound like I'll get much information from him, and since they don't talk, I doubt he knows anything going on with Trent now anyway.

Suddenly, I feel really stupid for this plan, and even though I wanted this tattoo I don't know what I expected out of this trip. Instead of trying to ask more questions, I go a different route. One I might regret, but I don't want to leave it at that.

"Do you think you could ever be close to him?"

Again, he doesn't answer right away. He wipes at the tattoo before looking up at me again. "No. Could you be close to your sister?"

I think about that while he continues to clean up the finished art on my arm. "Maybe," I practically whisper.

"You're all done."

I look at my arm, and love how it turned out, despite my reasoning for coming here in the first place. I thank Zander and pay him before I leave. I think I'm in over my head with this, and I need to quit while I'm ahead.

Before I leave Zander says, "I hope you and your sister can work it out and let me know if she wants to end up matching with you."

I give him a small smile with a nod. I won't tell him that isn't likely to happen, even if I still hold on to that small amount of hope.

I'VE JUST ENDED another class at the Wright House, and as usual I'm trying to get out of here as fast as I can to hopefully avoid a run in with Trent. Kylee comes up and taps me on the shoulder while I'm putting my things away.

"Hey, how's it going?" I ask.

"Can we talk again?"

"Of course."

We wait until everyone leaves because I can sense her uneasiness, and I assume she doesn't want to have an audience if it has anything to do with our previous conversation.

"How has it been going?" I ask once everyone is gone.

"It's fine," she says, but I can tell she doesn't mean it. I give her a look to show I know she's not being honest. She just sighs.

"You can tell me," I encourage.

She looks hesitant to go on, but finally she does. "I tried to take your advice about ignoring those bitches, but I feel like it's just getting so much worse."

I wince. I knew my advice wasn't great, but I don't like hearing that things haven't gotten better for her.

"I'm sorry I didn't –"

She waves her hands to cut me off. "No, no, I'm not blaming

you, it's just," she seems to groan. "I hate it here. I hate dealing with everyone and I'm sick of it."

"What happened?"

"Well, no one is talking to me, which I thought was kind of great. That was until my bed was covered in sticky notes with a bunch of mean shit written on it."

I don't need to ask what was written on there, I know how nasty teenage girls can be to each other.

"I'm really sorry, Kylee, what do you need?" I truly don't know what else to say.

She shrugs. "I want to run away, that's what I always do when I'm scared and overwhelmed. I run."

I think about that for a second before responding, using my voice because this conversation got a bit more serious, and I don't want anything lost in interpretation. "Are you actually planning on running?"

"Yeah? No? I don't know, I always do this," she shakes her head.

"Why?"

"I've never had a home, well not a real one, anyway. So, when I would be at a foster home, even if it was good, I still wouldn't feel safe, and it would just be easier to run."

I can't even begin to know how she feels, or know what she's gone through, but to constantly be in survival mode, that must be exhausting. She is also reminding me of Mila, and how she was right before she left me.

"I know you said before you didn't want to go to Travis, but I really think you should," I encourage softly.

Kylee shrugs. "I just think it'll just make everything worse, but I know if I run, I'll end up back in juvie. Though, that might be better for me anyway."

"Hey, I don't believe that. You can get through this program; you can get through this bullshit. You can do this. I know it. You're a smart girl, and even if it doesn't feel like it now, things will get better."

She still doesn't look sure, then I see her eyes look over my shoulder, and she smirks. *"That guy Trent is over there."*

I roll my eyes and refuse to look behind me. *"Ignore him. Are you going to be okay?"*

"Yeah, you know," she seems to think about how to say what she's going to continue with, *"I've seen him stare at you a lot."*

"I don't care about him. I care about you and making sure you are okay."

She gives me a sly look, and I think the conversation about her is over now, which makes me nervous because I really don't want her to run. I debate giving Travis a heads up anyway.

"Yeah, I'm okay. He's cute though," she smiles, and I know for sure the conversation is over.

"He's way too old for you. He's too old for me too." I roll my eyes telling a sixteen-year-old girl this.

She smirks, "Something tells me he wants you anyway."

I swing my head over my shoulder to make sure he didn't hear that, but he's not there anymore.

"Please tell me if you need anything, Kylee," I tell her before she has a chance to leave.

She nods. "I will."

I shake my head after she's gone. Teenagers are so weird. I decide to stop by Travis' office to talk to him before leaving. I won't tell him everything going on with her, but I feel like I need to give him the heads up if she's thinking of running. I don't want that on my conscience.

After a single knock on his door, I go inside. He greets me with a smile, and his obligatory ASL phrase, *"Hi, how did it go today?"*

"Good." I know I have to voice the rest because he will not understand anything I'm about to say. "I'm worried about Kylee."

His brows furrow. "Why? What's going on?"

"Look, she didn't want me to say anything, so I'm not going to tell you everything because it's not my place, but just maybe check in with her."

He nods. "I will. Is it something serious?"

"I think it could be."

"Okay, yeah. Thank you for letting me know."

I give him a small smile before waving, goodbye. I think he might try to talk to me more, but I've already turned around and started to walk away. As usual, I keep my head down as I leave to avoid any possible Trent sightings even though he supposedly already saw me, and according to Kylee he stares at me, and she's noticed. Which means I'm sure other people have too. *Great.*

Once I'm in my car, I pull out my phone to see a text from the asshole himself. It's been over a week since the concert, and I have done a decent job avoiding him. It seems like he's getting tired of waiting for me to reach out.

Trent: You look beautiful today, Flower.

Violet: Stop stalking me.

Trent: I wouldn't have to if you would talk to me.

Violet: Sounds like the mindset of a psycho.

Trent: Who says I'm not?

Without responding, I head back home. I know I'm going to end up seeing him again soon, I can just feel it.

28

5 Years Ago (Age 16)

I thought I was alone before, but I was wrong.

Now that Mila is gone, I'm truly alone.

We weren't close, we fought all the time, but when we fought at least she was talking to me. At least *someone* in my house was talking to me.

But now she's gone, run off to who knows where, with who knows who, and doing who knows what. And I don't know why. She left about a month ago and hasn't reached out to me since.

I avoid going home as much as possible, hanging out with Jenson as much as I can. My dad never asks where I am, doesn't reach out to me. I feel like some days he wishes I would just run away too.

When I started to realize Mila wasn't coming back, I tried to talk to my dad a bit more. I tried to look at her disappearance as a way to bring us closer. That might be a messed-up way to think about it, but I just wanted to hold on to the tiny thread of family I had left.

My dad was cooking, I sat down at the island, waiting for him to say something to me. He didn't.

"What are you making?" I sign when he turns around but keeps his head down. I know he can see me signing, so he knows I'm talking to him. He doesn't acknowledge me.

Eventually he puts food on two plates, taking his and leaving the kitchen while mine is left on the counter for me. I stare at it while the tears stream down my face on a silent sob. I stare at that plate for so long the food gets cold. I get up and leave without touching it and go up to my room.

After my door is locked, I turn on my stereo as loud as it will go, lay on the floor, and allow myself to fall into the music.

It's the middle of the night when I wake up to my smart watch vibrating on my wrist. Confusion takes over because I know it's not my alarm. I look to see that it's signaling a string of texts. From my sister.

> Mila: Wake up.
>
> Mila: Let me in.
>
> Mila: Violet.
>
> Mila: Now.

It takes me a second to realize she's actually texting me. I head to the front door, looking out to make sure it really is her. Sure enough, there she is. And she looks like a mess.

I open the door to let her in, she storms past me without even a simple "thank you". She's storming up to her room, and I follow. She tries to slam the door in my face, but I manage to stop it before it closes.

She turns toward me, but keeps her head down, her blonde hair covering her face as she signs.

"Go away, Vi, I'm not going to talk about it."

I wring my hands in front of me. I have so much to say, so much I want to let out and unleash on her. I want to tell her how hard it has been to be alone, how I hate that our dad doesn't talk to me. I want to make her feel horrible for leaving me. I want to ask why; I want to tell her she's an idiot for leaving.

But I don't do any of that. I can't see her eyes, but I see how red her cheeks are, and the smeared makeup on her face. Her hair is a mess and looks like it's been tugged and tangled even before she stepped out into the rain. She's shaking, I can't tell if it's from crying or from being cold.

So, instead of saying any of the mean things I want to say instead of hurting her and starting the fight I really want, I just say the one thing I never thought I would.

"I missed you."

I don't even know if she saw what I said, but I don't give her the chance to reply, as I give her my back and walk out of her room, shutting the door behind me.

    Clearly, she went through something while she was gone. I may never know what it was, but I know one thing. And that is that my sister is strong, it takes a lot to break her, but whatever she went through might have done exactly that.

29

Trent

Present

Violet can't avoid me forever; I won't let her.

I have been a bit busy cleaning up my businesses and making sure my dad has his nose out of all of it. Because of that, I gave Violet some space because I didn't have the time to give her my full attention, and I figured it would be good. It could give her a chance to think about me, and how much she wants to see me again. Despite what she may say, she wants me just as badly as I want her.

I saw her a couple days ago talking to one of the kids after her class, and I couldn't take my eyes off her. I've never been addicted to anything. I haven't tried drugs; I never get drunk. I remain in control, and I like to keep it that way.

But Violet may be the closest I've come to an addiction. When I see her, I feel like I need to be closer to her, surrounded by her. It's a new and dangerous territory.

We texted a bit after I saw her but continued to give her space for a few more days. Now, I can't take it anymore, and I need a fix. I will do whatever I need to make sure I get one. That's why I find myself outside her apartment building once again.

I'm trying a new tactic, which is why I'm dressed in dark slacks, a white button up, and leaning against my bike with my right leg crossed over my left.

> Trent: Put on something nice and come downstairs.

> Violet: Go fuck yourself.

> Trent: Gladly, but I'd much rather fuck you.

> Violet: You're disgusting.

> Trent: We both know that's not true.

> Violet: Stop. Stalking. Me.

> Trent: You like it.

> Violet: You wish.

> Trent: I don't need to.

She doesn't respond, and I think she might force my hand, and make me actually come up to get her this time. Now I know which apartment is hers so I wouldn't have to guess. I decide to give her a few minutes, and just as I'm about to head up to get her, she's walking out the front doors.

My breath is knocked out of me. She's wearing a dark purple dress that falls to her mid thighs. The top is tight to show off her perfect tits. The bottom flares out and swings around her thighs as she walks toward me. She has black heeled boots on her feet. Her blonde hair falls down her shoulders, and it tempts me to bury my hands in it. She has an adorable scowl on her face as she approaches me.

I smile as she approaches. She stops a few feet from me, crossing her arms across her chest, pushing up her breasts, making her cleavage even more obvious. I run my thumb across my bottom lip as my eyes continue to run all over her body.

"You're perfect." The words slip out of my mouth without even thinking as soon as my eyes meet hers.

She shifts on her feet. "Uh, thanks. Why are you here?"

"We are going on our first official date."

Her eyes narrow on me. "The concert wasn't a date?"

"You admit that it was?" I taunt.

She ignores my question. "What makes this count as an official date?"

I smile. "Because I'm going to make sure you actually like me by the end of it."

She snorts a laugh. "Not going to happen."

WE PULL up to the restaurant. I pulled strings to get us a reservation last minute. They book out at least a month in advance, but the owner has a few vices that I help supply him with. One phone call, and he was able to get us a table with a view.

Violet looks around as we step through the door and go right to an elevator. I keep my arm wrapped around her waist as we step inside. I press the button to take us to the top floor. Once the doors open, we are greeted by the open, low lit restaurant that is surrounded by panoramic windows that look out onto the Portland skyline.

I lead Violet forward, watching her reaction as we are brought to a private table with the best view this place offers, and away from the other patrons. We are sitting across from each other, and I can't take my eyes off her as she stares out the windows in amazement. I just watch her.

The waiter comes up to us, and I barely even notice until he starts pouring water in the cup in front of me. He asks what else he can get for us to drink. I order an old fashioned and notice that Violet is still staring out the window. Reaching across, I run my hand over hers that's flat on the table. She looks over to me, and then sees the waiter.

"I'll have a gin and tonic." I raise my eyebrows, slightly shocked by her drink choice.

He walks away to get our drinks, and Violet finally looks at me, taking in my shocked expression, and signing something.

"Show me some signs," I say suddenly.

It's her turn to look surprised. "Like what?"

I shrug. "Whatever you think I should know."

She seems to think for a moment, and I see when she comes up with something. The smile on her face lets me know what she came up with probably isn't a compliment.

"Okay, copy me," she commands before making different gestures with her hands.

I do my best to copy what she does, and I have no idea how I'm going to be expected to remember these. I've seen her sign all the time, even when she uses her voice, but I guess I haven't paid much attention to the specifics like I am now.

She shows me a couple times before telling me to do it on my own. I try to do it how she showed me, but I'm sure I botched it. My suspicions are confirmed when she covers her mouth after a soft laugh slips out.

"Not bad," she lies.

"What does it mean?"

The waiter returns with our drinks, so she doesn't answer me yet. I tell him we need another few minutes to look at the menu before looking back to Violet with my eyebrow raised waiting to know what she just taught me to say.

"It's how you should introduce yourself in ASL," she shrugs right before taking a sip of her drink.

"But what does it *mean*, Flower?"

"Maybe I'll tell you later, if our date is successful." She picks up her menu and attempts to ignore me while looking at it.

Reaching over, I push the menu down softly so she will look up at me again, this time with an annoyed face.

"If this date is successful, you'll be too busy screaming my name for the rest of the night to tell me. So, might as well tell me now."

"Trent," she feigns a gasp. "Do I seem like the type of girl that puts out on the first date because if so, you are very mistaken about that. I'm a lady."

I catch her sly smile before she hides her face with the menu again. I actually laugh. A genuine laugh, and I can't remember the last time that happened.

30

Present

I taught him to say, *"I'm Trent, and I am a little bitch."*

I have no plans on ever telling him that, though, so he can just sit and wonder. Or I'll just make something else up to tell him what it means. I doubt he will even remember the signs anyway considering how much he was struggling.

But I did like that he asked how to sign something.

I thought he might have been actually trying tonight until that last comment about me screaming his name. Though, I won't admit, I might like the night to end with that as well.

We both order once the waiter comes back. Without my menu shield, I go back to looking out the window. It really is a beautiful view. The sun is beginning to set, and it creates an orange and pink glow around the entire city. I feel his fingers graze my hand again to get my attention. The small contact makes my heart race, and I try to shut that reaction down quickly.

"Tell me something about yourself, Flower." Trent looks genuine with his request.

I shift in my seat suddenly, slightly uncomfortable with that look on his face, and my body's reaction to the minuscule contact we just had. I need to get myself together.

"Like what?" I don't want him to really know much about me, so I feel like I'm walking a fine line. This entire plan is to get to know *him* and his dirty secrets. Not mine.

"I told you about my family. Your turn."

I wince before taking a large sip from my drink, the alcohol burns my throat and I revel in that for a minute before I answer.

"Mom died when I was younger, dad doesn't really talk to me, older sister is a bitch."

He nods. "Makes sense."

"What does?"

"You having daddy issues. It's why you want a better *daddy*."

"Did you seriously just say something about me wanting a better daddy?" I verify I saw that correctly.

He nods.

"Gross, you aren't and would never be my *daddy.*'

He just smiles wider. "I could be."

"Pass. My turn." I think back about our past conversation when his family came up and he said he isn't close to anyone. "Why do you have mommy and daddy issues?"

His smile drops. "Because they suck."

"What about your stepbrother?"

"He sucks even more." Trent takes a large sip from his drink, imitating how I reacted earlier.

"Do you think you could ever get along?"

"No."

His response is immediate and firm. My eyes drop, I don't know why that bothers me, but I guess I don't like the finality his tone has. Obviously, I have issues with my dad and Mila, but somewhere in the back of my mind I have the smallest sliver of hope that maybe we could be a family again. I try not to think about it too much, but it's there.

"What about you? Could you ever get along with your sister?"

"Maybe. We live together, so I tolerate her." I down the rest of my drink, and immediately want another one.

"Family sucks." I nod in agreement. I don't dare tell him

that at one time my family didn't suck, and it was pretty great. He doesn't get to know about that.

"So," I place my elbows on the table, despite that being bad etiquette, and lean forward, "what exactly do you do for work, Trent?"

He smiles like he expected this to come up at some point. It probably should have, but every time we have been together, we are usually too busy fighting or fucking. This is the first real conversation we've had.

"I work at Wright House with you," he smirks.

I scoff. "I know that's just a part of your parole."

He smiles wider. "Someone has looked into me."

"How do you make money? Because it isn't there."

"I own a couple businesses," he leans back.

"What kind of businesses?"

"Sales kind."

"What do you sell?"

"Why does this feel like an interrogation?" He chuckles.

"Why won't you answer?"

"I sell a variety of items. Supply and demand and all that bullshit."

I go to ask another question, but he cuts me off before I get to say anything.

"What are you going to school for?"

"Teaching. I want to teach ASL at hearing schools."

"You can practice with me, show me more signs."

I can tell this is a diversion from me asking more questions about his businesses, and we are both saved when our food is brought to the table. We eat without any conversation, and I try not to focus too much on what he was saying about what he does.

It's not like he really told me anything, and he didn't mention his dad being involved in what he does. He even said before that they don't have a good relationship. Maybe Nate and Mitch are wrong, and it is all Trent, not his dad.

Or maybe, Trent really is just in sales and it's all his dad.

Not likely.

Once we are done, Trent pays for our meal and leads me out with a hand on the small of my back. We go back down the elevator and head to Trent's motorcycle and I'm suddenly uncomfortable not knowing what to expect next. He must sense it because he gives me one of his easy smiles.

"What are you thinking, Flower?"

"I just don't know what to expect from this version of you."

"There's no different version. It's all me."

I don't believe him but choose to drop it for now.

"Where are we going now?" I ask as he hands me the helmet I always wear with him.

"How about we just go for a ride," he suggests, and I doubt I imagine the innuendo.

"Last time we did that you took me to your house."

"Would that be so bad again?"

"I'm not sleeping with you, Trent."

He just smiles before putting his helmet on and straddling the bike, ending the conversation. Since I don't have much of a choice at the moment, I follow suit, removing my hearing aids before putting the helmet on then straddling the bike as well. My body is plastered against his, and he takes off.

Riding on Trent's motorcycle is such an overwhelming feeling. The wind whips at our legs, mine are exposed because I wore a dress like an idiot, but I kind of like the slight sting the wind hits me with.

We go from the freeway to deeper roads that lead into the woods, these aren't the roads that lead to his house, though. As we continue to ride through the now dark streets my hands on him start to wander. I can feel his muscled stomach underneath his shirt, and I run my right hand up and down slowly.

I feel his hand grip mine to stop my movements, and I smile because it wasn't a sweet hand grab. No, it was a "stop that shit" grab. He removes his hand again and after another few minutes I begin my wandering again. This time, I move down to the top of his pants, then lower. I feel his hard cock stretching the fabric. I rub myself slightly against his back while my hand rubs him through his pants.

His hand comes down on mine again to stop the movement. We continue to speed through the streets, taking turns too fast and I know he's breaking the speed limit, but I don't even find it in myself to care. I like fucking with him. I like knowing I can affect him so strongly. He's such a controlled man, and I like it when he loses it.

Suddenly, I notice a red and blue glow coming from behind us, I turn my head slightly and see the lights flashing in the distance, coming closer. My arms tighten around Trent's body, nerves taking over. I expect him to slow down, and pull over, just hoping I don't get caught up in whatever mess is about to unfold. I shouldn't have come out with him. I knew this, and yet I still did it.

Maybe, if we get arrested, I can mention Nate and Mitch, and they can help me. I don't know their last names, though. I begin to panic, and it only gets worse when I feel Trent speed up even more.

I shriek as he takes off. I'm completely wrapped around him, holding on for dear life as he is going at an obscene speed. Our legs practically graze the ground at how sharp he takes the turns.

The lights are still flashing behind us, and I know Trent is not going to pull over. He's trying to outrun them. I want to scream at him that he's being an idiot. I know he wouldn't be able to hear me through our helmets and the wind. Plus, I'm sure there are sirens going crazy behind us. I close my eyes, tighten my grip and hope if we die it happens quickly.

The bike underneath us continues to dip and turn as Trent races against the cops behind us. I feel it skid beneath us at one point when he takes an even sharper turn. I scream because I could swear for a minute we crashed, but he takes off again and I know we didn't.

I don't dare open my eyes to see if the lights are still there. I don't want to see where we are, or how close to death I potentially am. Adrenaline is taking over my body, I'm shaking with it, and I'm sure Trent can feel it in my grip.

After what feels like forever, suddenly, we've stopped. I open my eyes and look around to see we are in front of Trent's house. I glance around and don't see any signs of the flashing lights that were behind us. What the –

I rip my helmet off and swing my body around to straddling Trent before he's able to stand up. I don't know what I'm doing, I feel so out of control at this moment, I just want to feel something to reassure that we didn't die and I'm now in some sort of a weird limbo. I take Trent's helmet off quickly, and before he has a chance to say or do anything, I slam my lips down onto his.

He doesn't kiss me back right away, probably in shock, but once he catches up, he's attacking my mouth just as fiercely as I am. His hands grip my waist roughly as I start to grind my hips against his. I moan at the sensation, and it only spurs Trent on more. His tongue licks inside my mouth, claiming me. His hands on me guide my movements. I can't think of anything at this moment except *more*.

Reaching between us, I work his belt, and the button on his pants quickly. I'm fumbling around, but he doesn't seem to mind because once the button is free, he lifts his hips to help get the fabric off. Without wasting any more time, I pull my underwear to the side before sliding down onto him. I gasp at being so full so quickly.

Trent reaches his hand up to my face, brushing my hair behind my ear, and I look up into his eyes. The look there is full of his lust and desire, but there's also something…softer… that I refuse to acknowledge so with that I rise up before slamming back down on him again. He opens his mouth; I assume on a groan. I move my hand from his shoulder to his chest so I can feel any of the noises he makes.

I start to move my hips against him, hitting the exact spot I need, and it only makes me move faster. Harder. Trent is lifting his hips as much as he can while keeping his feet planted on the ground on either side of the motorcycle, so we don't tip over. I don't care though, I move on him just how I need, chasing my pleasure selfishly without caring where we are, who he is, and what we are doing.

I'm so close, I feel it about to slam into me as I continue fucking Trent right here on top of his bike.

"That's it, Flower. Use me to make yourself come." I think that's what he says, even if it's not, that's exactly what I intend to do.

His mouth finds mine again, and I bite his bottom lip. I feel his growl in his chest before he starts rising his hips more furiously. His mouth moves to my neck, biting and sucking every inch of skin there. Then, I feel the release within my grasp. I slam my eyes closed, focusing on purely that as I ride him harder and harder until I've reached the peak and I'm tumbling over the edge.

In the midst of my orgasm, Trent lifts me slightly and gets off the bike. I'm so lost in my pleasure I can barely tell what's happening until he walks us up to the front door. He's still carrying me as we walk inside, and I attack his mouth again.

Our tongues tangle together, teeth bite at each other, and I'm rubbing myself on him shamelessly. I still feel like I need more. I think Trent's original plan was to take me somewhere, but as soon as I let out another moan, he has me on the floor in the entryway of his house.

I'm on my back, my dress pushed above my hips, and underwear so wet it's useless. He sits up on his knees, looking down at me, and I'm sure I look like a mess.

He doesn't even seem to care as his fingers peel off the soaked fabric covering my center and throws them to the side. I reach for him, but my limbs are slow to catch up, and he's lying on his stomach between my thighs. His tongue licks my entire slit and I throw my head back from the sensation.

My still overly sensitive clit gets the most attention from his tongue before he's sucking it into his mouth. My hands find his short hair, and I hold on for dear life as he completely devours me. He's eating my pussy like it's his favorite meal and he's been withheld from it for years. I'm panting and when I feel him press a finger into me, I cry out. He doubles his efforts with his mouth as he adds another finger. My back arches as I feel another release beginning to take over.

I whimper his name and pull on his hair harder. My thighs wrap around his head, and I don't care if I kill him as long as I finish first because I won't let him leave the spot he's in right now. He can't stop.

My orgasm hits me so hard and fast as I scream and pull him even tighter to me. I feel like I just left my body, and I have no control over my reaction. I don't know what I'm saying, how I'm moving.

Once I come back down, Trent is crawling up my body, pressing his hips into mine before his mouth lands on mine again. I taste myself on his tongue as it slides into my mouth. I wrap my arms around his neck to pull him closer to me. His hips press into mine, and it's like he's trained me to need the orgasms he gives because I whimper with the need to have him inside me again.

He pushes my dress the rest of the way off my body, only breaking our kiss to pull the fabric over my head. He rips my bra down like it personally offended him before descending his mouth onto a nipple. He sucks the peak into his mouth before biting down. I grab at his head, but he's licking the sting away. Then, he moves to the other one and does the exact same thing.

My hips move beneath him, silently begging for him to fuck me. I need to finish what was started on the bike outside. As he raises up to kiss my mouth again, and the fabric of his shirt rubs against my wet swollen nipples, I groan at the need to feel his hot skin on mine. Without taking the time to undo the buttons, I rip at his shirt, so it bares his muscular chest to me.

While he's kneeling between my thighs, staring at me, I'm doing the same to him. He pulled up his boxers at some point, but his pants are undone and around his thighs. I can see his erection straining the fabric, and I reach out to touch him. He swats my hand away before leaning back down over me.

"Tell me what you want, Flower."

I go to open my mouth to tell him, but he presses his hand over my mouth before I get the chance.

"Tell me in sign language."

My eyebrows jump up in surprise. He won't know what I'm saying, but I guess that doesn't matter since he already knows exactly what I want.

My hands shake, but I manage to do what he's asking me to.

"Fuck me."

I barely finish signing when he grabs my hands and pushes them above my head, holding both my wrists in one of his hands. He uses his other one to free himself. I wrap my legs around his waist and push his pants down with my feet. If I'm going to be naked and fucked on the floor, then so is he.

He pushes into me roughly; I squeeze my thighs around his hips. I want to wrap my arms around him, scratch at his back, pull at his hair, anything. He won't let me, as he continues to hold my wrists down above me.

It's like he's making a point.

He's in control.

I took over while on the bike, my instincts took over, the adrenaline ruled my brain in those few moments, and I didn't even think I just acted. The fear of being caught, the energy the chase gave me, and the fact that Trent is the last person I should be doing this with was a deadly combination that has now led us here.

He pounds into me, the snap of his hips hitting mine hard, his pelvis is just at the right angle to rub against my clit with each thrust. I lift up to meet him each time. My throat scratches from all the screams and cries, but I can't help it. I don't feel like I'm in control of my body at all.

I can tell I'm going to come again, and it's going to be stronger than the two previous ones. I try to push my arms up as I feel like I need to hold onto something, but he won't let me. He moves his free hand to my hip, pushing it down onto the floor so I can no longer meet his thrusts, and I whimper. He continues his movements, and I continue my climb as he fucks me into the floor, completely held down by his powerful body.

My eyes close as the sensation becomes too much. I feel Trent's tongue peek out to lick at my lips, and I try to press closer to his face, but he pulls away and his thrusts slow. I want to scream at him. I open my eyes to see he's smirking.

"Keep looking at me, Flower. I need to watch you when you come."

"I – God," I practically scream as he goes right back to fucking me just as hard as before, but this time not only is he hitting my clit at the right angle, he hits that spot inside me, and it doesn't take long until I'm gone.

I keep my eyes open as long as I can, but soon it becomes too much, and Trent's hips lose their rhythm signaling his own release. He swells inside me, and I know he's finished too.

We lay on the floor, a sweaty, panting mess, when I realize something and push him off me.

"You didn't use a condom," I groan. I'm on birth control, but who knows all the nasty places he's stuck his dick.

I'm sitting up with a wince as I grab at my dress to pull it on, but he reaches out to stop me, forcing me to look at him.

"I'm clean, I got tested as soon as I was released, and I haven't fucked anyone but you."

My jaw drops slightly at that. I don't believe him, but the alternative of him telling the truth is just too much to consider right now. Instead of acknowledging it any further, I snatch my dress before he can stop me and pull it over my head.

"I'm on birth control so no worries for babies either."

We are both still sitting on the wood floor, and as reality starts to come back, it makes the situation weirder the longer we stay here, unmoving. My dress is back on, but I don't know where my panties ended up.

"Well, I guess you should take me home then." I try to break the sudden awkwardness I'm feeling.

He shakes his head before standing, and pulling his pants back up his hips, but not buttoning them. He stays shirtless, and I admire his body that is a pure work of art. The muscles on his arms covered in tattoos that crawl up to his neck, and across his chest. He is both beautiful and terrifying at the same time.

"No can do, we had the cops chasing us. I barely lost them to get us here, they probably have an APB on my license plate right now."

My jaw drops, and I stand up too. "What does that mean? I'm stuck here with you? For how long?"

He just shrugs like this isn't a big deal. "Dunno, but it's probably better to lay low for a little bit, less of a risk of running into them again."

My head is spinning, and it's no longer from pleasure.

"Why were they chasing you?"

"Speeding probably."

I roll my eyes. "That's it?"

"Can you think of anything else?" He raises his eyebrows at me. I could admit I know more about him than he thinks I do. I could use this time to try and get more information from him, but I don't. For some reason, I choose to stay quiet on the subject for now.

"No." I think of something. "If they know your license plate, couldn't they come here anyway? It's registered with your address."

He smiles, and I think lets out a small laugh by the way his chest bounces. "I cover all my bases, Flower, my bike isn't registered at this address. If someone needs to find me, it's a lot harder than that."

I want to ask more questions about that, but he gives me his back, and walks upstairs toward his room. I feel like I'm stuck in place as I watch him go. I feel like I have whiplash from this whole night, between seeing somewhat sweet sides to him, to getting a peek inside the criminal piece, I have no idea who Trent Moore really is.

31

Trent

13 Years Ago (Age 22)

I've been working on distancing myself from my dad throughout the years. I don't want to follow in his shadow forever, and I am fucking done with him telling me what to do.

The hardest part for me has been getting people to work with me. I don't have much to offer yet, not a lot of business or perks. It's not like I have many friends who I could ask. I've never really had friends, but that's by choice. People annoy me, and once they do something to piss me off, I stop being around them.

I'm the same way with women, always have been and always will be.

As much as I haven't wanted to admit it, my stepbrother, Zander, has shown some potential for me, but he wants nothing to do with it. Our parents moved away somewhere, but he stuck around here to help take care of his grandma.

He mentioned before after graduation he was going to move up to Oregon because he has something there, but he hasn't. And he's always a huge asshole when I deal with him. I'm usually trying to convince him to come work with me, but still.

Last I heard anything about him was from my mom while she praised him for being the golden boy, as always, she mentioned his grandma passed away. I know that means there's only a limited amount of time before he moves like he wanted to. I decide to go see him to try and convince him to work with me again.

That's why I find myself outside the house his dad bought for them when they lived here, that Zander has been living in with his grandma since they left.

"The fuck do you want?" he asks in greeting when he opens the front door.

I roll my eyes, how no one else sees what a dick he is just baffles me.

"Can I come in?"

"No."

"I just wanted to see if you've reconsidered what we talked about before."

"What? That bullshit about working with you? No thanks, I

know you're trying to be like your dad, and I have no interest in getting caught up in all of that. Fuck off, Trent."

He tries to shut the door in my face, but I put my hand out to stop it.

"I know you want to move to Oregon, how are you going to do that without money?"

He pauses for a second before opening the door again and leans against the doorframe with his arms crossed. Zander is a big guy, he has about three inches on me in height, and arms that look like he could knock someone out with a single punch. Which is exactly why I want him to work with me.

"I have money," he insists.

I know for a fact he doesn't have *much* money, despite what he wants me to believe. My dad always taught me to do my research, and I've always found a way to do just that.

"But is it enough?"

He shrugs. "I'll make it be enough."

"Work with me, just for a couple weeks, and you'll have more than enough."

I see the look on his face. He's considering it. Then, he shuts down again.

"No way."

"Whatever is waiting for you in Oregon can't wait a couple

more weeks?" I want a reaction from him. I want something to hold over him because despite all my research I have no idea what is there for him.

"Don't come back here, Trent," he says without acknowledging my question, and then shuts the door in my face. This time, I let him.

As I'm walking away, I see his car in the driveway, it's a black Subaru WRX. He loves that thing, is borderline obsessed with it if you ask me. The kid has a thing for art and cars. That's when an idea hits me. If he won't willingly come work for me, then maybe I just have to make it so he doesn't have any other option.

Zander has been arrested.

It was easier than I thought it would be to plant the drugs. He was caught and arrested. The amount he had was enough for an 'intent to distribute' charge. His dad is helping with a really good attorney so he's going to get a good deal.

I think my mom said something like a year. She was so surprised, she never thought Zander would do anything like this. Me, however, she wouldn't be surprised. She didn't say that, but she didn't have to.

Now, they can stop acting like he's this amazing person because he's not. Even if those drugs weren't his, he's still guilty of shit, we all are.

When he gets out, he won't have any choice, but to come

work for me. During that time, I'll continue to build my empire, and I'll be better than my dad. I'll be better than anyone else.

I want to be the guy in charge. I'm the one pulling everyone's strings while no one knows a thing about me. Everyone will be in my pocket while I'm in control. And I don't care who I have to step on, what lines I have to cross, or what I have to do to get there.

32

Trent

Present

I'm in my office while Violet continues to sleep in my bed.

I woke up early this morning to her laying across my chest, her hair fanned across me, hand on my chest, and leg tucked between mine. I would've thought that would freak me out, and I would rush to get her out of my house as soon as possible, but that's not what happened. I didn't want to disturb her when I got up. So, as carefully as I could, I extracted myself from her grip and came in here.

What I told her was partly true, if we left, there might have been a risk for the cops looking for me, and I didn't want to risk it. But in all reality, she could've had her friend or sister come get her, I wasn't going to force her to stay. But she didn't push it.

She willingly came up to my room with me.

She willingly put one of my t-shirts over her body.

She willingly crawled into my bed with me.

I originally came in here to look up some more properties, something that I could buy for storage or maybe to convert. I feel restless in the lack of growth I'm having with the business side of things, and I want more.

For some reason, though, that's not what I ended up doing. Instead, I found myself typing up a letter to Zander. I don't even know why but talking to Violet about family last night brought up the memories of what I've done. For some reason it doesn't fill me with pride like it used to.

No, when I think of what I did and then think of Violet I almost feel bad for all my past actions, and I don't like that feeling.

So, I typed a letter to Zander, printed it, and put it in an envelope with zero plans to actually send it. I shoved it in the top drawer of my desk before leaning back in my chair and running my hands down my face wondering what the woman in my house is doing to me.

There's a knock at the entrance of my office, and I look up to see Violet standing there in just my t-shirt, her legs completely exposed, and I know she's not wearing anything underneath the fabric that falls to her mid thighs.

I don't say anything, I just gesture for her to come over to me. She hesitates for a moment before pushing off the wall to walk toward me.

She stops when she's right in front of me, I spread my legs, and pull her to stand in between my thighs. I wrap my hands around the back of her legs, running them up over her ass up to her hips. I just look up at her.

"Say something, Flower."

She gives me an annoyed look, and I know she's about to sass me when she raises her hands, and opens her mouth, but I stop her by yanking her body down on top of mine so she's straddling me in the chair. Her warmth is pressed against the sweatpants I'm wearing. I'm instantly hard from the feeling.

"Say something in sign language," I correct.

I don't know what it is, but I like watching her sign. I like how natural it is for her, and it reminds me of when we first met when she refused to use her voice with me. I have no clue what she's saying, just like before, but I like seeing it.

She moves her hands around for a few moments before stopping. Plus, maybe I'll start to learn some. I know that would be the biggest surprise to her, if I actually started signing to her. I doubt it will happen any time soon, but I know it would make my Flower happy.

"What did you say?" I ask while I squeeze her hips.

"I asked what you are doing in here."

"I just wanted to get some work done." I lie.

She nods, looking around almost nervously. I look down at her arm where she has a tattoo that I know is new. I run my fingers over the slightly raised surface.

"When did you get this?" I ask.

She shrugs. "Recently."

"Why did you get it?"

I feel like she's not going to answer, and it's going to lead to another argument. "It's for my mom."

Instead of saying anything else, I cup her cheeks before guiding her mouth to mine in a soft kiss. Our lips barely graze each other when she melts against me. I kiss her without intention for more. I just want to feel her lips on mine. She tries to deepen the kiss, but I pull back.

"Someone can't get enough of me," I taunt, and it's enough for her to roll her eyes and get off my lap.

"I still can't stand you," she says definitively, but something about the blush that spreads across her cheeks, and the way her knees wobble makes me think she might not really mean it.

"Do you want breakfast?"

"You cook?" She looks surprised at my offer.

"How else did you think I've survived?"

"The blood of virgins, and animal sacrifices," she responds, deadpan.

I can't hold back my laugh as it rumbles out of my chest.

This is the second time she's made me laugh recently, and I don't hate the feeling.

I lead her out of my office and into the kitchen. She sits on one of the barstools at the island while I go to the fridge to get out the eggs, ham, cheese, and butter for bagel breakfast sandwiches.

I turn back around to see she's just staring at me.

"What?"

She shakes her head. "Nothing. Can I go home?"

"I'm not holding you hostage, of course you can."

"Then I want to go home."

"After breakfast."

She groans then gets up from the stool. I start to ask where she's going, but her back is turned to me. I debate following her because I don't really need her looking through my shit, but decide to give her some space. If she doesn't come back after five minutes though, I'm looking for her.

I put together the sandwiches on a baking sheet to put them in the oven when she enters the kitchen, taking the same seat she was in before. She's looking down at her phone now and typing something out.

Once the baking sheet is in the oven, I walk over behind her to wrap my arms around her shoulders. She locks and puts her phone down as I come closer. I turn her around in the stool with my eyebrow raised.

"Hiding things from me, Flower?"

She scoffs. "We aren't together, I can hide whatever I want."

"You might think that, but you're still mine."

I pull away from her to start cooking the eggs. She's quiet for a moment while I get the pan on the stove.

"What does that mean?" I can hear the nerves she tries to cover.

I turn around to face her. "Exactly what I said. You're mine."

She crosses her arms over her chest. She's not wearing a bra, so the action pushes her tits up. "I don't belong to anyone. Especially you."

I smile at her defiance. This is the Violet I enjoy playing with. As much as I do enjoy her submission, I will always enjoy her fight.

"You can deny it all you want, but you are mine. Do I need to prove it to you?"

Her eyes widen, and I see the indecision on her face. She's not used to someone like me, that has been clear from the beginning. She's much younger, and I know not very experienced, but I don't care about that because she's the only woman to leave her mark on me in this way. I've never needed to have someone the way I need to have her.

While she's staring at me, I make my way around the counter to stand in front of her again. She's looking up at me, her breathing has picked up, and I see how tightly her thighs are pressed together.

"Get on your knees," I command.

Her jaw drops slightly, and I know she's about to argue. I don't give her the chance as I grab a fistful of her hair and yank her head back. She yelps, and grabs onto the counter like I would actually let her fall.

"I'm going to show you what it means to be mine."

When she goes to reply I pull her off the stool, and into my body, slamming my lips onto hers. I kiss her hard, and she opens automatically. My hand in her hair tightens, and she whimpers in my mouth. I pull her waist into me so she can feel how hard I am for her already.

I pull away from her lips, and push her to the floor onto her knees, loosening my grip on her hair. She looks up at me with swollen lips and her eyes glazed over, I can't wait to see those eyes fill with tears when I fuck her mouth.

"Take out my cock, Flower." I run my thumb over her bottom lip. She peeks her tongue out slightly, and I push my finger in just barely. She nips at my skin before I pull away.

I expect her to fight back, but she does what I ask, and pulls at my sweatpants until my erection is free, and right in front of her face. She looks up to my face for the next command, and *fuck* if that doesn't make me even harder.

"Put me in your mouth, and don't stop until I pull you off."

She smiles with a glimmer of defiance in her eyes, as she leans forward to take me into her mouth. I yank on her hair again so she will look up at me.

"No teeth. And keep your eyes on me."

She doesn't say anything, just wraps her fingers around the base and squeezes enough to make me grunt. She pumps her hand up slowly, teasing, until I let up on her hair enough, she's able to lean forward to take me into her mouth.

I groan at the sensation of her hot mouth enveloping the tip of my dick. The vision is even better. Her blonde hair is still a mess from sleeping in my bed, and from my fingers. Her pink lips wrapped around me. Dark eyes looking up at me with lust and hatred. It's a heady combination, and one I want more of.

"Hate me all you want, Flower, but don't forget that you're mine." I tell her right before thrusting my hips forward so she's taking me further into her throat.

She gags, and I pull back slightly. Her eyes don't leave mine, just like I asked. Even as her eyes begin to shimmer with tears, she continues to look at me. Then, she's sucking me in herself, her tongue runs up the back of my shaft right before she sucks hard. I shout at the feeling, my hand in her hair gripping tight again as my hips push further on their own.

"That's so fucking perfect. You're so fucking perfect." I groan without even thinking about what I'm saying. She's looking at me, but I don't know if she can read my lips through the tears in her eyes as she takes me deeper and faster.

Her hand starts working me along with her mouth as her confidence increases, and I can't tell if she's trying to please me, or hurt me, but I let her because this is what I mean when I tell her she's mine. She gets to have some of the control. Whether she knows it or not, this is what I was trying to get her to understand.

I feel myself about to let go, my balls tighten, and I pull her off me quickly. I need to get inside her. I need to feel her squeeze my cock as she comes, and then I'll let myself finish.

She tries to take me back in her mouth, but I don't let her. Yanking her onto her feet I pick her up by her hips and plant her ass on the counter before attacking her mouth with mine again. Her lips are puffy and red. She has tears streaming down her face, I taste the saltiness in our kiss, and it only spurs me on.

I reach between us to feel how soaked she is, I tease my finger at her entrance, gathering her wetness before circling her clit a couple times. She whimpers into my mouth, pushing her hips toward me for more.

I break away from her mouth. "You get this wet from being on your knees, I should have you do that more often."

"I'm wet from the thought that I could have easily bit your dick off," she snaps.

I pull her to the edge of the counter, closer to my rock-hard cock which is now teasing her entrance. "You would never. You like coming on it too much."

Without giving her another chance to say something to me, I shove into her roughly. She cries out at the sudden invasion. Her nails grab at my shoulders, scratching down my back while I pump into her fiercely. I remove my hand from her hair to grab her hip with one hand, bringing my other around in between us to rub at her clit.

She cries out my name as her hips buck up, chasing her release. I know I won't be able to hold back once she gets there, but I need it to happen soon because I'm so close already from her mouth.

"Show me you're mine, Violet." I say her name, and she sees it on my lips because that sends her over the edge of her orgasm.

Her pussy strangles me as she screams her release, and I can't hold back my own any longer. My thrusts become erratic as I groan out my own orgasm.

We stay where we are, our breathing is heavy. Violet's head is against my chest, arms still wrapped around me. I haven't pulled out of her yet. I know that once I do, we are back to where we were before. She lifts her head, dark eyes looking into mine. She opens her mouth to say something, then furrows her brows and looks over to the oven.

I remember I was in the middle of cooking us breakfast. With a muttered curse, I separate myself from her and go to pull out the food. It's not too burnt, and luckily, I didn't start the eggs yet.

I turn toward her to see she's settled back on the stool.

"You still hungry?" I ask.

She smiles, and it seems surprisingly genuine. "Starving."

33

Present

After we ate breakfast, I asked Trent to take me home. He seemed reluctant but told me he would. I put my dress from last night back on, though I couldn't find my panties so riding on the back of his motorcycle was extremely uncomfortable to do commando.

The whole drive I couldn't forget about what happened on the bike, and then this morning. Which only made the drive more uncomfortable.

I'm thankful once we pull up to my apartment complex, I leap off as fast as I can to get away from him. I need to think. Of course, he doesn't let me get away from him, and at this point I shouldn't even be surprised. When I go to toss him my helmet, he grabs my arm and pulls me against his chest.

I huff out a breath when our chests collide. His hands move up to cup my face, forcing me to look at his face.

"Come over later."

I start to shake my head to deny him, but he doesn't let me move.

"I will come get you after I'm done with work for the day."

"No," I say quickly. "This was the second time I've been stranded at your house; I want to drive myself."

"Okay," he leans down to press his lips to mine gently. "But if you don't show up, I am coming over here to get you."

I roll my eyes. "Stop threatening me."

He smiles, then raises one hand, and signs, *"No."*

He kisses me again, briefly, before letting me go. I refuse to watch him drive away, so I head inside quickly. I need a shower, and to stare at myself in the mirror for a while, questioning my life choices.

Once I'm inside I see Mila in the kitchen, and my heart rate kicks up. I look like I did the walk of shame, there's no doubt about that. I'm wearing last night's dress, despite cleaning myself up after we fucked in the kitchen, I can still feel his cum in me. My hair is tangled, and my face is blotchy.

"Where were you?" she asks like she's my parent or something.

"Nowhere."

She steps in front of me, blocking my access to the bathroom. "*Were you with Trent?*"

My face screws up. "*Doesn't matter.*"

"Yes it does, Vi, he's dangerous."

I scoff. "*You would know, right? With all your secrets. I still don't know why those cops were here, and that's the only reason I'm even talking to Trent.*" That might not be entirely true, but whatever.

"*I didn't want you involved at all. You butt in and refused to back down because you're just that stubborn.*"

"So are you! You don't think I can do it; you don't think I can handle myself."

"Have you fucked him?"

I rear back at her question. "*None of your business.*"

"*I can tell you that's not the way to get the information that the cops are looking for.*'

"I'm supposed to get close to him, that's what I'm doing."

"*Spreading your legs isn't the way.*"

"Then what is the way? Since you haven't helped me at all."

"Because I didn't want you involved."

"Why are you involved in the first place? What all have you done to get information for these cops?" I fold my arms across my chest. I want an answer. I want her to just tell me something about her life because I know next to nothing.

"It doesn't matter! Stop seeing him and let this go."

I look at her for a moment, she's mad at me. She might be scared for me, but I know it's because she doesn't think I can handle it. She thinks I'm weak. She thinks I'm stupid. It only makes me want to prove her wrong. It also makes me want to fight back.

"Tell me what happened when you ran away, Mila."

She looks like I slapped her with my question. I've never asked. She came home that night, and I've never seen her so upset, not even when our mom died. We never talked about that night ever again.

"Doesn't matter," she won't look at me.

I wave my hand to get her to look at me again. "*It does matter. Does it have to do with those cops?*"

She throws her head back and takes a deep breath. "*Leave it, Vi. It doesn't matter. It happened. It's done. It'll never happen again.*"

"What happened?"

"Nothing. Go do whatever with Trent, but you're going to end up hurt, and I won't be able to help you."

She turns her back to me, and I call after her. "I don't need you to help me."

I can tell she wants to turn around and say more to me, but she doesn't. Instead, she goes into her room and slams the door.

As I go into the bathroom to finally shower, I think about how I wish she would tell me. I wish we could be closer, and actually help *each other*. Our mom wanted us close; she always encouraged us to talk through our problems with each other and make up. Ever since she's been gone, we haven't talked about any problems. Mila is like our dad and shuts down with her feelings. I'm like our mom, and I want to work through it.

I get in the shower as soon as the water is warm enough, and I feel like I'm washing away the entire night with Trent, the argument with Mila, everything. I miss feeling like I had control over my life because it is suddenly becoming harder and harder to feel like I have any.

I'M PULLING up to Trent's house, it's not quite dark yet because the sun sets so late in the summer. He has been bothering me through text to come over since he was "done with work". I plan to ask him what exactly that means for him, though I know he won't answer.

I also have a plan coming here today, unlike the last two times which were spur of the moment, and I was in a lust induced haze each time. At least, that's what I'm choosing to believe. I'm really not going to have sex with him tonight because I need to stop giving in so easily. When he goes to sleep, I'm going to go through his office to find anything that could give me information.

Trent greets me at the front door, and he looks too good just like he always does. His dark pants hug his legs while the white button up on his torso leaves nothing to the imagination. Even if I didn't already know about the ink covered muscles underneath, it wouldn't be hard to imagine. The sleeves are rolled up to his elbows, the tattoos on his thick forearms make my mouth water as everything that happened this morning flashes through my mind.

With a smirk on his lips, he leans against the door frame with his arms folded across his chest as I approach. I'm in cotton shorts and a t-shirt because I wanted to be comfortable and didn't want to bring a bag to make it obvious about my intentions to stay the night. Even if it isn't for the reason he would like it to be.

Once inside, Trent leads me to the kitchen where he has laid out a bunch of take-out boxes on the counter.

"I thought you cooked," I sass.

"I do, but it's been a busy day, and I wanted to offer you more than just something warmed from a box."

"Technically, this is warmed in a box."

Trent grabs me, pulling me into his body and kissing me with a nip at my lip. "You're such a pain in the ass."

"And yet you won't leave me alone." I push him away, and he lets me go with a chuckle.

We eat, and I wish I could say it's awkward being with him like this. But It's weirdly normal, and I wish he would piss me off again because fighting with him is what I know, and it reminds me of who he is.

"What did you do at work today?" I finally ask.

"Are you finished?" He nods toward my plate before taking it over to the sink.

I glare at his back. "Why won't you tell me anything about your work?"

He turns around to face me and grips the counter. "Why do you want to know so bad?"

"You want to know things about me, and I want to know things about you. That's how this works."

He smiles. "How what works?"

"A conversation."

"I think you like me, Flower."

I roll my eyes.

He chuckles before turning back to the sink to clean off the dishes. I take the opportunity to look around his house a bit more. I walk into the living room, and it's so bare. There's no pictures, no memories. Nothing that shows someone actually lives here, let alone anything about that person.

As I continue to look around, I notice it's the same everywhere. No pictures. No personality. Nothing. I feel Trent wrap his arms around my waist, pulling me back against his hard chest. His lips trail over my neck. I turn around in his arms.

"You don't have any pictures."

"I don't like them."

"Why?"

He shrugs. "There's nothing and no one that's important for me to stare at every day."

"Tell me something real about you, Trent," I say without even thinking. I don't know why, but for some reason I feel the need to know something about him that might make him seem more human to me, and not this evil asshole I know him to be.

He moves his hands to the side of my face, brushing my hair back while he seems to look behind me while he thinks. He opens his mouth to say something then stops himself. I shake my head, trying to pull out of his grasp. He doesn't let me.

"I hate what I do, but I can't get away from it."

I narrow my eyes. "What does that mean?"

He pulls his hands away from my face, and I know he won't say anything else about that. His cocky smile is back on his face. "Let's watch a movie."

"Netflix and chill, how original." I roll my eyes.

"You said it, not me, Flower."

WE REALLY DID JUST WATCH a movie.

I tried to keep my distance and had to remind him I need subtitles on. About halfway through, I took my hearing aids out after they started to be uncomfortable since I've been wearing them all day. The movie continued, and I found myself leaning more toward him. Then somehow, I ended up cuddled against his side. His arm around my shoulders, my head on his chest. My eyes start to drift closed, and I don't even realize I've fallen asleep until I feel Trent carrying me up to his room.

I pretend to still be asleep when he lays me down on his bed, gently covering me with his comforter. I try to stay as still as possible while I wait for him to lay down next to me.

Finally, the bed dips with his weight, and then I feel his hand slide up my hip, and around my waist before I'm pulled back against his chest.

This makes my plan a bit more complicated, but damn if I don't like the way he's holding me right now. Instead of trying to fight it, I find myself falling back into unconsciousness as sleep takes over once again.

I'm not sure what time it is when I open my eyes again, but the warmth from Trent's body is gone, and the room is still dark. Sitting up, I look around to make sure he's not hiding in a corner watching me or something. I wouldn't put that past him.

The bedroom door is closed, and when I open it, I see the glow from the lights downstairs. I wonder if he's working in his office again. I hope that maybe he's in the kitchen getting a midnight snack or something, and I can sneak in there under the excuse of looking for him.

My bare feet hit the hardwood stairs, and I feel a hint of vibration under them. I pause to confirm the feeling, and sure enough there's *something*. I continue down the stairs, the vibrations continuing as I descent.

I turn, and that's when I see the source of the vibration. Trent at the piano. And he's playing it. I asked him before if he played, and he didn't answer me. I have a feeling since he snuck down here while he thought I was sleeping that he didn't want me to know about this for some reason.

I stand in the archway, leaning against the wall as I watch him. His back is to me, he's shirtless, and I watch the muscles bunch as he moves with each note he plays. I feel the music under my feet planted on the cold floor. Whatever he is playing, it's powerful. Everything he does is powerful.

The only tattoos Trent has on his back are on his shoulders. I'm a little surprised, I would've thought he would be completely covered on his back, but he's not. I feel as the song seems to come to an end, and I shift my weight from one foot to the other. The slight movement makes him aware I'm standing here. He turns around quickly to face me.

"How long have you been standing there?" he asks, running his hand through his short hair.

"Not long," I answer easily.

"I didn't think that would wake you up. I'm done." He goes to close the top of the piano.

"No, you didn't wake me up. Keep playing."

I walk over to him and sit on the bench next to him.

He shakes his head. "I don't really play in front of anyone. Or ever really."

"How long have you played?"

"My mom made me start lessons when I was pretty young."

I choose not to ask him more about that because I know that will make him shut down, and for some reason I want to experience him playing more. He seems almost vulnerable like this, and it's endearing.

"Play for me." I sign.

He pulls me into his lap so I'm straddling his hips on the small bench.

"Teach me more signs."

I bite my lip before nodding. I repeat the phrase I just said before telling him what it means.

"Show me how to say, 'I want you to fuck me.'"

I narrow my eyes at him before showing him the signs.

"Now I'll know when you say that to me," he smiles, and I smack his chest. I go to move off his lap, but he stops me. "Show me more."

"*If you're actually interested in learning you have to learn more than just the dirty phrases.*"

"What was that?"

I tell him what I said.

"Fine, what about your name."

"In ASL, you have a sign name, and then your English name which is just the finger spelling."

"Show me."

I only show him how to spell my name in ASL, he doesn't get to know my sign name when I know he will never use it. I don't believe he's going to use any sign language outside of these times he asks for lessons anyway.

"How do you sign 'beautiful'?"

I scrunch my face before showing him the sign.

He readjusts me on his lap before raising his right hand, and finger spelling my name slowly. He is slow and doesn't seem sure, but he does it correctly. Then he points to me before copying the sign for beautiful.

"Was that right?" he asks.

"Depends, what were you trying to say?"

"Violet, you're beautiful."

I shrug to cover the blush I feel forming on my cheeks. "Yeah, I guess that's right. Your turn."

"My turn to be beautiful? I already am," he smiles wide, and I roll my eyes.

"Play for me."

"So demanding," he says, but then he's lifting me up off his lap, and turning me around so I'm sitting on his lap but facing the piano.

He puts his hands in a certain position on the keys, and I sit with mine in my lap. Before he starts to play, he picks up my hands and lightly puts my left one on top of his left one still resting on the keys. I copy the movement by placing my right hand on top of his.

His hands start to move, taking mine with him as he begins to play. I feel his leg move under me slightly, and I think he's pressing on the pedal underneath us. I feel like my hands on top of his is distracting for him, but when I go to move them away, he stops playing. I put them back, and he continues like he never even stopped.

I finally decide to lean into the music, relaxing my back against Trent's hard body under me, and feeling the vibrations from the notes mixed with the movement of his body. It's a heady mixture, I close my eyes to focus purely on the feeling of everything. I feel like I'm almost floating as he continues to play.

His hands hit the notes with emotion that's palpable, I almost believe it's actually real. I know a lot of musicians play off their emotions, but Trent doesn't seem like a person who has emotions, so to think he's using them to create something beautiful is doubtful. But as his hands move under mine, how his body flows with the music he plays, I start to believe it.

All too soon, the song is over, and I'm opening my eyes, turning my head to look back at him. He's already watching me, but without saying anything he lifts me up to place me on top of the piano.

I squeal at the movement, and I go to move off the instrument because I don't want to risk breaking it. Trent doesn't let me and holds me in place with his hands on my thighs.

"Lay back, Flower. I want you to feel every note."

I start to argue, but he squeezes my thighs to stop me from saying anything. I huff out a breath before doing what he says and laying back. He moves my legs up, so they are bent in front of me with my feet planted on the smooth surface I'm currently laying on. I rest my hands flat at my sides so I can do exactly what he told me to. Feel every note.

He runs his hands along my shins, up to my knees, and I hold my breath not sure what he's going to do next. Then he moves them back down until he isn't touching me anymore. I feel like my body is on fire where he just touched, and my breathing is choppy.

The piano shakes under me with the start of the song. It

was so powerful, it's almost like he hit the keys with his fists. As he continues, I can tell this song is more angry than the other ones he's played. My body shakes from each note as he keeps going. I can feel it down to my bones as he continues to play.

There's emotion. Power. Trent. He's creating this music; he's controlling my body with it without even touching me. The thought makes my core throb with need for him. I can't even explain why, it's like the adrenaline rush, but for an entirely different reason. He's pulling strings on my desire with each key he plays.

My thighs tighten as I think about his hands currently occupied by what he's doing and how they feel when they touch me. How he can play me so perfectly, and maybe this is why. To him, I'm just another instrument for him to figure out and to play.

I barely notice when the song ends, too wrapped up in my thoughts until I feel his hands on my legs again. This time he's pulling them apart, I sit up on my elbows to ask what he's doing. His amber eyes meet mine, and the look on his face is downright feral so I keep my mouth closed.

His hands slide up my thighs, leaving goosebumps on my skin when he reaches the waistband of my shorts, he starts to pull them down. I lift my hips to help as he takes my panties off with them, before throwing my legs over his shoulders. A shot of insecurity runs through me at how exposed I am with him just looking at my center that I know is unbelievably wet.

He runs his tongue along his bottom lip before looking up to meet my eyes again. "Such a perfect fucking pussy, Flower."

I want to say something snarky, but I don't get the chance before he pulls me forward so my ass is almost off the piano, and his face is buried between my thighs. My back arches at the first swipe of his tongue.

My hips buck on their own accord as he starts to devour me so fully, holding my body against his face so tightly there's no way he can breathe. My hands flail trying to find purchase for something to hold onto, but the shiny surface of the piano doesn't provide me anything. I reach down to grab onto his head, pulling his hair.

He's licking me so thoroughly I know I'm not going to last long before I'm coming. I want to enjoy this a bit longer. Everything he's doing is so fucking good, I never want him to stop. He flicks at my clit before sucking it into his mouth. I cry out, and yank his head harder. My thighs are squeezing tightly around him.

I reach up to roll my peaked nipples between my fingers while he continues working magic with his tongue. His hands hold my thighs so tightly I wonder if there will be bruises, I secretly hope there are.

Suddenly, he finds the perfect rhythm of licking and sucking, and I know I won't be able to hold back any longer. Especially when one of his hands moves from my thighs, and he presses a single finger inside me, I go off with a scream.

My legs are shaking violently as I come, and he doesn't let up. He continues to eat me with a purpose, his finger pumping in and out. I whimper from the oversensitivity, pulling at his hair to get him to let up.

He stands up, and looks down at me, sweaty and panting. I probably look crazy, but the way he's looking at me is all heat and desire. My release is covering his mouth, and I reach for him wanting his mouth on mine. He smirks while licking his wet lips, and I whimper at the sight.

His hands slip around my waist, pulling me up off my back to a sitting position. He leans toward me, and I think he's going to kiss me like I want, but when I close my eyes in anticipation for his lips on mine, he yanks me off the piano so I'm straddling his lap again.

"Show me how to say, 'I need to fuck you,'" Trent says as he raises my shirt over my head, followed by my bra.

"I need you to fuck me," I say instead.

He grabs a fistful of my hair to pull my mouth to his finally. I taste myself on him as he pushes his tongue into my mouth. I open eagerly, meeting his desperate kiss with my own. I grind my hips against him, feeling his hardness under his sweatpants, and even though I just had an orgasm not even two minutes ago, I'm desperate for more.

Reaching between us I work his pants off, he helps me by shoving them down his hips. He pushes me back so I'm leaning against the piano, the keys digging into my lower back. His mouth comes down on my chest taking my nipple in his mouth sucking hard. I arch my back trying to get closer. He moves to the other one, my nails are digging into his shoulders, and my hips are moving, searching for him, desperate with the need to be filled by him. The need only grows the more he plays with me.

"Trent," I gasp out desperately.

He releases me, and I whimper as the cool air hits my now wet and painfully pointed peak.

"Fuck me. Please. I need – " he grabs my hands in one of his before I can even finish, and holds them between our chests while he pulls my hips down onto his in one solid rough movement. Seating himself completely inside me with one single movement.

I try to break my hands out of his grip, but he won't let me. He holds my wrists with bruising force. He hasn't moved his hips, and I'm beginning to feel desperate, needing him to move. I grind my hips slightly to encourage him. He reaches up with his free hand to grab my throat. He uses his grip to push me back against the keys once again.

With his hand collar around my neck, and my hands held hostage by his, I'm completely at his mercy when he starts to thrust up into me. The angle instantly makes my eyes roll back in my head as I feel every single inch of him hitting me perfectly.

He squeezes my throat, starting to take away my air. I open my eyes in shock, and when I look at him, he lets up on his grip slightly.

"Keep your eyes on me. You need to remember I'm the only person who can fuck you like this."

I bite my lip to keep from crying out again with a particularly brutal thrust. Finally, he lets go of my hands so he can hold onto my hip while he drives into me so hard my back scrapes against the piano. I reach up to grip his forearm while his hand remains on my throat.

As he continues to slam into me, I scratch at his arm, and his grip tightens, taking my air once again. He's guiding my hips to meet him thrust for thrust as I feel the pleasure about to take over once again. The lack of air makes my heart race as I think I'm going to pass out before I reach the peak of my pleasure.

I gasp out his name with the last bit of air I have, my nails digging into his skin. My vision starts to darken as I gasp and claw at him, our hips slapping together roughly. Then right before everything goes completely dark, he lets up. I take a huge lungful of air while my body explodes in an orgasm so strong, I feel like I might pass out from that alone.

Trent yanks me up to a sitting position in his lap, our chests pressed together as his mouth attacks mine again. I'm still coming, the new angle resulting in my clit rubbing against him as he continues to thrust up into me with punishing force.

Our mouths battle with tongues and teeth as he fucks me from below. I wrap my arms around his neck to hold him against me as I feel his thrusts become erratic. He's close, I can feel it. I hold him tighter against me, crushing my chest against his, and buck my hips to gain the extra friction against my clit.

I feel his groan in my mouth while he comes and it triggers another smaller release of my own. We continue to kiss, breathing in each other's air like we need it until the kiss slows down as we come down from our highs.

Pulling away, we just stare at each other. I reach my hand up to run it across his jaw, the slight stubble there scratches against my finger tip. He really is beautiful. He has so much darkness surrounding him, and yet in this moment he looks like someone I could actually be with. And then he opens his mouth to speak.

"How do you sign, 'that was the hottest thing I've ever experienced.'"

Just like that, the spell is broken.

I wince from the loss of him from my body when I get off his lap. I grab my clothes off the floor and pull them on. Once I'm dressed, I look up to see Trent leaning against the piano, watching me with his arms folded across his chest.

"What?"

He doesn't respond, just reaches out to pull me against his chest. My hands fly up and press against the muscles there. I don't look at him right away, so he places a finger under my chin to force me to look up. He doesn't say anything, and I don't think he's going to, but I can see in his eyes he wants to.

"Where did you come from?" His lips barely move with the words, I almost don't understand them. I feel like he might not even want me to know what he said. I might not have even seen them correctly.

He crushes me to his chest before pressing his lips to my forehead briefly. Then, we are both heading back up to his bedroom. My plan for snooping is long forgotten, especially as I fall asleep once again with my head on Trent's chest, his arms wrapped tightly around me.

My last thought is that I need to end this entire thing before it blows up in my face because at this point, it's inevitable, this is a train wreck waiting to happen.

34

Trent

Present

Jason and I are at my warehouse again. Of course, I didn't get the money back that was stolen from me. I didn't expect to, it was more about sending a message. Just like I did.

Which is why I'm here making sure nothing else is stolen, and Jason is here because I wanted to talk to him about how things are running on the ground. I've been pretty detached from anything having to do with almost everything lately. I've been too wrapped up in Violet.

I haven't seen her since she left my house a few days ago, and I haven't reached out. I realize that I'm getting *too* involved with her, and it makes me uneasy. She's becoming a dangerous addiction I can't kick, and I can't have that. Not in this life. Not for me. I don't see women more than once. I'm in dangerous territory with her, and it's why I've chosen to back off a bit.

Of course, I still see her at Wright House when I have to go, but I don't make myself known.

"Looks like everything is here," Jason announces.

I nod, and glance around. "How are things at the club?"

"Fine, nothing really to report. I think maybe he's started to back off."

I scoff, as much as I wish that was true, I highly doubt it. It's not really the 'Chris Moore way' to just *back off*. "How is everything with the new suppliers?"

"Also good, we lost quite a few buyers because they started going to your dad's place a bit more since they get more...uh freedom."

He means sex. Considering Chris isn't above trafficking women, he expects them to sleep with the clients for a certain price. Add in the drugs, and access, it's a slam dunk for him. The girls at my club might sleep with clients sometimes too, that's their prerogative, but it's not what we advertise on the streets because that's not what they are there to do.

"I fucking hate this," I mumble.

"Yeah, it's a bitch to deal with, but it'll be okay, boss."

I run my hand down my face. "Do you ever want to try living a more normal life?"

He tilts his head to the side. "What do you mean?"

"Like be done with this bullshit. Be a fucking banker or something."

"Money isn't as good in that," he jokes.

"True." I realize at this moment I don't know much about Jason. Not that I've ever cared to ask. I just know he was friends with Zander and helped us get set up here, but other than that I know nothing about this guy. "You got any family, Jason?"

He looks shocked by my question, which I understand. I don't know why I'm asking. I don't know why I care to bring it up. I blame Violet. She's getting under my skin in ways I didn't even think was possible.

Reaching up to rub the back of his neck he hesitates before answering. "Uh, yeah. Just my mom and me, always has been."

"Girlfriend?" I really don't know why I'm asking this stuff.

"Not right now, no. I tend to pick the crazies who are just using me for shit."

I am surprised he admitted that, and I can tell he didn't mean to say that much. I've always wondered if Jason used product back when I first met him, he seemed like an addict, but lately he's seemed more…put together. He's still a skinny fucker, couldn't replace Zander in being an enforcer for me. But he has been helpful in getting information.

"You ever had one that might have been good for you?" I want to slap myself. This isn't fucking gossip time.

"Uh, yeah, I guess. I fucked up with that one though, and she won't ever talk to me again."

I stop myself from asking more about what happened. It's not my place, and this has already been way too fucking weird. Instead, I ask something I never thought I would.

"Have you talked to Zander lately?"

"Not really, not since you got ar – " he stops himself.

I chuckle. "You can say it. I was arrested. I went to prison. I did my time, it's not like it's a secret."

He just nods. "After you were arrested, he ran off with his girlfriend, and hasn't talked to me since."

I expected as much. I know he wanted to get away from anything and everything that had to do with me, and since Jason stayed involved, I'm not surprised Zander didn't want to be friends with him.

"Do you have an issue with him now too?" I wonder.

He shrugs. "Not really. I mean, he made his choices, I made mine. It's his life, I don't see the point in being mad at anyone for how they choose to live it."

I don't like that he has a point. I obviously still have anger toward Zander for fucking me over, but choosing to live a life free of me, and to distance himself away from me and in turn away from my dad. I can't blame him for that.

"Fuck, man." I laugh. "Let's close this place up, I have somewhere I have to be."

∽

I DIDN'T HAVE ANYWHERE to be.

I thought about showing up to Violet's apartment, and making her come with me again, but decided against it. For a couple reasons.

One, I don't like how much I'm thinking about her. I don't like how she's taken over the majority of my thoughts, and I need to get some distance to help with that.

Two, I need her to come to me. I'm always practically forcing her to see me. It's been fun, and there's some intoxication that comes from it. She needs to make the decision on her own at some point, though. I need to see that this isn't completely one-sided.

After another two days of not hearing from her, I decide to text her.

> Trent: What are you doing?

> Violet: Reading.

> Trent: What are you reading?

> Violet: A book.

> Trent: What kind of book?

> Violet: A good one.

> Trent: What is it about?

> Violet: An annoying older man bothering a twenty-one-year-old deaf girl.
>
> > Trent: That does sound good, does the girl happen to like this older guy?
>
> Violet: No. She finds him infuriating.
>
> > Trent: Does she feel that way when she's screaming his name while he's fucking her?

I did not intend to make this conversation sexual, but I can't help myself. This is my problem with her. I lose all sense of what I should do, and what I plan to do.

I plan not to contact her, I do it anyway.

I plan not to show up to her apartment, I do it anyway.

I plan to leave her alone for good, I can't bring myself to do it.

So now, instead of working or doing anything remotely productive, I'm lying on my couch, smiling at my fucking phone at our banter.

> Violet: What do you want, Trent?
>
> > Trent: I thought it was pretty obvious. You.

She doesn't reply right away to that one, and I toss my phone off to the side as I get up, and head to my office. I slump down in my desk chair, and open the drawer that holds the letter to Zander in it. I still haven't sent it. I'm not going to, but I debate it every time I see it.

I slam the drawer shut and lean back with my hands on my face. *Fuck.* This isn't like me. None of this is like me. I don't think about one woman. I don't consider sending a fucking apology letter to the man who fucked me over and sent me to prison. I don't question every single fucking thing I'm doing in my life.

"Fuck!" I yell, picking up the first thing I grab on my desk which is a tablet and throw it across the room. It hits the wall by the door, and I'm sure it's broken. I don't care. None of it matters. None of this fucking matters.

I used to believe I had a reason for doing all of this. The money. The power. The control. The success. I have reasons for it. Lately, I haven't felt any of that.

I don't give a shit about any of the money.

The power doesn't feel the same, the control I have over the people around me.

The businesses.

It doesn't feel like anything.

The only time I feel anything is when I'm around Violet. When we are fighting. Fucking. Texting. It's the only spike of anything I feel anymore, and it's driving me insane. Even right now, I want to go out to grab my phone to see if she replied.

I refuse to give in. Instead, I do my best to distract myself by focusing on the one thing I have a semblance of control over in my life, and its work. I throw myself into it, doing everything I can to not think about the little blonde woman who has taken over my life. And she doesn't even know she's done it.

By the time a few hours have passed I decide to stop working, even though I didn't do shit.

I looked at buildings, hated all of them.

Worked on some business plans to maximize profits with the new supplier's prices. It's shit.

Looked at exotic islands to run off to and debated it for way too fucking long.

Somehow, I also ended up looking up videos of ASL and watching for way longer than I care to admit.

I pick up my phone and saw she did reply over an hour after the text I sent her.

Violet: Why?

While I'm drinking the second glass I poured, staring at the single word trying to figure that out for myself. I finally reply with the only thing that comes to my mind.

Trent: I don't know.

35

Violet

Present

"He *doesn't know?*" Jenson scoffs, as he reads Trent's reply.

I'm not surprised, though I refuse to acknowledge the pang in my chest at his answer. It's not like I expected some big confession through text or anything, but I expected...something. Even a "I like fucking you" would be better than "I don't know." Clearly, I shouldn't have expected shit from him. I should know better.

"*You tell him he can shove his big dick in a meat grinder.*" Jenson tosses my phone toward me.

He came over earlier because I feel like I haven't hung out with him much lately, and I know it's my fault. I've been... distracted. But he also works, and so do I. Plus, Trent keeps practically kidnapping me.

"You have to appreciate the honesty," I tell him.

"I don't appreciate him using you for sex."

"Technically, I'm using him too. And you wanted me to sleep with him from the moment you saw him."

I haven't told Jenson everything I'm doing, and why, but he knows I'm not just doing this for fun.

He just waves me off while grabbing more snacks from the kitchen. We are having a movie marathon of our favorite old movies from childhood because I like the nostalgia. Mila left for "work" about an hour ago. We haven't talked about the other night, and it's actually bothering me.

I know something happened to her, and it changed something in her. I want to know what it was. I want to help her. I want to feel like I have her on my side.

"You're a woman, you're allowed to use men," Jenson signs once he's set the snacks down on the coffee table in front of us.

"That's an interesting take...from a man."

"It's true, though. Women are always the reason the bad guys turn over a new leaf."

"I really don't think that's true." I shake my head.

"It is. Think about it. Guy falls in love with the woman he never thought he would, and then suddenly he's a new person.'

"You watch too many movies. This is real life. And no one is falling in love."

He shrugs. "If you say so."

"It's true. He's a criminal!"

"And?"

"And an asshole that you wanted me to threaten bodily harm to, not five minutes ago."

"And you won't admit that you like the guy."

"Because I don't."

He just shrugs again.

"What?" I slam my hands down.

"Nothing."

"Tell me."

He looks like he lets out a sigh before putting the popcorn bowl down and facing me completely. I don't like that; it means he's about to give it to me straight. I don't want real talk right now. I want encouragement to continue to hate Trent.

"Have you considered the fact that maybe he's not a horrible guy?"

I laugh. *"He is. Trust me."*

I saw his charges for going to prison. Attempted murder is a serious one.

"Maybe he was. But what if he's changed? You said it yourself, you can't find anything on him right now."

I said I was having a hard time finding anything. To be fair, I haven't been the best at searching though, because I end up in his bed.

"I think he's good at hiding it. He's a professional at this stuff."

"Well then have you considered that maybe he actually likes you."

No because I refuse to think that, even if he told me previously that he does. I don't believe it.

"Wouldn't matter if he did."

"Why not test it then."

I narrow my eyes at him. *"What do you mean?"*

Jenson hands my phone to me. I don't take it from him, so he sets it in my lap instead.

"Text him back. Tell him you want to see him."

"Fuck no!"

"*Vi, just see what happens.*"

I hate this. I don't want to see what happens. I don't need to know if Trent likes me. He's going to want to see me just to sleep with me again because I've proved myself to be a sure thing.

God, I hate that. I feel like I'm whoring myself out, and despite how good it feels in the moment, I always feel like shit afterwards.

Despite all of that, I do what Jenson says and text Trent back. The only difference is, I'm telling myself I'm doing it to continue to get information on him. I'm going to follow through on this if it's the last thing I do. If only to prove to myself and Mila that I can do it.

> Violet: Maybe you should figure it out before seeing me tomorrow.

I toss my phone at Jenson so he can see what I said. He smiles while looking at the screen. I grab a bag of gummy candy and begin chomping at it like it's my lifeline. I see the flash on my phone go off signaling a text, and I chew faster. Jenson reads the text first. I glance at him from the side, and see his lips quirk up in a smile.

He slides my phone in front of me so I can see, and I almost kick it off the couch, but not before I see what he says.

> Trent: About time you asked me out, Flower.

"*Happy?*" I ask Jenson.

He smiles. "Yup."

JENSON LEFT after our movie marathon, and I pretended like I wanted to go to bed. I'm tired, but not enough to actually sleep. I keep staring up at the ceiling and can't stop my mind from running a million miles an hour.

I can't stop thinking of everything. Mila, what happened to her. Kylee and what is going on with her. Trent and whatever is going on with us. It's just too much for me to wrap my head around. I feel like I'm drowning, and there's no lifeline in sight. I am grasping for control, but it keeps getting further and further away from me.

Something has to change, and I know what that's going to be. I need to focus on me. I need to stop letting Trent get under my skin which is why tomorrow when I see him, I'm following through on my plan to get information on him, and then I'm walking away.

It's the only option I have. I miss when my life was uncomplicated. Mila and I co-existed as best we could, Jenson and I hanging out. I go to work. I go to school, and everything is just simple. In the matter of like a month, my life became unbelievably complicated, and I'm ready for it to go back to before.

I get out of bed; I need a snack. Once I open my door, I see Mila is in the kitchen, and I think about turning around and heading back into my room. But we need to talk. I walk into the kitchen, and she snaps her head up to look at me but doesn't say anything.

"*Hey,*" I finally try.

"Hey."

"Just get done with work?" I try to ease into it.

"Yeah."

"What...what exactly do you do for work, Mila?"

"We aren't doing this right now. I'm exhausted."

"I just want to know what you do."

She throws her head back and takes a deep breath. "I am a bartender."

"Then why – "

"I work at clubs known for some criminal activity and try to get information, okay? Is that what you wanted to know?" She's mad.

"I just wanted to know what my sister does, and why the cops are involved. So, yeah."

"Now you do. Are we done?"

I want to ask more about how she got started in this, but I can tell she's not going to talk to me about it. She's already irritated and even though I can't fall asleep, my mind is exhausted.

"Yeah. Night." I choose to forego my snack, and head back to my room.

As I lay my head on my pillow, I give myself a mental pep talk.

I'm Violet *fucking* Pederson. I am strong. I am going to do what needs to be done to get enough shit on Trent to send him back to prison, and then I'm going to live my best fucking life knowing I can do whatever I goddamn want.

36

Trent

Present

Violet finally initiated us seeing each other. I shouldn't have been as excited about that as I was. And yet here I am in my kitchen, cooking her dinner, like I should have the other day instead of getting takeout.

I tried to get her to agree to let me come over to her place, but she shot that down extremely quickly. She said it's because her sister lives there too. I don't even care about that; I just want to see what her space is like. I bet she has pictures from school, and that her place is decorated in a bunch of girly shit. I bet it feels like a home.

I see her car approach my house through the large windows. I rinse my hands before going to greet her at the front door. She's so fucking pretty as she walks up to me with a tiny smile on her face that I doubt she's aware of. Her blonde hair is in waves around her shoulders. My eyes rake up her legs that I know are extremely soft, and feel fucking amazing wrapped around any part of me. She's wearing jean shorts, and a t-shirt with Converse on her feet. So simple, and so perfect on her.

"You're beautiful," I sign since it's one of the only ones I actually know, and it's fitting because she is.

She asked why her, and I was honest when I said I don't know.

I don't know why she's different from any other woman I've been with.

I don't know why I can't get her out of my goddamn mind.

I don't know anything when it comes to her.

She rolls her eyes as she gets close to me, and I reach out to grab her hip to tug her into me. "I shouldn't have showed you that sign."

"Why not?"

"Because you're going to overuse it since it's the only one you know."

"Then teach me more." I nip at her neck.

"Feed me first," she gasps out, and I chuckle.

I lead her inside to the kitchen where I already have two plates set out. She signs something I don't recognize.

"What did you say?"

"Smells good."

"Well, prepare to be amazed by my chef skills because this is about to be the best spaghetti and meatballs you've ever had in your life," I say confidently.

She laughs. "I don't know, I've had some pretty amazing spaghetti in my life."

"This will be better," I tell her as I start to fill our plates.

She seems...different today. Less feisty with me which I can appreciate, but I also like her fire. She's also here, and I'll take that however I can get it.

After we are done eating, I clean up our plates, and end up finding her looking at the piano again. I was not planning on playing for her, ever. I don't play in front of anyone. I barely play in general, it's just when my mind is so out of sorts it's what I fall back into. Old habits die hard, I guess.

Of course, every time I see it now, I think of her, and how perfect she looked sprawled on top of it for me. How she felt the music I played, and then let me play another type of music with her body.

I come up behind her, wrapping my arms around her waist as I pull her back against me. She stiffens for a moment before leaning back. I run my mouth along her shoulder and up her neck. She tilts her head to the side to give me better access as my mouth skates along her soft skin. I nip at her jaw lightly.

She turns around to face me, and I almost forget what I was going to say.

"I want to show you something." I see her swallow like she's nervous before nodding her head.

I take her hand in mine as I lead her out to the backyard. We haven't been back here, there used to be a small fire pit and some benches, but I got the urge to make it...more. So, I hired some people to make it a more permanent fixture. There's a step down into the circular pit that is surrounded by bench seating, and in the middle is a built-in fire pit with a table around it.

It was just recently finished, and I realized I didn't have anyone else to enjoy it with. Only her. Something like that wouldn't have ever bothered me before, but lately it kind of has, and I don't like that.

"It's nice," she says, looking around. It's all open forest back here. Only trees for miles. No other houses or anything. "Kind of eerie back here, isn't it?"

I look around and shrug. "I've always thought it was peaceful."

Suddenly, she turns around, and wraps her arms around my waist. I'm a little surprised by the movement because this might be the first time she's willingly touched me like this. She leans up on her toes, face tilted up toward me, and I'm almost too stunned to move to meet her halfway. Her lips brush against mine softly, and I finally move to kiss her back. Gripping her hair, I tilt her head back to deepen the kiss, and as if this wasn't already confusing I am thrown off again when she whispers against my lips. "Take me upstairs."

I'm not one to question whatever is happening right now, so I do exactly as she says, scoop her up in my arms and take her upstairs.

37

Present

Trent dumps me onto his bed, and climbs up my body, but I have other plans. I came here with a purpose, and I'm not getting sidetracked. My plan included thinking about our first time together, how he fucked me within an inch of my life, and I passed out so hard afterwards. Now, I'm going to do that to him.

I thought about drugging him but couldn't figure out how to get the right drugs. The irony is not lost on me that I think part of his "sales" is drugs, but I don't know which kind.

I push on his shoulder until he's lying flat on his back, and I'm straddling his hips. He tries to sit up to capture my lips, but I pull back, not letting him. His hands tighten on my waist while I smile at his frustration.

"Remember what I told you I wanted?" I ask with a mischievous smile.

His brows furrow, clearly not remembering that conversation.

"I told you I wanted to tie you up and take away your senses. Your control."

Recognition flickers as he remembers that particular text conversation.

"You want to be in control tonight, Flower?" he asks, running his hands up my thighs, under the hem of my shorts.

I bite my bottom lip while I nod.

He smiles, and I thought this would be more of a fight. Instead, he lifts his arms above his head, and I take that as my cue to lift up his shirt revealing his chiseled chest to me. A chest I'm more than happy to get to explore tonight all I want.

I throw the fabric onto the floor, then get up off his lap to grab what I need from his closet. It's easy to find a black belt, and a tie. There's one more thing I need, but I'm going to do one thing first.

He watches me, the excitement in his gaze as I climb back over him. I grab both his hands, bringing them above his head by his headboard before securing them there with the belt wrapped tightly.

Leaning down so my lips ghost over his, I flick my tongue along his top lip before asking, "Where do you have headphones?"

"Office."

I smile because that's what I hoped he was going to say. "Don't move," I tell him with a nip to his mouth.

Climbing off him, I make my way to his office quickly. I don't have too much time to snoop right now, but maybe it'll help me when I'm back in here later. I start with drawers, opening the three on the left first, the bottom one is locked, which is annoying. I open the top right drawer and see an envelope with "Zander" written on it.

I pick it up, peeking inside to see papers. I pull them out, seeing it's a letter Trent wrote to his stepbrother. I am dying to read it but know I won't have time. I'll have to come back to it later.

I tuck the paper back inside the envelope, and luckily see a pair of noise canceling headphones in the drawer as well. I run to put the letter in my purse before going back upstairs.

Trent is exactly where I left him, shirtless and tied to his bed. It's quite a sight, and one I don't exactly hate. I push the letter I found out of my mind to focus on the task at hand, and how fun it's going to be to torture him a bit.

I lean over to kiss him, and he captures my lips like he's starving for them while I slip the headphones over his head, making sure his ears are covered then pulling back from his mouth. He tries to follow me, but can't due to the restraints and I smile down at him.

Moving to stand at the end of the bed, he has to strain his neck to look at me while I smirk at him as I run my hand down my chest, over my breasts, down my waist to the hem of my shirt. He won't tear his eyes away from me as I lift my shirt so slowly, revealing every inch of skin to him at a pace I know is driving him mad because he would have me naked already.

I drop my shirt to the floor to reveal my see-through lace black bra. I've never actually worn it before. I got it when I wanted to feel sexy, and then never ended up having a reason to wear it. Not until tonight.

Trent's eyes don't leave mine, and I slide my hands down to the waistband of my shorts, hooking my thumbs in them, and do the same move of pulling them down painfully slowly. I bend over to finish pulling them off my legs, standing to reveal the matching black lace thong that barely covers anything.

His jaw drops, and I see him pull at the restraints, which only makes me smile wider. I kneel on the end of the bed, picking up the tie I left there before crawling the rest of the way up the large body beneath me.

"You're so fucking beautiful, Flower."

I don't say anything as I take away his sight by tying the tie around his eyes, securing it in a knot behind his head. As I step back, I can't help the wide smile on my face as I think about this big powerful man now being completely at my mercy for as long as I want. And I intend to take my time.

I place my hand on his chest and begin to run my fingers down his skin. I trace the ink along his pecs before sliding them lower onto the muscles of his abdomen. I take my time just feeling him tense underneath my light touch.

I get down to the waistband of his sweatpants, and run my fingertips just inside the material, moving them back and forth, just enough to tease. He bucks his hips up slightly, giving me a silent cue to remove his pants. And just because I know that's exactly what he wants, I don't do it. Not yet.

Instead, I climb up on his lap, straddling him again. I watch him try to move his hands out of instinct to grab me, but he can't. I settle my weight down on his hips, and swivel once with my hands placed on his chest. I feel the vibration of his groan. I move my hips harder, enjoying the feeling of rubbing my pussy along his covered erection.

I start to rub myself harder against him, keeping my hands planted on his chest. I let out a moan, even though he can't hear me with those headphones on, but I don't care. It feels too good for me to care. I move against him in a way that it doesn't take long for the pleasure to begin low in my stomach and start to consume my whole body.

I look up to see Trent's face, and he looks like he's almost in pain. As I'm about to lean down to kiss him his mouth moves to speak. "Use me to make yourself come. I want to feel you soak my fucking pants."

I press my lips against his, and he devours my mouth at the slightest touch. He bites my lip before forcing his tongue in my mouth.

This angle is even better as I ride him harder, hitting the perfect spot while our mouths stay fused. I whimper into his mouth as I start to come with a small cry. Once the feeling subsides, I break away from his mouth, and slide down his body back to his waistband, this time pulling down his pants and boxer briefs all at once.

His rock-hard cock bobs free as I continue to pull his pants the rest of the way off. He lies completely naked, unable to touch me, hear me, or see me. The power I feel is extreme. Knowing I could just leave him like this, completely vulnerable and he wouldn't be able to stop me. It's an exhilarating feeling, and I think I understand why he likes to be in control at all times. Even though I enjoy his control too, this is something I could get used to.

I wonder how long it would take until he broke himself free. He probably could, fairly easily. He's *choosing* to be like this for me. And that unleashes an entirely different feeling within my chest. One I push away instantly.

Keeping up with my torturous pace as I run my hands up his thighs. Instead of wrapping my hands around his cock like I know he wants, I continue my journey up his chest. I feel the rumble of what I assume to be annoyance when I bypass his dick completely.

I pull back completely and watch as he shifts around trying to figure out where I went. I pull my hair back in a ponytail so he won't feel it, and so it won't get in the way. Crawling back onto the bed I settle between his slightly spread legs, but I still don't touch him yet.

His mouth moves, but I only catch the last bit of whatever he's saying. " – you don't touch me soon – "

I cut off his threat by grabbing onto the base of him and squeezing. He immediately bucks up slightly, signaling me to do more. I move my hand up his length just like I have done for his entire body, slowly. I can't help the laugh that bubbles out of me when I watch him throw his head back in frustration.

When my hand meets the base of him once again, I lean over, and take the head of him into my mouth. His hips shoot off the bed, and I pull back slightly. Then, finally double down my efforts, and slide down his length as far as I can until he hits the back of my throat.

I pull back and run my tongue up his entire shaft before licking around the head and pulling him back into my mouth. I am not a professional at giving head by any means, especially since the one in the kitchen was the first one I ever gave. But the way Trent responds to everything I'm doing makes me believe I'm doing pretty decent.

I always thought with my aversion to certain textures I would hate blow jobs. But when Trent forced me to my knees for him, I didn't hate it like I thought I would. I still think I would hate the feeling of him coming in my mouth, but that won't matter since I'm in control here.

Since I can't fit him entirely in my mouth, I continue to work him with my hand toward the base while I lick and suck at the tip. He keeps trying to push me to go faster, but I'm going at my pace. I rest my other hand on his chest to feel all the vibrations from noises and words that leave his lips.

I take my mouth of him again and continue to work him with just my hand as I look up at his face. He looks like he's mumbling, and I can't tell what he's saying since his lips are barely moving. I move my fist faster, squeezing harder before taking him back in my mouth and sucking hard on the head, tasting the saltiness of precum, surprising myself when I don't gag.

Then, I do what I know he wants me to, and hollow my cheeks out while working him hard and fast with my hand. I feel the bed shake from him pulling at the restraints. I know he wants to wrap his hands around my hair and force me to take him exactly how he wants, but that's not going to happen.

I gain confidence as I go, and I know he's right at the edge when I pull off of him. He's so hard, covered in my spit, and I've never been so turned on. The power I feel in this moment only adds to my arousal, and I like it.

Taking him back in my hand I work him with minimal pressure, and I move up to press my lips softly to his. He tries to kiss me harder, but I don't let him.

"Violet," he groans. I run my tongue along his lower lip before he continues. "Fucking fuck me, now."

I chuckle against his mouth so he can feel it before kissing him hard. He licks at my mouth like it's the greatest thing he's ever tasted and kisses me just as hard. It's the only control he has at this moment, and he's taking advantage. I start jacking him harder in my hand as I bite at his lips.

His kiss becomes even more frantic as I feel him swell in my hand, and I know he's about to finish, I pull back from his mouth just in time to see him explode all over my hand. That shouldn't be as hot as it was.

I get up to grab a towel to wipe us both off. He clearly expected me to untie him after that, but I'm not done with him.

He's going to pass the fuck out from how exhausted I make him. He's breathing heavily in the aftermath of his release as I wipe the towel across his lower stomach, and his oversensitive cock.

After I'm done, I throw the towel to the side, take off my thong, and pull off the headphones because they are going to get in the way for what I'm about to do. I climb on to straddle his large chest.

"Untie me, Flower," he says as I run my wetness along his chest, and I know he can feel it.

"I might. But make me come first," I tell him as I rise up to his head, kneeling over him, tucking my legs under his shoulders then sink down, and he clearly doesn't need to be told twice.

As soon as his mouth is within reach of me, he's eating me like it's his goal in life. I cry out at the feeling of his tongue finding my clit with scary accurate precision almost immediately. I rock against his mouth as he nips, licks, and sucks. I reach out to grab at the headboard, so I don't fall over.

He spears me with his tongue, and I practically lose it at the feeling. I feel the vibration of a noise he makes as he latches onto my clit and sucks so hard before flicking it with his tongue. I reach down to grab at his hair as I ride his face.

I doubt he can breathe well, but that doesn't seem to deter him as he continues to work me higher and higher perfectly. I press down hard to get the full pressure of his tongue on me. I wish he could touch me with his hands too, but I'm not letting him go yet.

Leaning back, I balance myself on his thighs as I roll my hips against his talented mouth. I dig my nails into his skin as the orgasm takes over. I buck harder against his mouth as I go off. It keeps going as his mouth doesn't stop, but I don't even want him to.

By the time it's finally subsided I don't know if I can stand up, my legs are so wobbly. I slide down to his chest again and watch as he licks his lips like he's trying to make sure he savors the taste of me.

"Let me go so I can properly fuck that delicious cunt of yours," he says, and I bite back the moan those words induce.

"I think I want to fuck you first," I tell him with a small smile he can't see.

"The longer you keep me tied up the worse it's going to be when you let me go," he threatens.

"That's what I'm hoping for," I say against his mouth.

I slide down further, and grab hold of his cock which is surprisingly hard again. I work him while I adjust my legs on either side of his hips. I hover just slightly above the tip, enough where he can feel me, but not enough. His hips buck up trying to push inside, but I keep myself just out of reach.

"Flower."

I hum as I tease the head of him along my wetness before positioning right at my entrance and sinking all the way down, so we are connected at the hips. I moan at the feeling of him stretching me in the best way. I roll my hips to adjust to the fullness. Leaning forward, I plant my hands on his chest again before lifting up and slamming myself back down.

His chest vibrates under my hands, and I don't think before ripping the tie off his eyes. I want him to see me fucking him. I lift up, and slam back down again as I watch his eyes adjust to the soft light in the room. As soon as he can see me clearly his eyes turn feral. He lifts up fucking me from below, and I dig my nails into his chest.

"You thought you could fuck me? I'm always in control, get used to it."

I raise an eyebrow at him as a challenge, then lift off him completely. I hold back the whimper from the loss as I slide off the bed.

"Yeah?" I ask. *"Then come get me."*

I turn and leave the bedroom. I probably don't have much time before he gets out of the restraints with the new motivation I just gave him. Despite my near nakedness I rush downstairs to find a decent place to hide, as I'm looking around, I feel strong arms grab me around my middle, hauling me back against a hard chest. He turns me around, and lifts me up, my legs wrapping around his waist.

"What were you doing, Flower?" I smash my lips to his to avoid answering. It doesn't seem to deter him as he kisses me back just as strongly.

Instead of taking me back up to his room, he throws me down on the couch in his living room. I've seen Trent in a lot of different lights, but the way he's looking at me right now makes me believe he's going to genuinely destroy me.

"You fucked up, leaving me like that. I hope you weren't planning to walk for the next week."

He forces my legs open as he settles his hips between them and thrusts into me so hard my back shoots up off the couch. I grip the cushions so hard I feel like I might rip the fabric. Trent grabs my legs and throws them over his shoulders before leaning forward to fold me in half. I gasp at the pressure. He starts pounding into me and I reach up to scratch at his shoulders.

He moves back again, taking my legs off his shoulders, and pushing them together while he continues to fuck me so hard, I swear I feel him in my stomach. I'm crying out, clawing at the cushions, at him, at anything I can possibly reach.

I'm flipped onto my stomach, my chest pushed over the armrest. I barely get a chance to catch my breath before he's pushing into me again. He grabs a fistful of my hair and yanks my head back. He bites the skin where my neck meets my shoulder, and I cry out. I reach back to pull at the hair at the nape of his neck while he continues to fuck me so brutally, I believe he might be right about me not being able to walk.

With his free hand he reaches around to rub at my clit, and it doesn't take long until I'm screaming with release. He pushes my chest down to the couch, holding my hips up as he continues to pound into me. I feel him adjust slightly the angle hitting me even deeper. I can't tell if my orgasm finished and I rolled right into another one, or he just prolonged it.

He's holding me down by my neck and holding my hips up as he fucks me hard until finally he loses his rhythm as he starts to find his own release. He collapses on top of my back as he lets it go. I'm completely surrounded by his warmth both inside and out while we come down. Breathing heavily, covered in sweat, I think my plan might have backfired because I'm suddenly exhausted.

It feels like we lay here trying to catch our breath for hours. I'm sure it's really less than five minutes by the time Trent stands up, scoops me up in his arms, and carries me up to his room again. He lays me down in his bed, I notice the belt on the floor, and look back to Trent who is climbing into bed next to me.

"How did you get out of that?" I ask.

He smiles. "I could've slipped out of it at any point, but I liked you thinking you were in control of me."

I huff out a breath, I assumed that to be the case, but still. He wraps his arms around me and pulls my back against his chest. I want to wiggle away, but as soon as his lips place a gentle kiss to my shoulder, I decide it won't hurt to stay like this for just a few minutes.

I DIDN'T MEAN to fall asleep, but I wake up, and immediately panic that I fucked up my plan yet again. Then, I feel the warmth still next to me, and see Trent is still passed out.

As carefully as I can, I slip out of bed and grab his shirt off the floor to slip over my body. I continue to keep my eyes on the sleeping man to make sure he doesn't stir. I slip out of the bedroom carefully before heading back down to his office for the second time tonight.

I lock the door before rushing over to finish looking in the drawers again. I open the last one and see a file. I pull it out to see what's in it. There just looks to be permits and building info. I shrug, I'm not sure if this will be something important, but it can't hurt.

Sighing, I stand up with my hands on my hips as I glance around the room. I don't know what I expected to find, it's not like illegal dealings include receipts or anything, but this is his house. He has to have something around here. I look down at the laptop on the desk. I know this will have something, but I'm sure he has a password on it.

Sure enough, once I open it, I'm met with a prompt for a password. Trent seems like the type of person to have some stupid random word as his password since he doesn't have any pets or important people in his life. I don't even know his birthday, for fucks sake so I can't even use that.

I try a variety of generic versions of "password" but am unsuccessful. I close the laptop and bite at my lip, thinking about another course of action I could take. I can try again to get him to talk about what he does.

Or I just hand over the file to the detectives, hope it helps, and cut my losses while I'm still ahead. Technically, then I didn't fail, and I haven't gotten too involved with Trent…right?

I emerge from his office, looking around to make sure he's not waiting for me out here. I shove the file into my purse, and glance at the letter in there already, debating on putting it back. I shake my head, I'm too curious and want to read it, then maybe I'll put it back. Maybe.

Once everything is securely hidden in my purse, I head back up to Trent's room, half expecting him to be sitting up, waiting for me. He's exactly how I left him, sound asleep, sprawled out on his bed, covers pooled around his waist.

I try not to disturb him as I lay back down, he pulls me back suddenly, and I stop breathing as he holds me tightly, his face in mine, but eyes are still closed.

"Where'd you go?" I'm pretty sure he mumbled because it was hard to make out what he said.

"Bathroom," I lie easily. I don't even think he's awake because he nuzzles his face into my neck, continuing to hold me to him as he drifts back off to sleep.

I have a harder time, as I continue to lay there thinking about this being the last time I'm going to be in this bed with him. I know it's going to be, and I mean it this time.

So, why does the thought make my chest hurt?

38

Trent

Present

I wake up cuddled up with a small warm body. Instead of jumping out of bed as fast as I can to go be anywhere else than here, I cuddle closer. Burying my nose in her hair that always smells so good, like coconut and flowers. I look down at the blonde hair draped around my arm. I run some of the strands through my fingers, enjoying how soft it is.

Fuck. I don't know what this woman is doing to me, and I don't know how to stop it. I've never felt like this before. I fucking *like* her. Like a lot.

I like being around her.

I like her in my space.

I like talking to her.

Fighting with her.

Fucking her.

Just lying here with her like this. I run my other hand over my face while memories from last night flash through my mind.

I have never let someone do that to me before. Have I tied up women and fucked them? Yes. The other way around? Fuck no. But I wanted to. I wanted that from her, and I loved watching her be so confident in everything she did. I even liked having my senses taken away from me while she took what she wanted from me.

What the fuck is happening to me.

Violet stirs, and I look down just as her dark brown eyes open and look up at me. For just a moment I feel like there's softness in them, like she's happy to be waking up here with me. I run my finger along the side of her face, pushing the hair away. She sits up, giving me her back that is sadly covered by my shirt, even though I remember we went to bed naked.

I sit up next to her and turn her face toward me to kiss her lips. She doesn't let me deepen it like I would like to as she pulls away and murmurs something about morning breath before throwing the blankets off and getting up and heading to the bathroom.

I watch the cracked door, waiting for her to emerge again, and when she does, I smile at her. She looks almost nervous, and I don't know why. Does she feel bad about last night? Because she shouldn't.

"What's wrong, Flower?" I ask, getting out of bed to walk up to her.

She shakes her head. "Nothing, I should probably head home."

I furrow my brows at her. "Why?"

She just shrugs. "I have stuff to do."

"Stuff," I shake my head. Why do I want to make any excuse to get her to stay right now?

"Yes, Trent. Stuff. What is going on with you?" She folds her arms across her chest.

I don't know.

I rub at the back of my neck. "Yeah, I have stuff too."

She just nods, and starts picking up her clothes off the floor, and pulling them on. I go into the bathroom to brush my teeth while she changes, because I know if I watch her, I'll end up wanting to fuck her, and clearly that's not what she wants right now.

When I come out, she's out of my bedroom already, I run downstairs to catch up with her as she's already walking out the front door. I grab her elbow as she's opening her car door and turn her to face me. Her face is blank, giving nothing away on how she's feeling.

"What is going on?" I ask, running my hand through my hair.

"Nothing, I just want to go home," she rips her arm out of my grasp as she signs.

"Did I..." I sigh, not sure why I even care about this right now. "Do something wrong? Hurt you or something?"

Violet shakes her head. "No. You didn't hurt me."

"Then, what is it?"

'Nothing! Why does something have to be wrong for me to want to go home?"

That's not why I'm asking. I just think she's acting weird, and it's bothering me not knowing why.

"You seem more like you're running away from me than just wanting to go home."

"What is wrong with *you*?" she snaps.

I open my mouth to say something, but nothing comes out. Because I don't know what to say.

"I just – " *Fuck, what is happening to me right now?* "I just like having you around I think."

She snorts a laugh. "You think."

"I don't know, Flower, I had a good time with you last night, and now you're running away like something is wrong."

She sighs. "Nothing is wrong. I just need to go home, okay?"

"Okay." I wrap my hand around the back of her neck and pull her to me. I press my mouth to hers; she instantly opens to let me in, and melts into me like she always does. I sweep my tongue into her mouth, and she tightens her fist against my bare chest.

I pull back, she gives me a small smile. "Bye."

"I'll text you later."

"I know you will," she waves me off while climbing into her car. I continue to watch as she backs up and drives off.

I feel like a needy fucking bitch right now. I shake my head as soon as she's out of my eyesight. I have no idea what came over me. I just feel like she was running away, and that it was my fault for some reason, and that just didn't sit right.

Or maybe that something was wrong. I shake off the weird feeling as I go back inside, determined to distract myself with something today because I need to remind myself why I don't do relationships or feelings. So, why is Violet making me question that completely? *Fuck.*

MY DAD WANTED to meet with me. I tried to get out of it, because I have nothing to say to him, but decided to bring Jason with me just in case I need help burying the body later. He told me to meet at his club, but I actively tried to refuse, but he wouldn't budge and had a cleverly disguised threat if I didn't meet with him.

"Why are we here? This place sucks," Jason says as we walk up to the back door of the strip club.

"Because he wants to feel like he has the upper hand," I tell him as we enter.

The place does suck. It's dirty, the stench is attempted to be covered with cheap perfume I'm sure all the girls that work here wear. Plus, all the girls are drugged up beyond belief, and are barely standing a majority of the time. I don't know why this is what he does. Plus, all the drugs exchanging hands in this place are laced because he has them cut to maximize profit.

We go straight to his office, where I know he will be waiting for me. I instruct Jason to stay outside the door because I know my dad will see it as a sign of weakness that I brought someone with me.

I storm in with a purpose, closing the door behind me before standing in front of it with my arms folded across my chest.

"What?" I snap at the man sitting behind the desk.

"Trent, take a seat, son."

"I'm good." I want to stay standing.

"Fine," he stands up as well, like I knew he would. He can't have someone, let alone his son, stand over him.

"What did you want?"

He sighs. "You know what I want. Can't we put this useless

feud to bed, and agree we have mutual interests, and would benefit from each other's connections."

I groan. "No. I have told you this. I don't want shit to do with what you do. And you need to watch what you're doing fucking with my shit."

He has the audacity to look surprised. "What do you mean?"

"Don't act like you don't know. You always taught me to own my shit. So, own it."

He smiles. "I taught you a lot, but it seems like not all of it stuck."

"The fuck does that mean?"

"You think I don't know what you're doing at any given time? Come on, son, I have eyes and ears everywhere."

"You might think you do, but I made sure to get them all out of my life."

"Don't be so sure about that. Tell me about that little girl you're seeing."

My blood instantly boils at the mention of Violet. "There's no little girl. I only see women."

His smile widens, clearly aware he struck a nerve with me. "She just seems a little young for you, my mistake for not knowing if she was of age or not."

I scoff. "Like you care if they are of age or not."

He shrugs. "So, tell me about her."

"No."

"A little protective, are you?"

"She's just a warm place for me to stick my dick, there's nothing to tell." The words taste sour on my tongue talking about Violet like that, but I'm not going to make it seem like she's anything to me. He will use that. Sensing weaknesses is his specialty. Something I learned from him.

"Best to keep it that way, bitches can't be trusted."

"I fucking know. Was there an actual point to me coming here, or are we done?"

"I just wanted to catch up with my son, is that so bad?"

I turn around, ready to storm out of his office when his voice calling my name stops me with my hand on the doorknob.

"Next time, if you're going to bring back up with you, make sure it's someone who can actually hold their own." He's talking about Jason, clearly he has cameras or some shit he can see.

"I didn't bring him as back up. I brought him in case I needed to deal with your dead fucking body."

As I leave his office, the laughter from my dad follows me

until I'm storming out of the suffocating building, Jason is close behind me.

"What happened?"

I shake my head. "Nothing. As always." I think about how he mentioned knowing about Violet, and I know what I'm about to ask might be stupid, but I feel like I'll regret it if I don't cover all my bases.

"I have something I need you to do for me for a few days."

Jason isn't intimidating, but he can look out for anyone who might be watching my Flower and let me know if anything raises any alarms. I know what I would do to threaten someone. Shit, I know what I *have* done. And I learned from the best, so I feel like it's better safe than sorry.

39

Present

I finish up class for the day at Wright House. I noticed Kylee wasn't here today, and it's making me nervous. I kept it together as best I can throughout class, and now I'm just waiting for everyone to leave so I can talk to Travis.

I'm also actively avoiding Trent once again. It's been four days since I left his house, he's texted me a couple times, but I haven't replied.

I'm meeting with Nate and Mitch later today to talk about what I've found. I also still have the letter to Zander that Trent wrote, and I haven't read it. I've opened it a handful of times but can't make it past the first line. I feel like it's something I shouldn't see so I end up shoving it away.

After what feels like forever, everyone has left the classroom. I grab my stuff, and rush to Travis' office. I knock once before entering, as I always do.

"*Hi,*" he signs.

"*Hi,*" I start, and skip all the niceties. "I didn't see Kylee today, is she...um okay?"

He drops his head before shaking it, and my heart rate instantly kicks up. "She ran over the weekend."

I shake my head, needing to know I misread his lips. "What was that?"

"Kylee ran."

"No," it's all I manage to say.

"Yeah, I hate to say these things happens, but it does, Violet. These teenagers have been through so much we don't even know about, and sometimes they just feel they don't have control, and do things they think will help that. It's a survival skill."

"She's a kid, how is running away good for her survival?" I'm irritated, especially since he seems too nonchalant about this.

"We made a report with law enforcement, and unfortunately that's the only thing we can do."

I shake my head. "There has to be more."

"I've been doing this for a while, there's not. I'm really sorry."

"What if she gets hurt, or kidnapped, or fucking murdered?"

"Violet, I know you were close with her. I'm really sorry, all we can hope is she comes back, or law enforcement brings her back."

I want to yell and scream more about how wrong this is. I want to yell at Travis for not doing more after I told him to check in on her. I want to yell at myself for not doing more. She came to me for help, and I didn't do shit other than give bad advice.

I'm mad at Travis.

Mad at myself.

Mad at the situation.

I think about how I'm meeting with Nate and Mitch later. They are detectives, maybe they can do something to help.

"Sorry for yelling," I tell him.

"It's okay, I know it can be hard. Don't let it bother you too much."

I nod, but don't say anything else as I leave his office. As I'm almost to the building exit, I'm grabbed by the arm, and stopped before coming face to face with the last person I want to see right now. Especially when he gives me that stupid cocky smile.

"Why are you avoiding me?" he asks.

I really don't have the patience for this today. "I've been busy."

"With what?"

"None of your business, Trent!" I yank my arm out of his grip and turn to leave.

I feel him follow me out to the parking lot, and I wish he would just fuck off, I have to go. Instead, he grabs me, pressing my body against the side of my car.

"What is going on?" he asks.

"Nothing. I have to go." I try to push him off me, but he doesn't budge.

"What's wrong?" He almost looks sincere when he asks.

I sigh, I know I'm not getting out of this without telling him something. "A kid, Kylee, ran and it's bugging me, okay?"

"Kylee?" He seems confused and trying to know who that is.

"Do you know any of the kids here?"

"Of course I do. Do I know all of their names? No."

I let out a humorless laugh. "Of course not. You're here because you're forced to be, not because you want to be."

"Hey," he grabs my face with both his hands, forcing me to look at him. "Is that the only thing that's bothering you? You were weird when you left the other day, and you haven't texted me since."

"Yes." I lie.

He searches my face, clearly trying to see if I'm lying, but I give nothing away. He finally drops his hands and moves his body away from mine. "Okay."

I take the opportunity to get in my car as quickly as I can. He doesn't let me close the door, and leans in, extremely close to my face. "You know I won't let you avoid me for much longer, right?"

I sense the threat it's meant to be, but I still manage to roll my eyes, not caring about his bullshit right now. He leans down to place a quick kiss to my lips. It takes me off guard, but it's so quick, I barely register it happened until he's pulling away, smirking and closing my car door for me.

"What do you have for us?" Nate asks as soon as he enters my apartment, followed closely by Mitch. Mila is standing off to the side with her arms folded across her chest.

I pull out the file I found in Trent's drawer and place it on the counter in front of them.

"What's that?" Mitch asks while Nate starts thumbing through the papers.

I shrug. "I found it in his drawer in his office, it was the only thing that looked like it could be of use."

"Looks like it's building permits, plans, and business outlines," Nate says.

"Is that helpful?" I ask.

"We can look into them a bit more, but technically you obtained these illegally, so they aren't admissible in court." Nate closes the file.

I sigh, sitting down in the chair in defeat. I suck.

"Hey, it's okay, have you gotten any other information from him?"

I shake my head. "No, he's a completely closed book. He won't tell me shit."

"Anything about his dad?" Mitch asks this time.

I shake my head. "Just that he hates him."

I see Mila push off the wall in the corner of my eyes before coming around to face me.

"Does this mean you're done now?"

I narrow my eyes at her. *"You'd like that, wouldn't you?"*

"Yes. Yes, I would."

"What is your deal with me?"

Nate waves his hand to get my attention. "Thank you, Violet. We will look into this."

"I'll keep trying," I announce.

Mila slaps her hands down on the counter.

"I think he likes me," I tell them. Mila's eyes narrow at me. "He's been...more persistent lately, and I think I can use that."

Nate seems unsure, looking at Mitch and Mila before speaking again. "Violet, the more you involve yourself the more dangerous it could be. You've been helpful, you don't have to keep doing this."

"I want to. I can do this."

"Vi – " I cut him off.

"I can do it. I also have something to ask of you guys."

"Anything," Mitch says.

"There's a girl at the program I work at, her name is Kylee. She ran away, and I'm worried about what might happen to her."

"Do you have a last name?" Nate pulls out a notepad and pen.

I think for a moment trying to remember. "I think it's Brown."

"Age?"

"Sixteen, I think."

"I can't promise we will find anything, but we'll try."

I nod. They don't stay for much longer, and then it's just Mila and me in our apartment, awkward as always. I really don't feel like fighting with her, so I head to my room. Not surprised at all to see Trent has texted me.

Trent: Come over.

Violet: Pass.

I meant what I said, I can tell Trent actually likes me, and I'm sure I could use that to my advantage, if he wants me to like him back. Which…I might, but he won't know that. Ever. I just like how he makes my body feel. I think.

Trent: Fine. I'll come over, then.

Violet: No.

Trent: Those are your two options. Better pick one before I pick for you.

I groan at the infuriating man. Then, decide to make sure I get something out of him today.

Violet: Fine. One condition. You are telling me something about yourself. Something important. Something real.

Trent: Deal.

40

Present

I let Violet in, enjoying the whiff of her unique coconut and floral scent as she walks past me into my house. I want to follow her like a puppy. It's disgusting, and I don't know what's gotten into me.

Everything about her pulls me in.

I want to be close to her.

I want to touch her.

I smile at her as she plops herself onto my couch, instantly stretching out.

Seeing her there makes me think of when I fucked her in that very spot not that long ago, how I had her bent over that armrest. Maybe I'll get a repeat of that here in the next...ten minutes or so.

"Well, I'm here," she finally says, glaring at me.

I smile at her before sitting next to her on the couch. I sit close enough that our legs are pressed together. I want to pull her against me, but I know she wants to talk, and she needs her hands free to sign while she speaks. I'm learning what my girl prefers.

"Tell me what you want to know," I instruct, waving my hand for emphasis.

"What is it you do, Trent?"

I've always been creative about diverting from questions like this. Strategically not answering but giving enough of an answer to placate. Now, there's just something with her that makes me want to let her in a bit more. Let her see parts of me no one else does. Which is why I answer.

"I used to be in business with my dad. He's always been very demanding in his work. When I became an adult, I started to pull away from his businesses to build my own. I didn't agree with everything he did, and didn't want to be involved, so I did things differently. I continue to do things differently. Lately…" I pause, running my hand down my face before continuing. "I find myself wanting to take a completely different turn. Start over from scratch and remove myself from everything I built while in his shadow."

She seems to think everything over a little before responding again. "What would you do if you could?"

I chuckle. "I don't even know, that's part of the problem."

"You didn't really answer my question though."

"Flower," I take her face in my hands, forcing her to look at me. "I can't tell you every single detail. I don't want you involved in it. Please believe that."

She looks into my eyes, and it's so hard to decipher what she's feeling. I open my mouth to say more, but she stops me with her lips on mine. I start to push her onto her back, but she stops me with a hand on my chest.

"You should do what you want to do. No matter what you have done in your past you can always change your future," she speaks so softly, almost like she didn't really want to voice that, and wanted to keep it to sign language only, but she didn't.

I can't help myself, I kiss her again, needing to feel her. She lets me push her back to the couch this time, my body over hers. As desperate as I am to feel her fully, there is something different in this moment that is less...charged. We aren't desperate to rip each other's clothes off. We aren't in a rush to have sex. We are just kissing. My weight on hers, hands on each other. Mouths moving slowly. Our tongues dance together, but it's seductive rather than hungry. We are just content like this, and I like it.

I like her.

I didn't see that coming, at least not like this. Obviously, I've been drawn to her since we met, but I didn't think it would reach a point like...whatever this is.

We end up breaking apart eventually without fucking, and

that is another new thing for me. I don't think I've just made out with a girl since high school, and even that was rare because if I could end up sticking my dick somewhere I would.

"I need to go home," she tells me while we are tangled up on the couch.

"Why?"

"I work tomorrow."

I want to push her to stay, but I know I'm already in way over my head with all the emotions running through my mind that I have no idea how to control. So, instead of fighting her on it, I just nod before walking her to the door.

Before she gets into her car I cup her face, and she seems just as conflicted as I feel. I know she won't voice it. Not my Flower. I feel like I should say more. I should say anything, but the words won't come out, and that also doesn't happen to me. I always know what to say, but everything that comes to mind scares me to say it, so I don't.

I kiss her again instead, and she opens for me easily. I say everything I want to into our kiss, I feel like she does the same. Things have shifted with us, and I don't know why or when, but it's uncharted territory for me.

When I pull back, I rest my forehead against hers, continuing to silently tell her everything I'm thinking before letting her go. I watch her drive away. Once her car is out of my eyesight, I realize there's so many feelings and emotions in my chest and my head that I don't know what to do with them.

I am so beyond fucked.

∼

JASON ISN'T ANSWERING ME.

It's the next day and I haven't heard from him in a while.

I need to know if he has learned anything about anyone watching Violet. It's driving me insane, and he won't answer his fucking phone.

After about the fiftieth time of trying to call him, I decide to go see if I can find him or ask around if anyone has heard from him. I'm at my club within thirty minutes and asking anyone I see if they have heard from Jason. Those that know him haven't seen or heard from him in a couple days, and others don't even know who he is.

I'm irritated, and continue to send him texts to call me, but get nothing. After a couple hours of asking anyone I see, I choose to put it on pause for now. That mother fucker will hear about it from me when I find him.

As I'm leaving the club my phone rings, and I go to answer, ready to rip Jason a new one when I see it's my dad. I debate running over my phone with my car, but I know it's only a temporary solution.

"You have three seconds to tell me why you're calling," I snap into my phone.

"Meet me tomorrow morning, we have things to discuss." He hangs up before I get to say anything else.

I have nothing to discuss with him, but just like everything else with him, I doubt I actually have a choice.

∽

I FEEL like my entire world just flipped on its head. I thought I was making progress with everything, getting my businesses back in order. Getting my dad out of my life.... Violet. Ever since I met with my dad earlier today, I've felt numb. I've resorted to how I felt as a kid when I learned my mom had betrayed our family.

Empty.

Stupid.

Out of control.

The vision of Jason's dead body flashes in my mind as I sit here waiting for my Flower to enter. His wasn't the first lifeless body I've seen. Not even close. And it's not that I even particularly care that he's dead. It's the words my dad said as an explanation.

"He was a rat. Just like your girl."

What? I know I thought that a while back, but she hasn't seemed like it recently.

He's clearly wrong because I know Violet wouldn't be a snitch. She can't be.

"You don't believe me, son? Ask her yourself. She's been working with the pigs, and she's just been trying to get close to you to send you back to prison."

I don't believe him. But at the same time, I can't help the thought that maybe he's right. Violet couldn't stand me at first. Then she...well she kind of started to like me. And I definitely started to feel *something* toward her. Something I can't name, especially now when the thought of her betraying me makes me feel like my chest is on fire.

I hear the door start to unlock before it opens. The light comes on, and I watch as she sees me sitting here for the first time. A yelp leaves her as she drops her keys on the floor.

"Trent, what the fuck?" she signs quickly, her words breathless.

"Hi Flower." I smile at her, and can feel the uneasiness coming from her.

"How did you get in here?" I see her look back to the door, and her keys, probably wondering if she locked it. She did. I just was able to open it anyway, then lock it again.

I shrug in response. "I learned something interesting today I wanted to talk to you about."

"You had to break into my house, and scare the shit out of me to do so?" she snaps. Her attitude affecting me in the way I'm used to, but I don't necessarily want it right now.

I shrug again, and she narrows her eyes at me in irritation.

"You know, Flower, you never really told me why exactly

you decided to give me a chance. I mean you *really* fucking hated me when we first met."

"Who says I've ever given you a chance? We've fucked, and you should know better than anyone you can fuck people you don't like."

She's right, but for some reason I don't like that she's downplaying whatever it is we've been doing to just fucking. I've never let anyone take control with me. *Ever.* But I did with her, and whether she knows it or not, that actually meant something to me. Which is why I hate this position we are in right now even more.

"What do you know about me?" I ask as nonchalantly as I can manage, watching her closely for a reaction. She's good at not giving me much of one.

"Not enough."

"I don't think that's true."

Her breath hitches.

"What are you getting at right now, Trent?"

"I told you I learned something interesting today."

"Then tell me what it is and give up this whole villain act you have going on right now." I watch her hands as she speaks, noticing a slight tremble.

"It's not an act, Flower, I am the villain and you're about to learn why."

Her chest rises and falls rapidly.

"What's going on?" she whispers.

I pull out my gun from my waistband and pretend to examine it. "One of my guys was killed today."

Her eyes widen. "I'm...sorry?"

"Turns out he was a snitch. He was working with the cops, and I'm sure I don't need to tell you that people like me don't take too kindly to people like that."

She visibly swallows, and I think this might be the first time I've seen Violet afraid.

And she's afraid of me.

I almost feel bad.

Almost.

"Did you kill him?" she asks, her eyes shifting from side to side, obviously thinking of running away.

I laugh. "No, of course not."

She seems to relax for a moment before I open my mouth to speak again. "My dad did. I wouldn't have made it so easy for him."

Violet tenses again. "Why are you telling me this?"

"Why do you think?" I stand for the first time since she walked in here and tuck my gun away once again.

"I-I don't know," she speaks so quietly I almost miss it. Her hands also shake around the sign.

I approach her slowly; she backs up until her back hits the door behind her. I don't stop my movements.

"Try again." We are so close, my chest pressed against hers. Her breathing is rapid, I'm calm.

"Trent," she doesn't even bring her hands up to sign my name. I slam mine against the wall on either side of her head.

"I fucking know, Violet. I know you're working with them too. You have been this whole fucking time." My voice remains even and eerily calm. I could yell or scream at her, but I don't need to. My tone isn't what's going to scare her, since she can't hear it, it makes no difference. No, It's my words.

"What are you going to do to me?" she asks, and I'm almost impressed that she doesn't try to deny it or try and plead her case. That's not how Violet is. She's going to face whatever I'm going to do to her with her head held high, despite the fear radiating off her body.

I collar my hand around her throat to feel her racing pulse as I speak, "I should torture you for days. I should keep you tied up somewhere, bring you to the brink of consciousness, then force you to endure more. Then, when I've finally had enough, I should watch the life drain from your pretty eyes."

She watches each word leave my mouth, her breathing is rapid, eyes shining with unshed tears.

"That's what I would do to anyone else who betrayed me like you did."

She swallows roughly against my palm. "So do it, then."

"I should," I say, pushing away from the wall, away from her. With my back to her, so she can't see when I say, "but I can't."

Once I'm facing her again, I study her. Once again, I feel a pang in my chest at the thought of causing this much fear within her, but I can't care. *I don't care.* Not anymore.

"Get the cops off my case, I don't care how, and you won't see me ever again," I tell her.

Her eyebrows furrow, clearly confused at why I'm letting her go like this, but I don't give her a chance to question me. I don't want to stay in this apartment with her anymore.

I can't look into her dark eyes anymore.

I can't be this close to her and not have her in my arms again.

I can't see her cry.

I storm to the front door, she practically leaps out of the way before I leave, slamming it behind me as I go.

As I get back to my bike, driving away quickly, I can't help the thoughts that invade my mind. The betrayal from yet another person in my life. I couldn't trust anyone after what Zander did to me all those years ago. Vowed I wouldn't let anyone do that to me again. Yet here I am. I shouldn't have gotten close to her like that. I shouldn't have begun to feel anything for her. She was just using me and fucked me over. Just like everyone else.

I really can only trust one person in this world.

Me. Myself. And I.

41

Present

I'm on the floor, knees to my chest, hands buried in my hair as I sob. I haven't moved from this spot since Trent walked out. As soon as the door slammed behind him, I dropped down here, first in panic, then the tears came.

I'm so fucking scared.

I can tell everything he told me didn't faze him in the least. He would do exactly what he said he would.

He would kill me.

I'm so fucking stupid to think I could do this without being caught. I don't know how he figured it out, but it doesn't matter much now. Now, I'm just worried someone is going to come kill me.

Maybe it'll be him. Maybe it'll be someone he works with.

Maybe it'll be his dad. It doesn't matter, all that matters is that my life is clearly in danger. That's why I can't stop crying.

At least that's what I tell myself. Because I can't admit that part of me is upset that things between Trent and I are done. I refuse to admit anything like that, even to myself.

All of it was fake for me.

I was pretending, playing a part, just trying to get him to trust me.

That's it. I swear.

But it doesn't feel like that right now.

I'm hit by the front door swinging open, and I scramble away, pressing myself against the wall, while I stay curled up. He came back or sent someone to get me. This is about to be it. This is the last day I'm going to be alive. I wish I did more. I should've made up with my dad, been closer with Mila, been a better friend to Jenson. My twenty-one years on this planet is about to end in tragedy.

My spiral of thoughts ceases when the hands shaking me aren't doing so because they want to hurt me, but out of concern.

I look up to see Mila looking at me, terror in her eyes as she takes in my appearance. I'm sure I look like a mess, tears are everywhere, bright red face, tangled hair from my fingers.

"What happened?" she asks.

It takes me a few moments to slow my racing heart before I can stabilize my hands enough to answer.

"Trent was here," I pause, "he knows."

"He knows? Knows what?"

"He knows about me, Mila."

"About you...Fuck!" she exclaims the last word with her voice before standing up and pacing around our small apartment. "What did he say?"

I really don't want to tell her. If I tell her then I have to acknowledge what he said, and I really don't want to do that. I feel like it's going to make me look like even more of a failure to my sister, and I don't need more heart break right now.

"He said he should kill me, but he's not going to."

Mila runs her hands through her hair before clearly yelling out, "Fuck!" again.

"What do we do?" I ask her, feeling so small.

"We need to call Nate and Mitch." She grabs for her bag, dumping all the contents on the floor before grabbing her phone, and instantly dialing it.

I watch as she calls one of them, she's continuing to pace, so I can't read her lips through the whole conversation. I stop trying and put my head down again. I don't want to see the explosion I've caused. I don't need to see her to know I've disappointed her and proved her right all at the same time.

Her hands are on my arms again, softer this time, rubbing them until I raise my head to face her.

"Are you okay?" she asks.

I want to lie. I want to say I'm fine, but I can't. So, I shake my head, "no".

Then I'm taken completely off guard when she sits next to me against the wall and pulls me into her for a hug. I don't know the last time we hugged, but it feels nice. I start to cry again as she continues to hold me in silent support.

Once I don't feel like I can cry anymore I lift my head and look at my sister who looks like she's been crying too.

"Why are you involved in this?" I ask her what I've wanted to know since the beginning. I don't understand any of it, and I doubt she's going to tell me anything now, but I want to know.

She hesitates, and it looks like she's thinking about her words carefully before she begins. *"We would have to start from what happened when I ran away."*

My breath hitches at the mention of that. She's never brought it up to me. Never. I give her a small nod, silently telling her to go on.

"I was..." I see her struggle. Her hands shaking, and she doesn't look at me when she fingerspells the next word, *"R-A-P-E-D."*

I gasp, my hand flying to my mouth before frantically

signing everything I wish I could have said to her back then. "Are you okay? Who was it? Where did this happen?"

She looks back up at me again before continuing. "I needed a job. I found one at a club, and thought it was for a waitress job, but it wasn't. It was stripping. I figured I would make enough money in a short amount of time, so that's what I decided to do."

I stare at my sister as she signs her story. I feel like I'm seeing her in a completely different light than I ever have. Not in a negative one, but my respect for her growing at her strength.

"Guys were always handsy, but one night one guy wanted a VIP dance, so I went to the back with him, and...he wouldn't let me get away. I ran off and hid in a hallway. I didn't know what I was going to do, then Nate found me."

"Nate, the cop?"

"Yes. I thought he was just another guy there to hurt me, but he wasn't. He told me he was undercover, and told me to go see Mitch, and they would help me. They did, and I wanted to return the favor which is why I agreed to be a confidential informant."

"How was Trent involved in any of this? Oh my God, Mila did he — "

She grabs my hands, cutting me off. "No. It wasn't him. It was his dad's club where it happened, but I don't know who the guy was that hurt me. I just...Nate told me about Trent and what he did before. I didn't want you involved. I didn't want you to get hurt, Vi. It was never about not believing in you, it was about loving you, and not wanting this exact thing to happen. Or worse."

Her words make my tears start to come again. She hasn't told me she loves me in years. I can't help the emotion that breaks free at this entire conversation – shit – this entire day at this point.

"I love you, Mila. I'm sorry for everything."

"Don't be sorry."

She pulls me in for another hug, and this time I wrap my arms around her as well. We may have a long journey of healing our relationship ahead of us, but this felt like a massive step in the right direction. If only, I could get my dad to speak to me. Maybe we have a chance of having our family back.

Unless Trent has me killed first.

I doubt this is even close to being over.

42

Trent

Present

I slam down my fifth glass of whiskey since I walked out of Violet's apartment.

Maybe it's my sixth.

I'm not keeping track, I just know I came home, and started drinking instantly. Doing anything I can to numb the feelings stirring inside me saying that I've made a mistake. I don't make mistakes, and I don't give second fucking chances.

The betrayal I felt when my dad told me Jason was a snitch burned slightly, but only because I trusted him with keeping an eye on Violet. Which was all for nothing apparently because they were working together. That's what he told me at least. My dad said they were both planted in my life to try and get close to me for information for the cops.

Of course, I didn't believe him, then he convinced me. Even

when I confronted her, I expected her to deny it, beg me to believe her and say she didn't want me to leave.

That's not what happened. Not at all.

And that betrayal is the source of this constant pain I'm feeling in my chest that I'm actively working on eliminating with obscene amounts of alcohol. Which is why I pour myself yet another glass and gulp it down. I never get drunk. I don't like feeling out of control, but at this moment, I feel so out of control anyway I might as well drink it away.

With yet another full glass in hand, I sit down at my desk. I stare down at the clean surface, my laptop sits where I always leave it. There are a few pens, and papers with nothing important on them.

I wonder when the cops are going to come breaking down my door. I don't know what info either of them got they could have turned in. Jason would have had much more than Violet, since I didn't tell her shit. Unless she found something on her own.

Ripping open the drawers of my desk I look to see if anything is missing. The first thing I notice is the letter I wrote to Zander is gone. I didn't send that shit, so I know she has it. If she read it, she would know...*fuck*, she would know we weren't just fucking. Not to me.

That's what she told me.

We were just fucking.

The other thing I notice is a file with my *legal* business

information. Buildings, permits, business plans. Nothing illegal. My little Flower tried, but clearly didn't get anything important. Except that letter, but that won't mean shit to the cops. It would to her, though. It would matter that I look like an idiot, clearly feeling things I shouldn't feel for a person I never should have been with in the first place.

"Fuck!" I yell out while pushing everything off my desk until it all flies onto the floor. My laptop hits the floor with a thud, and I don't give a shit.

Everything can break.

Everything is fucked anyway.

I don't give a shit.

As soon as my glass is empty once again, I throw it across the room, shattering once it hits the wall. I run my hands through my hair, pulling on the strands that have grown since I was released.

Ironically, I feel more trapped right now than I did when I was in prison. At least when I was there, I was angry, and had revenge on my mind. Now, I'm not even thinking about that. I'm just thinking about how to make the pain go away.

I LET myself get too drunk and passed out last night.

Today, I woke up feeling like shit, but determined to move forward. Violet is in the past. Jason is in the past. Zander is in the past. Every fucking person that thought they could fuck me over is in the past.

Except the one I still need to take care of because I tried to leave him in the past, and he keeps coming back.

As I pull myself together, showering, shaving, and pretending like last night never happened, I get a message from said person telling me to meet him later this evening. This is the opportunity for me to be done with him once and for all. It's time for me to take my life back, and that might not be here in Oregon, that might not be what I'm doing with my life now. But it's going to be mine.

I feel like my old self as I arrive at my dad's club. I got dressed like I didn't pass out drunk and heartbroken last night. I look like I have all my shit together, and that's the way I'm going to act. Which is why I barge into his office without knocking, instantly leaning back against the door with my arms folded.

He sits behind his desk, as always, thinking he's invincible. There's a girl in the corner, her head is down, wearing only a bra and underwear. I can't see her face; her dark hair hides it from view.

"Son," my dad greets, pulling my confused eyes from the girl back to him.

"Who's that?" I ask.

"New girl, have to break her in, you know how it is," he winks at me, and I grimace.

"No, can't say I do. Can we speak alone?"

"We are." Those two words prove even further what I've known about my father for the majority of my life. No one else actually matters to him, not even me. Lives are disposable, especially those he deems unworthy, like he thinks he's God.

"You can wait outside," I tell the girl, she looks up slightly, but not enough for me to see her face.

"You don't tell my girls what to do, that's not your place, son."

Instead of saying anything else I go over to grab the girl by the arm and pull her out of the room. As soon as my hand latches onto her, she looks up, so much fear in those green eyes, and a flash of recognition hits me. I've seen this girl before, but where? She opens her mouth to say something, as I pull her out of the room trying to place why she looks familiar.

As soon as I have her out of the room, and am about to close the door she speaks, so softly I can barely hear her. "Trent?"

Her saying my name has me instantly realizing where I know her from. She's the girl I've seen talking to Violet at Wright House on multiple occasions. Kayla...Kyla...Ky...

"Trent," my dad snaps from inside his office. I go back inside, closing the door on her face while wondering what she's doing here.

"Seems as if you want to boss my girls around, you should get over yourself and work with me."

"That will never fucking happen. I have no interest in dealing with underage girls, which she is by the way."

He just shrugs. I know he doesn't care, but I felt the need to point it out anyway.

"Did you handle your own girl?"

My heart kicks in my chest at the mention of Violet. I refuse to let it show, so I keep my face blank while I answer him. "It's done. And so am I. I'm fucking done with you, *Dad.*"

He frowns. "The fuck does that mean?"

"It means exactly what I said. I'm done. With all of this. Get out of my life, and don't bother reaching out to me ever again. I want nothing to do with you from this point forward."

I turn to leave, and as soon as I have my hand on the doorknob, he speaks up behind me.

"You sure this is how you want to do this, son? You walk out that door, I will no longer consider you my family."

"We haven't been a family for a long time."

I walk out, slamming the door behind me. To my left I see the girl flinch, and I remember her name, "Kylee."

Her eyes shoot up to mine, the fear is so prominent in her red rimmed eyes, she flinches away from me as I approach her, but I'm not going to hurt her.

"What are you doing here?" I ask her, quietly.

She shakes her head. "He said he would help me."

"He's not, Kylee, you need to get out of here."

"I can't."

"Yes, you can." I run my hand down my face, not wanting to say what I'm about to, but at a loss for what else to do right now. "I can help you. Come with me."

She shakes her head furiously. "I can't."

"Yes. You. Can." I say through gritted teeth, not even sure why I'm so determined. I don't give a shit about any of the other girls my dad takes in, but this one was close with Violet. She would want me to help her. Even if I'll never see her again.

The door slams open, and my dad comes out. "Trent, you need to leave before I have your ass kicked out of here."

I look to Kylee, but she's not looking at me anymore.

"Stop trying to take my girls for your own personal use and get the fuck out."

Kylee reacts to his words, clearly believing that's what I was trying to do, when she slinks back against the wall. I shake my head; this is why I don't help anyone.

Without another word I walk out, leaving my father behind for the last time.

43

Violet

Present

I don't sleep. I can't, and it's been days since I've last seen or heard from Trent. I'm too paranoid to let myself fall into a deep state of unconsciousness because I'm preparing for someone to come knock down my door and kill me.

Plus, I'm angry.

At myself.

At Trent.

At his dad.

At the situation.

At my life.

Everything.

I'm just fucking mad.

The only bright spot is the fact that Mila and I are closer than we have been in what feels like ever. We don't avoid each other when we are in the same room anymore, and we actually talk. The lingering awkwardness that still surrounds our family is our dad.

He invited us – Mila – over for dinner again tonight. Instead of trying to get out of it, I'm going over with a purpose. I'm going to get our dad to talk to me. To acknowledge me. We are about to hash this out one way or another.

I'm done being ignored and acting like it doesn't bother me anymore. I'm done not speaking my mind. I'm. Done.

Mila and I arrive at our dad's house and are greeted how we always are. Her being greeted by him, and me being treated like I'm invisible. Mila knows my plan, so when I nod to her, she takes it as the signal it is and leaves the room. Our dad is facing away from me, as always, while he prepares dinner.

"Dad," I say in an attempt to get his attention.

He stiffens slightly but doesn't turn around. I haven't spoken to him with my voice in years.

"Dad," I say louder. He still doesn't turn around.

"Look at me please," I try.

Nothing.

I take a deep inhale, preparing for this confrontation before I yell out. "Fucking look at me, Dad!"

His head snaps up, he stopped what he was doing, but still isn't looking at me.

"Look at me," I say again, softer this time.

He's still, and after what feels like forever, he still hasn't moved at all, I shake my head. Maybe this idea was stupid after all, and as I'm about to walk out of this house he turns to look at me.

The look in his eyes kills me. They are red rimmed; the brown is dull and he looks like he's aged twenty years since my mom died. He's a broken man, who is stuck in his grief for his wife, so much so, he neglected the two daughters he still has.

"Violet," his mouth barely moves, but I recognize my name on it.

"Dad," I whisper. "Why?"

He doesn't say anything and opts to pull me against his chest while the tears start to run down my face, despite my effort to hold them back. He's so much thinner than he used to be. Nothing was better than hugs from my dad, he could engulf me, make me feel so safe. Now, it feels like I'm the one holding him up.

He pulls back, and looks at me, tracking the tears still falling onto my cheeks.

"I'm so sorry, Vi."

"Why?" I sob, unable to stop the tears that keep pouring out.

He shakes his head, taking a breath. "I couldn't...you're just so much like her."

"You wouldn't acknowledge me because I look like Mom?" My anger is quickly coming back, I don't think that's a good excuse to ignore your daughter for years.

"It's more than that. It's everything, you look like her, your attitude. Everything reminded me of her, and it was just so hard to face it."

"That's not good enough, Dad," I snap, pulling out of his arms completely. "I needed you. I fucking needed you! Mila needed you! We just lost our mom, and we needed our dad, and you shut down. You abandoned us."

"I know," he lowers his head, but I won't allow him to look away from me anymore.

"Don't look away. We need our dad back."

He nods, bringing his head back up to look at me. "You are so much like her, Vi. She would be so happy with the person you turned into."

"*Would she be happy with who you've turned into?*" I don't know if he will understand, it's been so long since we've communicated in sign.

He raises his hand, and I know he remembers, at least enough to understand. "*No.*"

"*Then why not try to make her proud?*"

"*I want to,*" he signs slowly, cautiously, unsure.

I give him a smile. This feels like progress. It's small, but that's okay. It's progress. And with something so simple, it feels like my dream of once again having my family doesn't seem so far-fetched anymore.

Especially when the three of us sit for dinner and have a conversation that includes all of us. Our dad tells us more stories of our mom. When he looks at me, I still see the battle he's fighting. I know I remind him of her. I resemble her in more ways than just one, and I know it's something he needs to work through. It doesn't make what he did right by any means, but it gives me hope.

And I find myself smiling, and for the first time in days, the constant fear isn't the prominent thought in my mind. It's replaced by the safety and happiness of my family. Especially when my dad brings out the old photo albums we haven't looked at in so long.

Mila and I are cuddled up on the couch looking at our parent's wedding pictures. They were both so young, so happy.

"*You really do look just like her,*" Mila tells me as we flip through the book.

I nod. I don't have anything to say to that.

As we smile and laugh at some of our ridiculous baby pictures, our dad comes back with more albums.

"I am really sorry for abandoning you girls. I just...I don't have an excuse. I want to be better. For both of you."

Mila and I look at each other before we both jump up and wrap our dad in a hug. We hold on for a long time. He said he wants to be better, and that's all I can ask of him.

It's late when Mila and I decide to head home. I feel lighter in a way I didn't think was possible. Mila even blasts music on the way home, loud enough for me to feel the vibration from every beat. She's always hated loud music, so the small act from her is so special to me.

We say goodnight before going to our separate rooms, and when I get a glance at myself in the mirror, I see I'm smiling, when I didn't even notice I was doing it. I continue to smile while I put on my pajamas, and when I pull out my phone to plug it in for the night the smile quickly fades as my stomach drops.

There's a message request from Kylee. I open the app and see it's her profile and the message has me stop dead in my tracks.

> Kylee: Violet, it's me. I really need your help.

> Violet: Where are you?

I chew on my thumb nail as I wait for her response.

> Kylee: I don't know. Some warehouse thing. I'm so scared. Please.

I shake my head, that is so not helpful. That's when I remember the file I had from Trent. I took pictures of the papers before I gave the file to Nate and Mitch because I wanted to go there myself at some point. It's probably a complete shot in the dark, but when I googled the address of one of the places it looked like a warehouse.

My blood turns to ice as I think of what this means. She's with Trent, or somehow Trent has her, and why the fuck would he want to do that? That's if this is the right place, and I refuse to believe that right now.

> Violet: Is there anyone there with you?

> Kylee: There was, but not anymore. Don't tell the cops though, just come alone I don't want to make it worse.

I don't like the idea of not telling anyone where I'm going, but it probably would make things worse. So, without saying anything, I just start sharing my location with Mila. Just in case.

I throw on some leggings, a black sweatshirt and Converse before making my way out of the apartment, careful not to alert Mila.

As soon as I'm in my car I reply to Kylee.

> Violet: I'm on my way.

44

Present

Something is off. I can feel it as I pull up to my warehouse. I'm here to clear out. I'm taking the last of the cash, and I already have the few guys I have left coming by to get the rest of the product, and they get to keep what they make off it. I don't care. I'm done.

As I make my way inside, the uneasiness I've been feeling the entire drive kicks up even more. The door shuts behind me, and I turn the lights on illuminating the large space, and I instantly know why I had a bad feeling.

"The fuck are you doing here?" I snap, instantly reaching around for my gun.

My dad raises his hands up to show me they are empty for the moment. "I was wondering if you were going to make it in time for the show."

"I have no interest in whatever the fuck you're doing."

Fuck the money. Fuck everything else right now. I turn to walk away when he calls out, "Kylee."

I stop in my tracks and turn back around just as Kylee comes over to my dad, standing there with her head down. At least she's wearing more clothes this time. A tiny fucking dress, but it is still more than the last time I saw her.

"You seemed interested in this one so I thought I would give her to you as a parting gift."

There's a catch here, I know there is. He knows I don't want Kylee for that, and he wouldn't willingly give up one of his girls. They are products for him which means they are valuable, and he is a greedy bastard.

"But of course, first, you'll need to stay until your girl gets here. You need a proper goodbye to her as well, I'm sure."

I stiffen at his words. He can't mean Violet. She wouldn't come here, not willingly, and definitely not alone. Not if she has already been working with the cops.

"See, I thought you said you dealt with her, then I found out that wasn't true. And why is that, Trent? Why isn't she buried in a ditch with that other fucking rat?"

"Wasn't worth it. She didn't have any info, and she was never going to get it. She was someone I fucked, that's it." The words taste gross on my tongue. She wasn't. Not at all.

He laughs. Not a soft chuckle. He full on laughs. "That was

a good attempt, but I know you have feelings for the bitch. That's why you couldn't do it."

I clench my fists at him calling Violet a bitch.

"No, I don't. I don't have feelings for anyone." I don't believe the words coming out of my mouth. They are so far from the truth.

I do have feelings for her, even now. I never knew what that was like, and I never thought I would. Yet here I am, so sure that I do, and she will never get to know.

"Great, then you won't mind watching while I take care of her for you." He pushes Kylee in my direction as he starts walking around, examining the room. Kylee stumbles into my arms, and I right her, before quickly letting go. "You can entertain yourself with Kylee while you watch."

I look over to the scared girl. She's shaking, and I think back to those sign language videos I started watching so I could learn for Violet and rack my brain for enough to convey what I need to. I tap Kylee lightly, and she shoots her terrified eyes to mine.

"You need to run."

Her eyes go wide, and I really hope I signed that correctly. She doesn't say or sign anything back.

"Do you understand?" I ask.

She nods.

Just as I'm about to give her the perfect opening to run away, I hear the same thing my dad does. Car tires on the dirt outside, and our eyes meet across the space.

People always thought I looked like him, and I've always seen it. Until now. Sure, our physical resemblance might be there, but right now we could not be more opposite on anything. He wants to hurt my Flower, and I want to see the life drain from his eyes.

"Looks like she's here," he smiles at me as he situates himself near the door.

"*Hide,*" I tell Kylee before rushing toward my dad and wrapping my arm around his neck from behind.

I hold on as tightly as I can as he thrashes in my arm. We are similar sizes, but I have significant strength on him due to working out every single day for five years when I was locked up. He's able to get an elbow into my abdomen so hard it has me loosening my grip as he turns around to face me.

"Wrong move, son," he gasps out, still catching his breath.

"I'm not your son. Not anymore."

I cock my fist back to hit him directly in the face, he turns to miss the brunt of the hit, but I still hit his cheekbone. He comes at me and tackles me down to the ground. Fists are flying as we grapple with each other. I've been in my fair share of fights, Zander and I used to attack each other constantly, plus I had to throw my weight around a few times in prison. But this is the first time I've come to blows with my own dad. And I hate to admit the asshole can fight.

Blood is spraying as we each get hits in, and I wrestle out of his grip, only to see Violet at the door, looking fucking terrified. I want to scream at her to get out of here, but I'm hit across my face with a fist once again. We continue going at each other until finally, I yank out the gun from my waistband and point it at him.

As carefully as I can, I look around, but I don't see Violet or Kylee, and I hope that means they got out of here, but I don't dare to pull this fucking trigger without being sure. I'm a good shot, but I don't want to risk hurting either of them.

My dad spits blood onto the floor as he laughs. "You going to shoot me, son? You wouldn't. You're fucking weak."

"Shut up. You're the weak one here. You were never a fucking dad to me. Mom couldn't stand you, that's why she cheated and left."

He smiles, the blood staining his teeth. I'm subtly trying to look out for Violet and Kylee, and as I turn slightly, I see them. I'm fully intent on keeping this asshole distracted long enough for them to leave.

"And yet, you hated her just as much as me," he says smugly.

"That's because I was young, and you brainwashed me."

"Maybe, but you made decisions, Trent. Everything you've done has been on you, not me."

"Yeah, but it's because that's what I was taught. I didn't have a family; I only knew control so that's what I wanted."

"You fucking loved it."

"I did, but not anymore. It's not worth it."

"And what is? That fucking cunt? She *lied to you. Used you.* You think you...what? Love her?" He barks out a laugh. "She doesn't feel the same. She never would, and you know it."

"You don't know shit about her. Or me."

"No? Let's ask her then."

45

Present

I have no idea what I just walked in on, and I freeze at the doorway. Trent and another man are fighting. I get brief flashes of his face, and I can tell that's his dad. Trent is punched right in the face as soon as he sees me, and I dart my eyes around until I see Kylee crouching in a corner behind some boxes.

Racing over to her, I skid my knees as I fall so fast in front of her. She's sobbing, clearly so scared. I touch her chin slightly so she can look at me.

"Are you okay?" I ask, even though it's stupid to ask. Of course, she's not okay.

"Trent said to run."

"Did he bring you here?"

She shakes her head furiously. "*He was trying to help me.*"

We clearly don't have the time to delve into this right now, especially since I look up and see Trent pointing a gun at the man, I believe to be his own father. I hold back my gasp as they talk to each other. I can't focus enough to watch what they are saying, but it doesn't matter. What matters is the fact that we need to get the fuck out of here.

I'm trying to come up with an escape plan, but they are close to the only door I know of here. I think we are going to have to do what Trent suggested to Kylee. Just. Fucking. Run.

She has her hand over her mouth, clearly trying to control her cries. I look at her, trying to remain calm as I give her the half-cocked plan.

"*Stay close to me, we are going to run as fast as we can. My car is outside. Understand?*"

She nods, and I look out, hoping for an opening. I see the moment Trent's eyes meet mine. I expected hatred, anger. I thought he would take the opportunity to do what he told me before. Keep me, torture me until I'm dead. That's not what I see, not even close. He looks almost worried for me, and there's not a trace of anger as he looks at me.

Clearly, I don't have time to dissect that. I betrayed him so massively I don't expect to ever get his forgiveness or see him past tonight. He looks like he's trying to help us escape, and I'm going to take the opening he gives us.

As soon as I see it, I grab Kylee's hand, and we start to book it toward the door. I'm not a runner, never have been, but in this moment, I feel like I could run a fucking marathon if I needed to.

We are so close, just about to be free of the stuffy building when a hand wraps around my upper arm, and I'm yanked back. I scream as I look toward Kylee. She's out the door, and she stops, looks back at me with wide eyes.

"Go!" I yell at her. I left my keys in my car for a quick getaway so at least one of us will be able to get out of this.

I fight against the hold I'm in, but strong arms hold me hostage. I look forward, seeing Trent who looks murderous. Then, I feel something hard press against the side of my skull. I know exactly what it is without seeing it. Not that I've ever had a gun held to me before, but it's not hard to guess. The cool metal and pressure are distinct.

Trent stands in front of us, his gun pointed above my head.

"Let her go," he says.

I can't tell what his dad says behind me. I feel the vibration in his chest as he speaks, despite wearing my hearing aids I know he's speaking, but I'm too focused on the gun currently pressed to my head to try and focus on what he could be saying.

"You first," Trent nods slightly, and I assume his dad told him to put down his gun.

"Let her go, and I'll do what you want."

I shake my head slightly but am stopped by the pressure increasing on my temple. More vibrations behind me.

Trent lowers his gun slowly, and my panic increases. I suddenly feel like this was all just a game, and I walked right into it with both of them. My body sags slightly in defeat at how stupid I was to walk right into this.

My eyes meet Trent's again just as he tucked his gun back in his waistband again, and he does something I never thought I would see from him.

"Flower."

My eyes bulge as I watch his hands move around the signs. It's not perfect, not even close, but I understand what he's saying, even as my eyes fill with tears and the gun stays pressed against my head.

"You're going to be okay."

More vibrations at my back.

"I'm not mad at you. I want you to know that."

The gun presses harder, and I wince, closing my eyes briefly. He speaks behind me, and when I open my eyes, Trent is finishing whatever he just said to his dad.

"I have so much to tell you." I think that's what he's trying to say, and then everything happens in slow motion.

The gun moves from my head, but the arm that's banded around me tightens, I watch as Trent pulls his own gun out again, I close my eyes, feeling the moment the gun goes off. The feedback from my hearing aids makes me want to rip them out, but I can't move. I can't feel anything beyond the ringing in my ears.

Then, I don't feel anything at all.

46

Present

The first thing that registers is the pain in my shoulder. I groan, which results in an immediate cough, making my throat burn. My mouth is so dry, and my eyelids are heavy. I fight to open them, needing to see where I am.

The last thing I remember was my dad holding Violet against him, I was signing to her. I saw someone enter the door but didn't get a chance to see who it was as I reached for my own gun because then there was just...pain.

I finally manage to open my eyes and realize I must have died when I see who is sitting in a chair across the room from me. Phone in hand, looking down at it. I try to get a glance at my shoulder, but I'm unable to move enough to see it. I know I was shot there. And by my own father. The panic takes over when I realize I don't know if Violet got out.

"Fuck," I groan, and Zander looks up at me. Eyes narrowed, and a smirk on his lips.

"You know, I really thought I would be pretty fucking satisfied seeing you in a hospital bed this time, but it really doesn't feel as good as I thought it would."

I cough. "You're an asshole."

"So are you, and I really thought it would feel good to see you get what you deserve for once, but this is pretty underwhelming if I'm being honest."

"Why are you here?" I manage to croak out, despite my desperate need for water.

Zander drops his arms and leans back in the chair like he plans to stay for a while, though I don't know why.

"I got your letter. Real old school."

"I didn't send it. Violet did. Where is she?"

"You don't get to know shit about her right now."

I groan, already tired of this conversation, in pain and so fucking thirsty I'm about to actually ask Zander for help but refuse to do so.

"Again, why the fuck are you here?" I snap at him, but I know my gravelly voice doesn't have the same effect it normally would.

"I have connections and heard about what happened.

Figured you being strapped to a hospital bed would be the perfect place for us to hash this shit out."

"What connections could you possibly have?"

He smirks, "Detective Nate Greene is a close friend of mine."

"Let me guess, you also knew about Violet playing me?"

Zander chuckles. "Actually, I didn't, not until I learned about this. But you were right in your letter. I do like her."

I sigh, fatigue is threatening to take over, but I don't want to pass out again. Not without more answers.

"If you know about everything, then you can fill me in."

"Nate got a tip on where you guys were and seems like he showed up at the perfect time, saw you get shot, and was able to shoot your dad before he was able to hurt Violet or get away.'"

"Is he…?"

"He's dead."

I almost thought hearing those two words would hurt me. I thought I might have some sort of reaction to them at least, but I don't. The only thing I feel is relief.

"Where's Violet?" I try again. I don't blame her if she chooses to keep her distance from me forever, but I just need to know she's safe.

"We aren't done. Tell me about her first. Do you love her?"

My already dry throat feels like it closes with the question. I haven't admitted that to myself, let alone to anyone else. Especially my estranged stepbrother who would have been more than happy to see me die along with my dad.

"Yes," I croak out before coughing again to clear my throat. "Yes, I love her. But I can never have her."

Zander sighs, running his hands along his thighs. "Look, I'll be honest, when I got your letter, I was fucking livid. I thought you were going to come after us again, and this was one of your stupid power plays. I came here to tell you to stay the fuck out of our lives, and while I will fucking castrate you if you threaten Mel again, I actually think you might have been genuine in what you said."

I think back to when I typed those words to him. I don't remember what all it said, I just know I rambled on like a fucking idiot which is why I never was going to send the thing in the first place.

"I get that you had a shit hand dealt to you, Trent. You didn't have to turn into the person that you did, though, and I hope that maybe you're going to turn your life around. That maybe she's worth it to you."

I shake my head. "It doesn't matter anyway; she won't want anything to do with me."

"You don't think you'll be able to get her to forgive you?"

"No, I don't."

"Well, for what it's worth, I know I shouldn't, and don't question what I'm about to say or I'll have them come in here and make you pass out again. But I forgive you."

"You what?"

"I said don't question it. And I seriously will fucking kill you if you try to hurt my wife again."

I want to laugh, especially at the ridiculousness that is this conversation. Zander is forgiving me. I wouldn't even fucking forgive me.

He doesn't let me say anything else before he's pulling a curtain I barely noticed aside, and revealing a sleeping woman, curled up on the bench that does not look comfortable. Her blonde hair is fanned out around her, and she looks so at peace. My heart drops at the sight of her.

"She's been here the whole time," Zander tells me, and I don't even know what to say. "She refused to leave, even when the doctors were trying to get her out of here, she started signing, and they left her alone."

I choke out a small laugh at the visual. My Flower can be so feisty when she wants to, and I remember when I was on the receiving end of it at the beginning, and I miss that more than I even realized.

"I met her. I didn't know who she was, obviously. I did that tattoo on her arm."

I want to be mad about that because I don't doubt that she

went and saw him with the intent to get information on me. For some reason, I just can't find it in myself to be mad. All that shit before doesn't matter. She's here now and hasn't left. It's the only thing that gives me hope.

I FELL ASLEEP ALMOST IMMEDIATELY after Zander left earlier. I wanted to stay awake until Violet woke up. I wanted to talk to her. I needed to talk to her, but once I wake up again it's not her face that I see, it's my mom's. Her red rimmed eyes greet me, and she looks genuinely upset, which surprises me.

Without saying anything to her I look over to the bench where Violet was sleeping before, but she's not there.

"She will be back," my mom says softly.

I turn back to her. "How do you know?"

She gives me a small smile. "I met her earlier. She's sweet, Trent."

I want to ask what they said to each other, ask where she went. I have so many things I want to know, but none of them end up coming out. My thoughts completely derail as soon as my mom starts sobbing next to me.

"I'm so sorry," she cries.

"What are you sorry for?" I shake my head and look around to see if there's any water because my throat still hurts.

She must notice because she asks me what I need before rushing out of the room and returning with a cup of ice water.

I gulp it down, despite her telling me to drink it slowly. It feels so good, instantly soothing my dry mouth and burning throat, I drink the entire thing.

My mom takes the cup from me, setting it off to the side before taking my hand in hers. I flinch, but then decide to hear her out. I don't have much of a choice, being stuck here, but I think back to what Zander said about turning my life around. I feel like this is one of the steps to do so.

"I'm sorry for what happened when you were younger, I didn't..." she pauses, looking for the words, "I didn't mean for things to happen that way, and all I wanted was to shield you from the life your dad lived."

"You knew?" I was always under the impression she didn't know about my dad's less than legal ventures. He painted her as a ditsy housewife my entire life. Turning a blind eye to the way the money came into their bank account, but more than happy to spend it while it was there.

"Of course I knew. I never wanted that for you, Trent. Never. I thought if I could find a way out, I could get us a different life. A better one."

"You thought cheating with your friend was the way to do that?" I can't help the venom in my tone. We've never talked about what happened. I never brought it up, and of course she never admitted it.

She shakes her head. "No. I know that wasn't the right way

to handle anything, but I was young. I was stupid, and I guess I wanted to hurt him in some way like my own 'fuck you.'"

I think this is the first time I've heard my mom cuss, and it makes me quirk a smile.

"You let me go with him, though."

"No, I didn't. He didn't give me a choice. He threatened me with everything if I tried to take you, and then my entire plan backfired. I wasn't there to protect you anymore, and he was able to tell you what he wanted you to believe. There was nothing I could do about it. By the time I could, it was too late, you already hated me."

I don't like the way my heart hurts at her tone when she says that. I did hate her. And she knew it. Hearing her side for the first time, and realizing she was just as much of a victim as I was in this fucked up situation hurts. Then at the end of the day she lost me, her son, her only child, and there was nothing she could do about it.

I turn my hand over to squeeze hers. "I'm sorry, Mom."

She sobs harder, pressing her forehead to our clasped hands. Just like with Zander, I know everything isn't fixed, but maybe I'm not as alone as I thought I was.

I hear a small gasp over the sound of my mom's cries, and I look up to see Violet at the doorway.

Our eyes meet, and I see the fear in hers as she looks from me to my mom, then around the room as if something is going to jump out at her.

"Flower," I smile, but she turns and walks away. My smile drops quickly.

My mom looks up, and over at the now empty doorway. "She's not sure what to do or say to you."

"What do you mean?"

"She's been here since you were brought in, and I spoke to her briefly. She said she doesn't know what she's doing but can't find it in herself to leave you."

"Violet said that?" I clarify to make sure we are talking about the same feisty flower I know and…love.

My mom nods. "Yes. She said you had things to talk about, and she wants to know what they are, though she doesn't know why."

"I don't either. I don't deserve a chance with her again."

She reaches her hand out to run it down my cheek softly. "That's not true. Everyone deserves a second chance, and I think this might be the time for yours."

"I've fucked up a lot, Mom," I admit.

"I know. Everyone does. It's how you choose to fix those things that matter, though. I hope you make the right choices this time around."

"Me too."

47

Present

I've slept on this uncomfortable bench seat for the last three nights, and it keeps getting worse. I'm always able to wake up when Trent is still sleeping, and avoid the inevitable confrontation this entire time.

I don't know why I'm even still here when I dread this so badly, but I can't bring myself to leave for more than an hour or so to go home, eat, shower, and change.

Zander showed up after the first night, and I was surprised to see him. He said he's friends with Nate, so he heard about the whole thing from him. Turns out his wife is best friends with Nate's girlfriend, and they are all really close.

I talked to Nate about what is going to happen from here. He told me I was brave for doing what I did and helping Kylee.

To be honest, I don't feel brave for anything that happened.

I feel like a fucking idiot. But Kylee is safe, so I guess it wasn't all bad.

Then, I unexpectedly met Trent's mom. I was reading while Trent was sleeping, and she came in. I tried to rush out, but she wouldn't let me. She seemed really nice, and I'm still not sure why she and Trent have such a strained relationship. She told me it was her fault, and she made a lot of mistakes she wishes she could take back. I let her have time alone with her son, unsure of where I stand in this weird position, I've found myself in.

I open my eyes, fully intending on sneaking out of the room like always, but I stop dead in my tracks when I see Trent's amber eyes on me. My heart drops to my stomach at the overwhelming feelings that take over at the view I didn't realize I missed. I've been in this room with him for days, but the last time I saw those eyes he was signing to me, and then there was nothing.

I passed out after the guns went off, and woke up in an ambulance, insisting I was fine, and I was told about what happened. Until this moment, I didn't think I would see those eyes again, the feelings that would overtake me. I don't even realize what I'm doing until I'm standing at Trent's bedside.

"Flower."

The tears come out on their own, and I don't know why, or how to stop them. Trent reaches for me with his good arm and pulls me down next to him. I can't stop crying, and I can't control it. I bury my face into his side while he soothes me with the gentle touch of his fingers running along my back until I'm finally able to pull myself together.

Sitting up slightly, I look at him. Despite all the sleep he's been getting he looks tired, bags under his bloodshot eyes. He looks miserable, but my heart still leaps at the way he's looking at me right now. He reaches his hand that was rubbing my back around to move the hair out of my face.

"You're here," his lips quirk with a small smile as he speaks.

For the first time since I've met him, I'm actually nervous about talking to him. "Do you want me to leave?"

He shakes his head, and I sit up more fully, crossing my legs in front of me, as he scoots over to give me room. We need to talk. I know this isn't the ideal situation for it, but so much has happened, and I just need to know what is going to happen moving forward. For both of us.

"Kylee is okay," I start off with.

He nods.

"Your dad is not."

He nods again once. "I know."

"I – You were right, about me. I was working with the cops. I was lying to you, and I know that's probably unforgivable to you, but I want you to know it wasn't all a lie. I don't know when it switched for me because I refused to admit it, even to myself. But it did."

Trent stays quiet, softly running his fingers along my leg, mindlessly, and I feel like he's just waiting for his turn to talk, but I keep going because I have more to say, and this might be the only time I can get it all out.

"I don't know why I'm here. I don't know why I've stayed. We don't work. We shouldn't work. That has been clear from the beginning. We are too different and both too stubborn to do anything about it. There's no future for us. I know this. But I wanted you to know that it wasn't all a lie on my end, despite the fact that you probably think that."

I go to get off the bed, but he stops me with his hand on my leg.

"Are you done?"

I sigh, and nod.

"Good, because you're right about everything except one. There could be a future for us. Only we get to make that decision, despite all the reasons we shouldn't work. We do, Flower."

I rear back like he just slapped me. "What?"

"We both have our flaws, we've made mistakes, we have reasons not to trust each other, but we could start over. Start fresh, both of us being completely real with each other. And if you're willing to look past my flaws and all my mistakes and can stand the thought of being with me, then that's what I want. I don't fault you for what you did, not one bit."

"You don't?"

"No, I don't. I've lived a shit life, hurting people for the majority of it, and it's driven away every single person who could have been important to me. I didn't want to give anyone that power over me. But I don't want to do that anymore."

The tears start to come again, and I wipe them away to see what he says next.

"Unless I'm going to prison, again, then I really don't have a future, and I wouldn't expect to hold you back."

I can't help the chuckle that comes out. "You're not."

He doesn't look convinced, so I continue.

"They tried, but I talked to Nate and told him you were just trying to help Kylee which is why you were there. And with your dad…out of the picture, everything could be blamed on him. That's who they were after anyway."

"But that was my building, and I know they knew that," he gives me a pointed look that says he knows what I took from his office.

I just shrug, "I didn't question everything, I just know you're not getting in trouble for this."

He laughs lightly before it turns into a cough. I jump up to grab a cup of water for him, which he drinks down quickly.

"You're a much better teacher than you are an undercover cop," he says, and I feign offense before he pulls me back down next to him.

"I think that's something I can accept," I say, pressing myself against his side while his arm comes around me again, holding me tightly.

Neither of us say anything as he continues to run his fingers down my back, and I get the feeling he's tracing out words on me, but I can't tell what they are. I'm so consumed in being in his arms again I don't question it.

When he learned the truth, I didn't think this would be where we ended up, and even before that, I knew at some point, I would be saying goodbye to him. The fact that we are here, like this, has so many emotions flowing through me.

I can't help but think about the fact that things don't always go how you plan and can happen so suddenly they take you off guard. I guess that's why people say you fall.

You fall in love.

Things fall apart.

Falling can be good or it can be bad. And sometimes you need to fall face first in the good or bad for things to happen. That's when everything can fall into place.

48

Present

I've been out of the hospital for a couple weeks now. It's been a whirlwind and a major adjustment. Despite what Violet and I talked about in that hospital bed we haven't been able to see each other much since I was released.

She started school again, and I had to organize my life. I had a lot to explain to my PO, but for some reason Nate was able to vouch for me and ensure I didn't get any violations when I really should have. I'm not sure why he's helping me, but I'm not one to look a gift horse in the mouth.

I put my club up for sale. I want to distance myself from everything I was doing before. It might be stupid, but I keep going back to what Zander said, and I know that's what I want to do.

I want to turn my life around.

I want to give Violet something my dad never gave mom or me.

Stability.

Love.

Family.

A life without fear.

It's what Zander did for Mel, and I'd be lying if I said I'm not a bit envious of what they have.

I've even put my house up for sale, because it has too many memories from the life, I'm trying to distance myself from. I rented a condo near Violet's apartment, and now I'm packing up the minimal belongings I want to take with me to the new place. I stare at the piano and find myself sitting down at it as I begin to play.

I close my eyes, reminiscing on the night I played for Violet while she had her hands on mine. Then, as she laid down on top of it. I couldn't keep my eyes off her, every subtle movement she made like she really was feeling the music through her entire body. I try to do that now, feeling the vibrations of each note as it flows through me while I play the song by memory.

This is how it feels to be completely wrapped in the melody, feeling it down to your bones. This is how Violet feels every time she experiences music. I get it now. Once I'm finished with the song I open my eyes and know what I need to do. I haven't told Violet the extent of my feelings for her, I haven't known how. I wasn't sure if she wanted to know, but I need to.

I come up with a plan, one I know she will appreciate more than anything.

THIS TIME as I wait for her in her apartment, it's for a good reason. And her sister knows I'm here. She was not thrilled with the idea of letting me in at first, because despite Violet forgiving me, her sister still has her hang ups. I can't blame her, though. And the fact that she relent, and I'm here now gives me hope for the future.

Plus, I told her my plan, and the tiny smile she graced me with made me feel better. Both of these Pedersen women are feisty, though. She threatened me with severe bodily harm if I hurt her sister again, and I don't blame her, which is why I accepted the threat before promising her I wouldn't.

Unlike the last time I sat here waiting for her to come home, I'm extremely nervous. My leg is bouncing as I sit on the couch until I hear the lock on the front door click, signaling she's home. As soon as her eyes land on mine she shrieks and drops everything.

"Trent, what the fuck?" I smile as I stand to greet her.

I see her hesitance as I carefully take her backpack from her hand and shut the door behind her before scooping up her keys and water bottle, she dropped.

"What's going on?" she whispers.

I still don't say anything as I lead her to the couch, trying my hardest to give her a reassuring smile. I'm sure my own nerves are probably making me look more unsure than anything. She watches me skeptically as she sits down, staring up at me. I back up a few steps because I need the distance not to touch her. I need to get through this first.

I've been practicing for a couple days now, and I know it's still not going to be perfect, but I hope it at least portrays what I want it to.

"Flower," I start, and hear her small intake of breath. "*We didn't have the most normal beginning, or middle.*" She snorts out a small laugh, and it gives me a shot of confidence to keep going.

"*When I first saw you, I never thought we would be here. I never thought I would feel the way I do for you.*" I take in a large lungful of air before continuing. "*I love you, Flower. I have never felt this way before and didn't know what it meant to be in love until you. You make me better. You give me hope. And I hope you give me the chance to love you how you deserve to be loved. Because that's what I plan to do for the rest of my life.*"

I slowly lower my hands, watching her face for a reaction. Her jaw is slightly dropped, and it brings me back to the first time I saw her. Plush pink lips, straight nose, dark eyes, and light hair. So. Fucking. Beautiful.

When she still doesn't say anything, I try again, "*I love you, Violet.*"

She looks so confused, surprised, and I can't tell if she's happy or not. I close the distance between us, sitting on the couch next to her. I want to take her hands in mine, but I want her to say whatever it is she's thinking, so I refrain. Instead, I run my knuckles across her cheek, down the side of her neck before pulling away.

"*Do you – Really?*" she signs slowly.

I nod. "*I want a life with you.*"

I wipe the tears just as they start to fall down her cheeks.

"*Trent, I –* "

Cutting her off with my mouth on hers, I don't want to know if she was about to reject me. She opens automatically, letting my tongue slide against hers. She fists my shirt, pulling me tighter against her. I move my hands to her hips, lifting up so she's straddling my lap. Her hands delve into my hair, pulling at the nape of my neck while I grip her hips tightly as she starts to grind against me.

Violet bites at my bottom lip, sucking it into her mouth before coming back and kissing me deeply. I want to ask her what this means, but I can't bring myself to stop kissing her. I fucking missed this. I missed her, and if this is some sort of goodbye from her, I won't be able to take it.

She slides off my lap, onto her knees on the floor between my legs. She looks up at me, her eyes shining with mischief as she slides her hands up my thighs without breaking our eye contact.

"What are you doing, Flower?" I ask softly because I forgot how to move my hands.

She doesn't answer me, instead moving to unbutton my

jeans, pull the zipper down, and guide them off my hips. I lift slightly to help as she pulls them down to my knees. My cock bobbing free right by her face. She runs her tongue along her lower lip before taking me in her soft hand, and my hips shoot off the couch. She smiles.

"Tell me how you plan to show me how I deserve to be loved," she says, pumping her hand slowly.

"I – " Suddenly, I'm unable to get a single word out as her mouth is on me, and my words die on my tongue with a groan as I'm surrounded by the wet heat of her mouth.

Her eyes look up at me while my cock fills her mouth, and she releases me. "Tell me."

"But you – " I don't get to finish what I'm saying again as she's taking me into her mouth once more. Further this time, and I fist her hair in my hand.

She continues to look up at me while working her tongue on the underside of me and sliding her mouth around me as much as she can.

"I'll wake you up every morning with a reminder of how much I love you." I manage to say right before she drops her mouth even further on me.

"I'll make sure your happiness always comes first," she hums around me, and I fist my hand tighter, making sure her eyes stay on me.

"I'll worship you in every single way you deserve. Both with my words and my actions."

She pulls her mouth off me and runs her tongue along the head of my dick before dropping back down again.

"I'll make sure every night before you go to sleep, I have done everything in my power to make you feel loved and if there's anything you're doubting, I'll fix it however I need to so you can know that you are everything."

She pulls off me again, pumping me in her hand while I loosen my grip on her hair and I continue as she watches my lips.

"Because you are everything, Violet. Everything to me, and I hope you give me the chance to prove that to you."

Violet stops moving her hand, and I feel like this was some sort of trick on her part, teasing me only to turn me down, but then she stands up in front of me. She moves her hands over her hips as she starts to speak.

"That sounds like a lot of work for you, do you think you're up for it?" she taunts, while unbuttoning her own jeans. I sit up straighter watching her intently.

I nod as she starts to slide the fabric down her thighs. I fucking love those thighs. I love everything about the woman standing in front of me.

"Are you sure?" she asks, kicking the jeans the rest of the way off, leaving her only in pale pink underwear.

"Yes," I practically choke on the word, my mouth is watering so much, dying for a taste of her.

She pushes on my shoulder so I'm leaning back completely, still staring up at her face and the tiny smirk on her lips as she climbs back on top of me.

"You better. Because I love you, and I'm not sure I want to see you walk away from me again." She rubs her fabric covered pussy over my solid erection, and I feel like I'm about to lose it if I don't get inside her right now.

"I could never. Say that again." I command, gripping her hips tight enough to bruise.

"You better?" She teases with another slow movement over my cock, and I start to move my fingers toward her center, ready to rip the flimsy fabric.

I shake my head.

"I don't want you to walk away again."

I narrow my eyes at her as my fist tightens on her panties.

"I love you," she gasps out the second I rip them from her body, instantly flipping her underneath me on the couch.

"One more time," I tell her, hovering just above her, the very last shred of my self control is the only thing holding me back.

She smiles, so wide it takes over her whole face as she raises her hand, "*I love you.*"

My mouth crashes down on hers the second I thrust inside her. She gasps into my mouth, and I pull out completely before slamming into her once again. I rip my mouth away from hers to sit up on my knees, pulling her hips up with me, angling her body as I pull her into me with every thrust.

Her arms flail, seeking something to hold onto as I pound into her. I feel her getting close, tightening around me, and I fuck her harder until she's squeezing my dick so hard, I almost explode, but hold back. I need more of this with her right now.

I pull her up onto my lap as I slide off the couch onto the floor with her still impaled on my dick. She's panting hard from how close she is, and I cup her face, bringing her lips back to mine as I thrust up into her from below.

She moans into my mouth as I hold her hips to pull her onto me with each thrust, making sure she's rubbing her clit along me as I fuck her. Our mouths stay fused, but I hear her breathless confession, "I fucking love you, Trent." Right before she drives her tongue into my mouth, and I flip her onto her back on the floor.

I hover above her as she writhes, begging for me to move. "I fucking love you, Flower." I tell her before pushing inside her once again. I don't let up, our hips slap together as she moans beneath me, and I know I'm not going to last much longer. I reach between us to rub at her bundle of nerves before whispering, "Come for me," right before her eyes slam closed, and she's screaming out her release.

The tightness around my cock is my undoing as I spill inside her before collapsing on the floor next to her. We are both breathing heavy as I pull her body against mine while we come down from the pleasure high.

I press a soft kiss to the top of her head as we lay on her living room floor. She sits up, running her hand along my chest, I realize neither of us have our shirts off, and I desperately want her skin completely on mine, but something about this is even better. We couldn't handle another second without taking what we both needed so badly.

"Now what?" she asks with a small smile on her lips.

I pull her against my side tighter. "Now, we have the rest of our lives. Together."

EPILOGUE

Violet

5 Years Later

I remember when I met Mel and Aylin for the first time, I was so nervous. I've never been great at making friends, hence why Jenson has been my best friend for so long. They surprised me when they were so quick to extend their friendship and my fear went away easily. They also accept Jenson when he's in town. After we graduated, he started traveling all around the world. He's a photojournalist so he gets to go wherever his company sends him.

It was really weird the first time I experienced Zander, Nate, and Trent in the same room together. The tension was so thick you could cut it with a knife, until Mel announced that everyone needed to put aside their differences and move on because we are all family.

There have been a few times over the years some arguments between the guys have progressed where I thought fists were about to fly, but they were always able to work it out. Trent and Nate had a hard time finding any common ground, but Nate's girlfriend Aylin helped them communicate a bit better. It's a perk to her being a therapist, I suppose.

Nate was extremely hesitant to let Trent and I meet their daughter, Layla. I understand it, but once again Aylin helped smooth everything over.

Now, Christmas at our house in Bend is a tradition. Trent's birthday is December twentieth, and everyone comes here early for that, then Christmas, then New Year's all together. It's my favorite time.

Once I graduated, I was offered a teaching job here, and Trent was more than happy to move to the mountains. Since we get snow here, everyone enjoys the holiday here with us. Including Mila and I's dad, and Mel's dad. Sometimes Trent's mom, and Zander's dad come as well, but they like to travel. It's a full house. Especially including the kids.

Nate and Aylin's adopted daughter, Layla, is sixteen and she loves to help out with the younger kids. Plus, they always bring their Bernese Mountain dog, which we have to remind the kids is not a horse they can ride.

I've taught Layla some ASL, she has gotten really good, and is able to have full conversations with me in my language. Everyone knows a bit, but she's the best. Other than Trent, who is fluent at this point. I never thought I would see the day.

Right now, it's Christmas Eve while we all sit around our

large fireplace in the living room, and get to open one present each. It's tradition.

Layla hands Mel and Zander's daughter, Bryce, her present. The two-year-old ripping at the paper, furiously as her mom holds her in her lap. I can't help but get emotional when I see them. Mel and Zander struggled with getting pregnant for years. She opened up to me about it one night, and I cried with her as she confessed, she didn't think she would ever get to be a mom. Then, they did IVF and got pregnant the first round with Bryce, and I have never seen such doting parents.

I had a hard time telling her when I got pregnant with our first son. It was while she was six months along, I found out, and told Trent I wanted to hide it from her forever. He asked how that would be possible, but when I told her she was happy for us.

I continued to feel bad, but she wouldn't let me. Then Bryce was born, and only three months later our son Charlie was born and she was so happy Bryce would have a cousin so close in age since they wouldn't have anymore.

And I thought we wouldn't either. Until I got pregnant again only six months after Charlie. We had another boy, Emmett. Two under two is a bit of a nightmare, but Trent is an amazing dad. I feel like he's making up for the shitty dad he had and determined not to be that to his sons.

Nate and Aylin decided not to have any other children and focused all their love and attention on Layla. She's growing up to be such a smart and caring young adult, it seems like they made the right choice. I've heard about some of what she went through when she was younger, so it's amazing how she is now.

"Aunt Violet, it's your turn," Layla signs to me, bringing me out of my thoughts as Trent takes Emmett out of my arms and puts a present there. It's a tiny bag with white tissue paper sticking out of the top.

I pull out the paper until I see a small velvet box at the bottom, and I automatically know exactly what it is. I look up at everyone who is watching me intently, I glance over to Trent who has handed Emmett to Layla and is smiling as he drops down to one knee in front of me.

"Take it out, Flower."

I shake my head, no.

He chuckles, and takes it out for me, opening it to reveal a beautiful ring. It's white gold with three large diamonds in the middle with smaller ones surrounding them. I'm not a jeweler, and never pay much attention to things like this. I'm pretty simple, but I should've known Trent wouldn't be simple with the ring he gets me.

I watch as he slips it on my finger before I can even accept. He runs his finger along the diamonds before flipping my arm around to run his hand along the tattoos on my forearm including the "I love you" sign for my mom, and the two overlapping keys I got for Charlie and Emmett.

"I didn't think I could love you more, and then you brought our sons into this world, and I fell more in love with you. And I continue to fall more every single day. I told you before I would continue to show you how you deserve to be loved, and I know I should've done this sooner, but I'm doing it now. I wanted everyone here with us so

they could see this promise. I will love you forever, wife or not. But I would really like it if I could officially make you mine forever."

I'm crying, and it won't stop so I just nod before throwing my arms around the man in front of me and kiss him like we are alone. We pull apart, and I see everyone is doing the sign equivalent to clapping by waving their hands in the air, and I laugh.

I love every single person in this room so much. Five years ago, I barely had a family with the people I'm blood related to, and now I'm in a room full of people who I consider family, and the amount of love I feel is overflowing from me.

Charlie throws his little arms around both Trent and me and I laugh as we attack his cheek with kisses.

Every single person in this room went through something that shaped them as a person, but it led us all to this moment. Right now. Together. And I know I wouldn't change a damn thing.

THE END

TRENT'S LETTER

Zander,

I can honestly say I never expected to be writing this shit down, and I still don't know why I'm doing this. It's stupid, and I'll probably never send this to you. I just wanted to say...I get it. I get why you did what you did. I get why you chose Mel.

See, I was taught to never have a weakness, especially a woman. No woman was worth risking everything to me, and maybe that's because my mom fucked my dad over, and I figured that's how it is for everyone. But I know that's not the case, and the right woman is definitely worth it.

You'd like her. She doesn't put up with my bullshit. She calls me out, she isn't afraid to fight with me. She's tough, and I know that despite everything I've done, everything I've put you through, everything I've seen, I would do anything for her. She doesn't know that, and I don't know how I would ever tell her, but I would.

I didn't start this to be a cheesy fucker, and I still don't know why I'm choosing to tell you all this. Maybe because I'm so convinced I'll never send this. But I do want you to know that I get it.

I also wanted to apologize. And you of all people know how fucking hard that is so wipe the smile off your face, fucker, I don't apologize for all of it. I still think we had a good thing going, and we could've been extremely successful. I do apologize for how I handled everything at the end. Obviously, what I did to you wasn't the right way to handle anything. I didn't know Mel was there with you, but I'd be lying if I were to say that would've changed anything. Because at the time it wouldn't. But like I said before...I get it.

You'll never forgive me, and I don't deserve it, but on the off chance I do send this, I wanted you to know that I have changed, and I want to be better...for her. She asked if I ever thought we could get along again, and I told her no. Something about how she reacted to that made me want to at least try. I don't have any real family, and not that you ever have been, it might be somewhat...nice if maybe we could get along. Not for me, but for her.

She's...everything. I've never felt like this before for anyone. Never thought it was possible, and it scares the shit out of me. Both how I feel and the thought of anything happening to her. I can only imagine this is how you feel about Mel, and I was your worst nightmare come true with the shit I did. So, I'm sorry.

This will never see the light of day, but at least I've gotten the words out somehow.

-T

ALSO BY MADI DANIELLE

Read the entire Falling series:

When They Fell (Book 1) - Mel and Zander

Who They Are (Book 2) - Aylin and Nate

What They Feel (Book 3) - Violet and Trent

Follow me on Instagram @madidaniellewrites for updates on what is next!

If you loved Trent and Violet please leave a review on Goodreads or Amazon, it really helps as an indie author!

ACKNOWLEDGMENTS

It's so crazy this series has come to an end. I started Mel and Zander's story in November of 2021 after a horrible year in my personal life, and I wanted to escape into a different reality.

Now, it's been over a year, two more stories that came out of creating the world I did with Mel and Zander I also have made friends, become part of a community and had experiences I never thought I would. It's been an amazing ride and I'm so excited to see what else is to come!

I have to thank the friends that have been here from the beginning, Ashley and Julia. You two are my ride or die and you know this. Also, Sarah Beth, you are one of the many people I've met on this journey and you can never escape me now! Thank you for being the best friend, beta reader and graphic maker!

Thank you to Leah Dawsey and Aisling Cousins for reading to make sure I properly portrayed Violet in all her glory.

Thank you to Kay Morton with Morton Editing services, I'm so glad to have met you and become friends with you. You're so amazing and we are going to have so many more projects together, so get ready!

And of course thank you Cat from TRC Designs for the beautiful covers you created for this whole series. Your talent always amazes me, and you are also the sweetest person ever and I love you!

If you got this far, just know this is only the beginning and I have many more stories to come, so prepare yourselves and I love you all!!

ABOUT THE AUTHOR

Madi is 20 something trying to figure out what "adulting" is. Madi has been writing stories since she was a teenager she continues to express all her emotions in her writing. She's also an avid reader, especially of dark romance. Madi lives in the PNW where she attended college after moving from the unforgiving heat of Arizona. Madi spends her free time with her husband and family of pets (4 dogs and 2 cats).

If you want to be kept up to date on news regarding my next release, follow me on Instagram, TikTok and my Facebook reader group!

www.ingramcontent.com/pod-product-compliance
Lightning Source LLC
LaVergne TN
LVHW011942060526
838201LV00061B/4185